Voices of the Hive

ROBERT LILES

iUniverse, Inc.
New York   Bloomington

iUniverse books may be ordered through booksellers or by contacting:

iUniverse
1663 Liberty Drive
Bloomington, IN 47403
www.iuniverse.com
1-800-Authors (1-800-288-4677)

Because of the dynamic nature of the Internet, any Web addresses or
links contained in this book may have changed since publication and
may no longer be valid. The views expressed in this work are solely those
of the author and do not necessarily reflect the views of the publisher,
and the publisher hereby disclaims any responsibility for them.

ISBN: 978-1-4401-3811-9 (sc)
ISBN: 978-1-4401-3812-6 (ebook)

Printed in the United States of America

iUniverse rev. date: 05/13/2009

I

Flight 36 from Atlanta began its descent into the city's international airport. The blue lights on the runway glimmered, inviting the airplane into the metropolis. The sun set over the city, marking the end of the day and welcoming the night. The vast sprawl of the area began to twinkle as the lights relieved the sun of its duty of illuminating civilization. Tall skyscrapers stood towering over the flat terrain, staring toward the great horizon, though not to the extent of suburbia's grasp. Freeways glowed like rivers of headlights, as commuters battled on the pavement to be the first home. Gridlock overcame the city streets and arteries, the angry sound of curses and horns rose from the impatient motorists. The on-ramps were clogged as each impatient driver fought for a spot on the freeway. Traffic oozed like halogen lava to the distant bedroom communities and miniature cities throughout the metropolitan area. Every commuter focused on each respective, stressful life they lived, ignoring the decaying urban core around them.

On the outskirts of downtown, many communities of ethnic groups and sub-cultures clustered. One neighborhood bore *carnicerias*, *curanderas* and abundant billboards in Spanish. Several communities were peppered about, bearing signs in the languages of eastern Asia. Each satellite of the Pacific Rim flaunted its home culture. One part of town flashed colorful signs with the syllabic blocks of *hangeul*, as the locals conversed in Korean. Another served citizens with menus and services scribed in Japanese. Yet another provided its locals with weekly publications in the ornate Chinese characters.

Lofts and galleries meshed in an artist commune flanked by a huddled collection of boutiques, bars, clubs, restaurants and housing, marking the city's gay district. Spiraling farther from downtown proper, a synagogue adorned with Hebrew lettering faced the Jewish Community Center. Several blocks of the city acted as a small-scale Europe, presenting the languages of Rome, Berlin and Warsaw.

Other such neighborhoods stood within the borders of the city. Each was a bastion to its people, offering them comfort and a sense of belonging. But most importantly, they provided them with a degree of protection. The inhabitants felt a greater sense of security in a place with a common, cultural foundation than in other parts of town. They were quasi asylums from the wilderness, the hinterlands of this vast metropolis. Far from the urban core, other denizens of the more homogenous suburbia surrounded the city like a pack of feral wolves, mostly not welcoming to the central city's people, yet willing to venture within its diversified innards to bring food back to the den, preying upon its resources. The suburbs were truly the deadliest, most vicious areas of the great city.

The sun had fully set and lights across the city burned brightly. Closer to the urban center a mass of people walked on the sidewalk in a unanimous direction. They came from all over, flocking to a central point. A haunting call beckoned them like a widespread hypnosis. They followed suit as lemmings to a cliff, closing in on this common location. It was a call to prayer, preached in Arabic. The masses came to worship Allah. The stately mosque was a jewel of the city. It was the only worship center for the city's Muslims. A golden dome capped the white building and multiple minarets pierced the sky. Elaborate designs graced the house of worship. People filed into the mosque to pray in uniformity, Soon, the building was filled with over a hundred of Islam's faithful.

Pedestrians walked by outside, paying little attention to the mosque. The road outside was less trafficked this time of day and only an occasional car passed by. The mosque itself, though large, was situated roughly a quarter mile off the nearest major street. The nearby shops and restaurants offering Middle Eastern goods and fare had closed. Less the chanting followers inside and a few passers-by, the area was deserted and the seclusion of the mosque left the area quiet and peaceful.

A roar rang out over this quiet neighborhood, as though thunder had fallen to Earth. The streetlights became dull in comparison to the bright burst of light. The mosque shattered as the explosion broke free from the walls of the building. The minarets toppled and large slabs of the building fell to surrounding grounds while lighter debris was flung high into the air and far from the disaster area. The force exerted from the blast shattered windows of nearby buildings. Flaming pieces fell all about like brimstone. A plume of thick smoke rose from the burning remains of the mosque as ash and cinders fluttered downward like hellish snow. The few survivors within screamed as their bodies burned. The fires within devoured the interior and all the followers of Allah. Those still inside, not instantly killed, who could divert their attention from panic prayed for the burning to cease. At last realizing they would be afforded no mercy, they prayed for a quick and painless death.

Within minutes, the emergency forces of the city were dispatched to the flaming chaos. The deafening scream of the fire truck rang in the call to action. Firefighters acted quickly to extinguish the flames, which, due to the scattering from the explosion, had spread to nearby buildings. It was set to be a conflagration if immediate action was not taken. The sirens whined and blared as the police and medical teams came. Another fire truck raced to the devastation. The horn trumpeted, signaling its approach. The orchestra of horns and sirens played a horrific symphony of disaster, with the inner city as its audience. Following the emergency teams, members of the press flocked like vultures with pads of paper and pens, recorders, microphones and cameras. They preyed upon the scene like ghouls, each journalist competing for the better coverage. In the end, the destruction and tragedy was all the same.

After an exhausting campaign against the flames, the fire had been defeated, the mosque was left in ruins and only a burnt mass of rubble was left in the fire's wake. A group of onlookers gathered as a morbid audience to see the extent of damage. Though the mosque had been obliterated, the emergency team managed to save nearby houses and properties from the same fate, though there was damage to several other buildings. The scene continued late into the night as an investigation into the explosion began immediately. The crowd had rotated, some left and new viewers came, the paramedics found no survivors and the police coverage of the area thinned, leaving a barricade of yellow tape and a smaller force on guard. The initial belief had been arson, though the crime had been sickeningly intertwined with mass murder. Authorities continued to piece the puzzle together. Only a few hundred feet from the mosque was a vending machine, which sold newspapers. The day's paper still sat in the box with the latest news. The headline read, "Car bomb in Iraq kills 6 US Troops."

The story of the explosion at the mosque attracted the attention of millions nationwide. The initial hunch gave way to confirmation that the event was an act of terrorism. Investigators discovered that a crude bomb had been placed in the ceiling and had been set to detonate during a prayer service to ensure mass casualties. Most sadly, not one faithful soul had survived the blast or fire. The mercy of Allah was naught amongst the followers within the mosque. Within a couple weeks it would become old news, and the public, having satisfied their sadistic craving for televised bloodshed, would grow bored of the devastation and all but forget the tragedy. Though for those who lived within the area it became an event, in the very least, as a backdrop in their lives.

Judy

Despite the gloomy air about the city the day after the bombing, it was a beautiful autumn day. It was in the peak of the season and trees boasted the fiery colors of fall foliage. The limbs of the trees reached above the houses and from their twigs burst forth vibrant hues of the warm end of the rainbow's spectrum. A sea of oranges, reds and yellows lined the sleepy streets of one suburb, being the most attractive aspect of the mechanical conformity of homeowner housing. Generic abodes sprawled for miles with nearly identical floor plans, brown-tiled roofs and wooden walls painted in shades of white. Garages were strategically built into the houses so that the houses' residents could pull in and close the door behind them to protect themselves from a conversation or mere friendly greeting from their neighbors.

The local elementary school's bell rang. A single school bus sat before the school, leading a convoy of shiny sports utility vehicles and sedans. Children spilled from the cinder block walls of the school, racing to the bus, impatiently waiting parent or crosswalk to be led across the street by a guard dressed in a bright orange vest. The nearby high school would let out in half an hour. At that time, the streets would become a chaotic mess of adolescent drivers attempting to impress each other with reckless driving. Naturally, the younger children had to be cleared from the streets before the teenagers stampeded from the doors.

Within the walls of the high school, one seat remained vacant in six separate, overcrowded classes. It was the seat assigned to Judy Rowan, who had been absent that day, leaving one open spot in algebra, biology, English, a seat with friends at lunch, home economics, music and government. She left her house early that morning as usual to meet with a Christian group to pray before school, however she left them to their worship and the teachers to their academics while she took a day off. It was not a day of relaxation and laziness, nor was there an engagement of entertainment or personal desire. Judy now walked quickly back to her home. Her backpack bounced with each rapid step she took. She made her way home, hoping to beat the school bell so that no classmate would see her in transit. Her parents would not be home for two more hours at least.

Judy had a radiant beauty and warm glow to her. She was relatively tall with cream-colored skin. Her soft hair was a light brown and helped to accent her angelic eyes of the same color. They were capped with thin eyebrows and framed by long, striking eyelashes. She was thin and adequately proportioned all about her body. Today she masked her physical beauty with clothing and accessories. A loosely flowing skirt flapped about her quickly moving legs in a flurry of brown, floral print. A black sweater two sizes too large left an unflattering image of her torso. Her hair was tied up and covered by a red scarf and her beautiful eyes hid behind a pair of large, round sunglasses. The most distinctive feature of her conservative wardrobe was a large, golden cross, which bounced on her chest as she hurried home. She would be at her house within minutes, barely enough time to hide away before the high school let out. The entire race home, she was overcome with guilt and prayer to God for forgiveness. The situation of a mere hour ago haunted her mind.

Judy left that morning to deflect concern from her parents by faking an illness. She needed the day off and could not have them believe she needed medical help, thus simply skipped school altogether. The day's plans frightened her enough already. The last thing she needed was a couple of concerned parents. Rather than walking to school, she headed to a nearby park and waited until well after the first class started. Then she began her trek to the main road, away from the vast acreage of housing. In an hour she had reached the main road and saw the long stretch of commercial outlets and churches. Her heart beat harder at seeing this sight. She stopped and stared at the store she sought once reaching it. The drugstore stood there appearing forsaken and frightening in her frenzied state of mind. She trembled in its presence. It had always been a corporate outlet set conveniently in the sleepy suburbs to accommodate the residents with its proximity and services, but now it seemed to be the forbidden spot in paradise.

Judy slowly approached it, not noticing customers moving in and out the doors with ease. A breeze rustled her scarf and she held herself tightly as though the wind's chill had been an omen of misfortunate things to come. She breathed heavily. Her stomach turned sour. Her body shook and shivered. Step by step she approached the entrance, though too terrified to walk in with comfort and confidence. In her mind she could see herself marching through the automatic glass doors, selecting her purchase and laying it down before the clerk, then returning home and it would all be over. However, in reality, it was anything but an easy task. Judy closed her eyes and prayed to God for the strength to enter the drugstore.

She still stood before the store, but had just returned before it. She had left the spot earlier, too frightened to enter and walked away to mentally motivate herself to enter. Now she paced before the store, peering in through the glass doors hoping to get a good evaluation of the place. Judy had been around the building for nearly two hours, too nervous to enter. She still tried to ease herself into entering, but so many scenarios and questions came to mind. What if she saw someone she knew? What if word of this got out? What if her parents found out about this? Is this a test from God? The

Almighty had been such an important factor in her life, yet she was desperate for guidance and found none from above. If only she could talk to the church's youth minister to interpret the word for her. She was unsure if this was a test or in the end what God would want her to do. It had become quite frustrating, but she maintained her faith.

Judy realized that she had been here for too long. It was essential that she proceed. If she spent only five minutes inside and took the hour long walk home, she would still have over an hour before the high school let out. Surely some friends from the Christian group would come to her door, concerned as to why she had not been at the morning prayer. She took a deep breath and dashed for the front doors.

The automatic doors opened and Judy flung herself inside. She stopped and froze, closely looking around for anyone she knew, unaware of how ridiculous and suspicious she actually looked. There were only a few shoppers and the cashier paid no attention to her. Judy moved toward the aisles to begin shopping. She started at one end and scanned the aisles as she moved to the other end of the store. The first aisle had only cosmetics. The wall was lined with nail polishes, lipsticks and eyeliners while the facing side of Aisle 1 bore powders. It was a sea of reds, browns, purples, blues and all other colors to paint the face. The next row was home to hair care products with shampoos, conditioners and dyes filling the shelves. Judy moved on to see a row of dental care followed by first aid, then a combination of soaps and lotions in the next. Her heart beat faster as she eliminated each aisle and closed in on the product she needed.

Judy then came upon an aisle of laxatives and anti-diarrheals, followed by an aisle of feminine hygiene and contraceptives. She stopped at the next row. It was stationery and the remaining aisles were simple medicines and snacks. She slowly walked back and looked at the previous two rows. It had never occurred to her before, though she had been in this store several times before today, but the most embarrassing goods on sale were lumped together in two consecutive aisles.

Judy stood back, narrowing down her search in her mind. It would have to be with the feminine hygiene and contraceptives. She walked down the aisle with medicines for the stomach and bowels, hoping to peer over the shelves onto the other aisle. She passed antacids and a range of laxatives of all sorts of brands, generic and name brand, powdered, capsulated and liquid, but paid little attention to them. She focused instead on the next aisle, hoping to find what she needed from the comfort of standing before medicines to relieve constipation. She could not see everything though and shuffled to her left to scan the opposite aisle. She came across the bulky package of adult diapers, which startled her as it appeared right before her face after the row of laxatives. When she realized what it was she was now facing, she blushed. She left the aisle and circled around to the drugstore's monument to safe sex.

Judy's eyes darted up and down, trying to find her item in the shelves, searching hard in this row for her objective. Then Judy came to a large wall of condoms. She had known of them, but did not know there was such a variety. So many brands hung from the racks on little plastic hangers and came in a great palette of colors. Although she was ignorant on how a person used them, Judy knew these were for sex, which made her more embarrassed. Her face grew red and a surge of heat came over her. She dashed out of the aisle, but still wondered what use condoms were and what the terminology on the boxes meant. For what exactly was "lubricated" and "ribbed" used? Perhaps if condoms were truly important they would have discussed the matter in school or church.

Finally, Judy walked around through the stationery aisle and around to the other side of the row, with the prophylactic devices at a safer distance. The linoleum floor was colored by the light reflecting off the packages. Though white throughout the drugstore, the floor here appeared pink and blue from the glaring glow of fluorescent light on plastic. Judy cautiously crept along as though a creature were lying in wait for her behind the tampons. She wondered how some girls used those. She had only used the pad equivalent. Out the corner of her eye, Judy caught a glimpse of what she had been searching for all day. Just seeing it made her heart burn in fear. It was surprising that something that small made her feel so scared. It was a home pregnancy test. With her eyes fixed on the box, she approached it like a cat stalking a bird. Every nerve in her body tingled and she became increasingly nervous.

"Can I help you find anything," a voice blurted out quickly behind her.

Judy sprang like a frightened gazelle and she whipped around with a startled scream. The worker jumped back and put his arms up in defense letting out a little gasp. Judy's breathing became rapid and she clutched her heart. She recognized him instantly. He went to her church, but she was almost sure he had no idea who she was. "You scared me," Judy said. The young man held back laughing, seeing she was clearly embarrassed.

"Sorry," he said, cracking a smile.

"It's okay," said Judy, "but no thank you, I'm fine." She could not smile back, though she tried.

"Just let me know if you need anything," the young man said with a smile. He did not immediately move, which upset Judy. Why would he not just leave? The situation was humiliating enough as it was. She may have disgraced herself in the eyes of God and her family and now this man might realize who she was if he saw past her crude disguise. This could get around her church. It would be so tragic. She wanted to be around other Christians only and such shame could have her cast out to the brutes and whores outside the pure Christian circle.

"No thank you," she said again. "I'm doing just fine." She was unintentionally angry and said her words quite rudely.

"If you say so," the man said snidely. He walked off and then murmured, "you've been here over an hour already. Just get the damn things."

At first Judy was angered, but then glanced down at her watch. She really had been in the store for over an hour. She would have to get the test and get home quickly. She snatched the box and turned toward the cashier. It was the same, sour-faced woman, but still, Judy could not go on. She became frightened again and felt sick to her stomach. She looked about the ceiling, and seeing only a few security cameras, all pointing to other locations, she impulsively stashed the box into her sweater. It rolled down her body and stopped at her waist, where the sweater had been tucked into the long skirt. Judy walked quickly for the door, the cashier did not even bid her a goodbye, then she set a fast pace for her home.

This was the incident of only a short time ago. The repetitive images of the day and feelings of guilt scrambled all other thoughts. She could not believe that she had been so quick to steal something. It was something she needed. Would God punish the poor for stealing food? Theft was a direct violation of Mosaic law, but to what degree? Was stealing a damnable offense to God under such circumstances? Perhaps stealing for desire or greed is what this particular Commandment meant. However, the scripture stated stealing in the vaguest sense. Had someone she had known seen her question her maternal status, she and her family would be frowned upon in the church. Judy figured God had let her steal the pregnancy test as she needed it and wanted her to continue going to church each Sunday as she always had before. Judy smiled, relieved by the logic and clutched the shiny cross about her neck.

She reached her house and fumbled with the keys. By her watch, the high school had let out three minutes ago. Surely her friends would flock to her house, because she missed the prayer that morning. Judy hoped they would not. She hoped they would not come to her door and barge into her privacy, simply for not coming to worship God. She knew they would, however. Her only hope was to ignore them.

Judy opened the door and entered her house, pivoting around to slam and lock the door. She ran up the stairs, tripping once, but quickly regained her footing. She ran into her private bathroom and slammed that door as well, just in case one of her parents was to come home early. Clumsily she attempted to unzip her backpack. In her frenzied state, Judy had trouble opening the bag. After clearing the drugstore, she removed the pregnancy test from her sweater and put it into her bag. Blood seemed to gush from her heart every which way as it beat, sending wave after wave through her veins. At last she opened the backpack and pulled out the box. The bag fell to the floor with a thud as the books slammed onto the tiles. She held the pregnancy test in both her hands before her face. The trembles in her limbs stopped. The fear and guilt left her. All was silent as she stared at the box. She gazed at it as though looking into a tiger's eyes. The contents within would determine her fate at her young age. Slowly Judy opened the box and prepared to administer the test. Meanwhile, a small group of her friends set their course for Judy's house and would arrive within minutes.

Judy stared at the stick intensely, impatiently awaiting the indicating mark. The air became tense. She had to remind herself to breathe. Her hands indicated her anxiety as she watched the stick, drumming the counter with her fingers. She bit her nails, nearly tearing them off. Then she put her fingers back to the counter to drum some more. She hoped for a negative result. The climax seemed so distant though the instructions stated to wait a mere minute and a half. It was unbearable. So much concentration had been put into hopes of not having a child that she gave no consideration to any plans with the baby if the unfortunate were to happen.

Judy screamed and clutched her chest. The ringing of the doorbell sliced through the thick tension in the bathroom like a machete through jungle foliage. She panted and tried to calm herself. The bell rang again. She knew exactly who it was. Her friends had come in fear of her well-being. Judy knew their reason for concern. She had a perfect record of attendance in all her years of high school. Though her friends were loyal, today she wanted only peace and freedom from human contact, at least until the test confirmed that she was not a mother, which she was fairly confident she was not.

She relented to compassion toward her friends and walked down to the front door. Perhaps it would do her good to get away from the test. Surely it would be ready by the time she finished talking with them. She could see the four young women through the glass still standing there awaiting an answer. Judy unlocked and opened the door slowly. Before her eyes, four of Judy's friends stood, each with an expression of concern. On the left was Linda, a girl with puffy blonde hair and a face of utter despondence. Her makeup always appeared as if she had been crying. Next to Linda stood Sandra. She was a large girl and all the world's sadness loomed in her eyes. Joan stood next to her. She had jet black hair and pallid skin. Joan always seemed nervous and spoke in the same way a rat runs through a maze, coming to dead ends, backtracking and taking an alternate path. On the right stood Anna. Though worry was present in her eyes, her face maintained an eternal grin. It was large and toothy, with an eeriness like a joker on a playing card. Likewise, it was often misleading.

"How are you feeling?" Sandra asked in her soft voice.

Before Judy could answer, Joan cut in, "we missed you at the prayer at the flagpole this morning."

"I'm fine," Judy said slowly. She tried to think of an excuse quickly, her mind trying to separate from the pregnancy test, still processing results upstairs. "I just need a day off, that's all."

"Ah," Anna said with a wink. "Just wanted to start the fun early. Didn't you?" Judy looked at her with a confused gaze. "Don't tell me you forgot already. Remember? Your parents? Their little getaway? Our sleep-over tonight? We've been planning it for weeks now." It all came back to Judy. In the bewilderment and panic of the uncertainty regarding the potential pregnancy she had forgotten about this particular weekend. Her parents must have left between the time she left that morning and when she got home. They had gone to a marriage retreat sponsored by their church, as they needed a bit of counseling. Judy proposed a sleep-over for that very night.

"Oh yeah," Judy said. "No, I didn't forget. All this stress with my parents... you know." She bit her lower lip hoping that explanation would suffice.

"It's okay," Linda said with a sigh. She attempted to smile, but could barely crack one. Neither Judy nor any of her friends had ever seen Linda smile. It raised concerns that she was suffering from depression. None took it too seriously, however, as Linda was a devout Christian, with a potential network of friends in church. With her faith and love in God, it would be impossible to be depressed. The other girls all knew that no Christian could be depressed, as they had the comfort of knowing they would someday die. That day they would go to Heaven.

"Well," Sandra said, "we just thought we should check in on you. We'll get going and come back tonight, unless you want us to stay." There was an intimation of hope in the latter part of her statement.

"No," Judy said, "I'll get things ready here. You guys go on and get ready. I'll see you tonight though."

"Okay," said Anna, still bearing that large smile of hers. "Maybe I'll invite some boys. I can always try to get Josh over here tonight." The girls all laughed. All except Judy, who became unsettled further by that remark. "Well," Anna said, "we should get going. See you tonight."

Judy had become instantly distant. "Bye," she said after the girls had walked off. Her eyes fixed into a stare as she closed the door. The physical images of the real world blurred and faded in her vision. Her intense gaze shifted from the entryway of her house to the skeleton in her closet. She looked into her own mind. The memory of a night just two months ago overtook her vision. She became locked in a trance. Everything from that fateful night that plagued her for two long months came to her now. It was overbearing and at that moment, Judy sank deep into thought and to the shameful experience that brought her to this point today.

Anna convinced Judy and the other three girls to a party. Naturally, Judy saw no harm in it as the attendees would all be people from their church. She had faith in God and faith in the faithful that it would be harmless fun and interaction with more people much like her. However, as the party grew bigger, greater numbers of sin appeared. Judy was tempted to leave, but there were people from her church and she did not want it believed that she had to run from the party in fear. So she sat on the couch, not talking to anyone.

Soon her eyes locked onto a boy across the room. She could not take her eyes off him. He was an attractive specimen of the other gender. On the whole he was thin, but Judy could see well-developed muscles in his chest and arms. He had short, dark brown hair and a face so finely chiseled, it paled any sculpted artifact from the world's finest museums. He stood just over six feet tall. His eyes were a piercing green. All others at the party disappeared from Judy's sight. This young man was surely a trophy buck for any female hunter. A smirk came upon her face, followed by a bashful smile as carnal thoughts entered her mind. She caught herself and shook her head to purge such impurities. Surely that was a sin in the eyes of God she thought. But she questioned the vulgarity of it. If not for such thoughts, how would mankind thrive and continue to populate the planet?

The young man looked over toward her and Judy diverted

her eyes, afraid he saw her. She hoped he had not caught her gawking, but deep inside she knew he had. She glimpsed upward again to see if he was still looking and the two locked eyes. Judy smiled again, baring her row of lily-white, perfectly straight teeth behind her glistening red lipstick. She closed her eyes and turned her head away, embarrassed. She was tempted to look over again, but before she could, the young man now stood before her with two cups in his hand.

"Hi," he said with an irresistible smile, "my name's Josh. What's yours?"

She blushed and replied shyly, "Judy."

He smiled back at her. It was a sexy smile, one that made her heart flutter like butterfly wings. "Hi Judy. I got you a drink," he said extending his hand, bearing a red plastic cup. Judy took it and thanked him. She looked into the cup and saw the dark color of cola with clear cubes of ice and small bubbles clinging to the sides. She was flattered that he had shown her this attention. She was quite thirsty and too shy to get something for herself. Her other friends were nowhere to be found. Judy sipped the drink, then slowly pulled her head away and gulped noisily. She looked at the drink disgustedly.

"I think this coke is bad," she said looking into the cup. Josh was drinking it next to her and did not seem to mind its odd taste. "I mean," she said, "it has some strong flavor in it that doesn't taste like coke. Is this some weird brand or something?"

"No," Josh said laughing, "there's some rum in it."

Judy frowned. "I thought you were a Christian," she said disappointedly.

"I am," he said. "I was invited here through friends at church. I'm a good Christian too." He took a swig of the drink.

Judy felt upset. "But drinking is a sin. They taught us that in Sunday school."

Josh laughed. "No way. Drinking can't be a sin." Judy

looked puzzled and the expression on her face demanded an answer without her verbally asking. "Look," Josh said to placate her concern, "they say that because they don't want us drinking too much, too often. I mean think of it this way: if drinking were a sin, why did Jesus do it? "Judy did not answer, but contemplated his logic. Josh continued, "don't forget the 'water into wine' miracle or the wine at the Last Supper. That's not to mention communion either. You know? They say drinking wine becomes the blood of Christ and they do this at services." Josh watched her, waiting for her decision. Judy realized that it made sense. If Jesus lived his life without sin, surely a little alcohol was permissible. The church and communion promote drinking wine, as it became the blood of Christ. In that regard, it almost seemed ghoulish and vampiric as well. Perhaps he was right.

"I guess you're right," Judy said and took another drink.

A couple hours later Judy had consumed more than enough alcohol. Her speech slurred when she spoke and her motor skills had been severely hindered. She was a mere shadow of her sober self now. Josh had a winning combination of pacing himself better and a higher tolerance of alcohol. Judy was slumped over and her eyes were closed. She was quickly falling asleep. At that instant, Anna appeared again after her long absence and approached Josh and the most inebriated Judy. "Looks like she had a good time," Anna said grinning, her eyes half-opened. She had also imbibed plenty of booze.

"Yeah," Josh said looking over at Judy. "I guess she's just not used to drinking."

"Probably not," Anna said. "She needed to loosen up a little though. She always has such a big stick up her ass." Anna sipped the drink in her hand and then said to Josh, "how's she going to get home? I don't want her puking in my car."

Josh said, "I'll take her home. She's a good girl. I don't want something happening to her. You know how people can be. Drunks."

"Well, whatever," Anna said. "Watch out for her parents though. They're going to kill her when they see her like this." Then she abruptly walked away.

Judy moaned and adjusted her position on the couch. Josh shook her arm, "you all right?" Judy just grunted and did not open her eyes. The world was spinning and she felt nauseated. "Come on," he said standing up, "let's get you out of here." He pulled Judy to her feet and she whined. "Let's go. I'll take you home. Can you tell me where you live?"

It was nearly 3 AM when Josh pulled up in front of Judy's house. He took her to a greasy fast food restaurant to help her sober up. Fortunately for the interior of Josh's car, Judy had not vomited. "Here we are," he said. Judy was half asleep. Josh had been trying to keep her awake. "We need to get you inside into your bed." Judy rolled her head toward the driver's seat and slowly opened her eyes. She could see the figure of the beautiful man, but could not focus on him. There seemed to be two of him now.

"Thank you for bringing me here," she murmured. "It's sweet of you."

Josh smiled at her. "Are you going to be okay?"

"I'll be fine," she said flirtatiously. "I just need to get upstairs and into bed."

"Do you need help?"

"Well, you can come in if you like. My parents should be sleeping." Judy giggled. "I told them I had to study for a big test and might be late."

The two got out of the car. Judy stumbled and fell, but caught herself. She jumped up before Josh could see her fumble. He came to her side and they walked hand-in-hand to the door. Judy walked side-to-side like a crab, still highly drunk. She dug through her small purse, searching for her keys. She pushed a miniature New Testament out of the way and pulled out her keys. She struggled to unlock the door, even with the bright porch light left on by her parents. Josh smiled and took the keys, unlocking the door with ease. He held the door open for his lady and put his hand on her back, guiding her into the house. They walked upstairs to her room. Judy sighed. Through the blurry haze of drunkenness she had a battle between morality and desire.

"Well," Josh said, "I should get home. But I had a great time with you tonight."

"No goodbye kiss?" Judy said with her head cocked slightly and with a seductive look glowing on her face.

"Maybe one," he said. "But as we discussed at the party, we're both good Christians. We'll draw the line there." Josh walked over to her, knelt down to the young woman on the bed and gave her a warm, passionate kiss. Both their mouths tasted of liquor, but neither cared. Judy felt so alive within and for the first time, infatuated giddiness. The two parted lips and looked each other in the eye. "I'll talk to you later," he said. "You should get to sleep now. Maybe I'll see you at church."

"Okay," Judy said smiling. She leaned over and put her head on the pillow. She closed her eyes and smiling said, "good night."

Josh paused and replied, "good night. Sweet dreams." He turned the lamp off on his way out of her room and quietly shut the door. Lying on the bed, Judy's head spun. Part was the alcohol swimming through her blood, part was fantasy floating through her head. She thought of Josh and how wonderful she felt at the moment. She thought of Anna and how glad she was to have her as a friend. It was Anna, after all, who convinced her to go to the party. The pleasant thoughts soon gave way to sleep. The alcohol defeated Judy, sending her to sleep soundly with a smile on her face.

As Judy slept, her door opened quietly. An arm extended into the room, feeling around in the darkness. It caressed the lamp and glided to the switch. The light clicked on, illuminating the dark room. Josh stood there, having not left. Judy slept still, unawakened by the light. He looked upon the beauty asleep in her bed. The divine powers of Bacchus had overpowered her, leaving her soundly asleep and defenseless. Josh bit his bottom lip and stared at her eagerly. He moved toward her, slithering upon his feet and moving in toward his prey like a feral predator. He knelt down and kissed her cheek. Judy remained motionless. He jiggled her hard and still she slept. Josh moved toward her waist and unfastened her jeans. He grabbed their sides at the hips and pulled them down. Judy grunted and her eyes opened. She took a deep breath and closed her eyes again. Josh stood up and unzipped his pants. He lay on top of Judy and covered her mouth, proceeding to rape the young woman.

After awhile, Judy noticed strange differences from her normal life. She tried to put the pieces of the puzzle together, reflecting back to the night of that party. Eventually she came to the conclusion that because of the alcohol, she had given herself over to Josh. She was ashamed, but she could not remember everything, only isolated parts of the night. She cried and prayed to God for forgiveness. She consented to intercourse out of wedlock. Hopefully it would get no worse. Perhaps the sickness she felt was a punishment from God for doing such a thing.

Judy wiped tears from her eyes, which poured down her face. The pregnancy test had given a positive result. The instructions claimed the test was 99% accurate and in the event of a positive reading, she should consult a doctor to verify. Hope faded fast though. She wanted that small margin of error in her favor. She hoped it was a defective kit. In her panicked state, she could only hope. She had been crying for twenty minutes now and logic began settling in. Odds were against her that the test was wrong. There were now two challenges before her now. First was what to do with her child. The second obstacle was getting through the night without this getting to her friends, for she knew this would consume her mind and feed on her emotions for quite some time to come.

Later that night, the top floor of her house smelled of pizza and a romantic movie flickered on the television screen, casting a pale blue light throughout the room. The floor was a huddled mess of blankets, quilts and comforters. The girls sat and talked, only partly paying attention to the movie. Judy had been rather quiet this evening. Her maternal state festered in her mind, feasting upon it like maggots on carrion. She felt sick and had forced herself to eat a few slices of pizza. Sandra had devoured an entire pie alone and the other girls managed to reduce the three they ordered into four pieces of leftovers. Judy noticed her hands had been shaking and placed them between her legs to hide them from her friends. Luckily it had been dark and for the most part, her friends seemed oblivious.

Judy's thoughts drowned out her friends and the movie as she sat hypnotized by the nagging voice in her head. She now needed a form of release. She had to vent this out somehow. She knew she could not just admit to being with child and needed guidance as to what she should do with it. If only there were some way that she could ask her friends. It must be inconspicuous and must not raise suspicion in the least. She thought harder. How could she go about asking for advice on this issue?

"Well, what do you think?" Sandra said shaking Judy's shoulder.

Judy snapped free of her trance and said, startled, "about what?"

"Hello," Anna said snidely, "about what the Christian Club should do to help save the school." The Christian Club was merely an external club, though it was large in number and stronger backed by supportive, tax-paying parents. The club had to meet after school on Wednesdays off campus, though they met around the flagpole each morning to pray.

In recent weeks, circumstances arose and the Christian Club decided to step in and urge the school to take action against these programs. One such case was a pending government issue at the state capitol. Abstinence only sex education was being challenged. Judy was not quite sure what this issue meant, but supported teaching abstinence only in school as the rest of the Christian Club supported it. Surely they would know what God would want, thus Judy would follow their opinion and support teaching abstinence as the only method of sex education.

Similarly, the child development classes offered daycare services. A few were children of some students. The club felt the school should in no way offer support for teenage pregnancy. This alleviated the students' mistakes, but the club felt a child born out of wedlock should not be given such support, only the parents should provide, even if it meant dropping out of school. The club also rallied against a forming club on campus. Several of the braver students petitioned and pushed for the school's first club for gay and lesbian students. They felt gays and lesbians should have a place to make friends and find support. The Christian Club, however, was in a fierce battle with the school, claiming this club would be a way for gays and lesbians to have sex on campus and would promote this sort of lifestyle. The list went on, fighting the library for carrying some controversial books while not allowing the Bible, the science department for teaching evolution as a theory and various other extracurricular activities they considered to be undesirable.

"I don't know," Judy said. She thought about the school's daycare and the abstinence only controversy. If only she knew what the latter meant. "Maybe we should talk to some of these people. You know? I think we should hear their side of things."

The other girls were quiet. Their jaws hung loosely in shock and they stared at Judy blankly. "How could you?" Anna asked. "These people are totally against our Lord and challenge our way of life. They want to destroy our values. We can't have our club in school because of those kinds of people. If good Christians like us can't have a club in school, why should they? And why should they promote bad lifestyles?"

Judy looked at her and replied, "but the school lets us pray before classes. Isn't that enough? Why don't we just leave them alone? We can believe what we want."

"Because," Linda said shocked, "they're not normal." Anna looked over at Linda, then back at Judy with that trademark grin of hers.

"That's right," said Sandra.

"What about 'love the sinner, hate the sin?' I know you've heard that before," Judy said.

"Oh screw that," Anna barked. "It's all their poor choices anyway."

"I don't know," Judy said sheepishly. Then it hit her. This was her chance to get the advice she sought. "Take these teen mothers though. What if one were raped, or the boyfriend ran out on her, or she was forced to a party she didn't want to go to in the first place and got drunk and couldn't control herself?" Judy stopped herself there. She was becoming too heated, but she realized the truth and bias was coming into her argument.

"First thing," Sandra began, counting her rebuttal on her fingers, "if a boyfriend ran out on her it would still likely be born out of marriage. What guy our age would stick around for that? Second of all, drunkenness is a sin, you should know that. Besides a girl should still be able to control herself. Third, why should they be in our school? They messed up, not us. It should be their responsibility, not ours. All in all, a child not born between a husband and wife is a sin. You should know that. There are other options you know."

Judy whispered, "you mean like abortion?"

The girls gasped and recoiled like vipers darting back before they struck. "No," Linda said disgustedly, "adoption."

"What if the girl doesn't want it?" Judy asked. "What if it would ruin the girl's life to carry it to term? What should she do then?"

The girls were quiet. "Beg God for forgiveness." Anna said at last. "What else can she do? People would be right to look down on that slut. An abortion is murder too. The best she can do is either care for that bastard child herself or give it up for adoption. That pregnancy *should* embarrass her. If God forgives her, that embarrassment would be a small price to pay to get into Heaven."

Judy was hurt by that remark. She remembered once hearing an argument for abortion that she decided to bring into the debate. "But about abortion, don't they issue a certificate of live birth, not conception? I mean, that says it's not a baby until it's born." All other pro-choice arguments were unknown to Judy, besides, of course, rape and loss of inhibitions.

"Whatever," Anna hissed, "listen to that whole Roe vs. Wade thing if you want. The government and good morals are two different things. Who else do you want to defend? Those gay perverts? Those anti-God science lessons? Think we should hear about evolution and their way of thinking how the universe was created? I can't believe you Judy."

Deep into the night, Linda, Sandra and Anna slept. Judy could only stare out the window as she sat on a chair in a separate room. She rested her chin on her palm, with her elbow on the windowsill. The pale moonlight colored her face the eerie blue shade of night. She felt hurt and betrayed by her friends. She felt as if they were against her. Maybe God too was against her. She thought He loved all His creations, yet her stray from the flock and her unborn child were both apparently atrocities in the eyes of God. She thought hard for the best moral option, hoping for the chance of redemption. Religion aside, she came to the impending reality. She was pregnant. In months to come her stomach would swell with the fetus as it gestated inside her. Eventually she would grow so big, no larger-sized bit of clothing would conceal her shame.

In roughly eight months she would be a teenage mother. It was ironic. For so long she degraded these mothers, dismissing them as strumpets. The Christian Club resented the school's daycare support of these bastard children. Most of all, she worried about how she would be viewed by her fellow members in the Christian Club and in the church. She had to get rid of the baby. She thought about carrying it to term and giving it up for adoption, but still, it would soon become obvious that she was pregnant. She looked away from the moonlit homes of suburbia spreading across the landscape and caught a glimpse of the portrait of Christ on the wall. She moaned, wanting everything to be normal again. If only her Savior would come to her and give her the advice she needed. If only her sweet, forgiving Lord would help her in this time of need. Then it hit her. It all became so clear. She knew what to do. She ran to the portrait and kissed it, then scurried to her room where all the girls were sleeping. She crawled under a pile of the bedding on her floor and soon fell asleep, smiling.

The next morning the girls awoke one by one. Downstairs, in the kitchen, a makeshift breakfast took form. Judy was the first to awake and began the morning feast. She poured herself a glass of orange juice and fixed a bowl of sugary cereal. Brightly colored shapes sweetened the milk in her bowl and floated like lily pads of sugar, oats and dye. As the other girls came downstairs, they joined her, each pouring a bowl of cereal accompanied by a breakfast drink. Anna poured the cereal into the bowl, then faced Judy. "Look," Anna said through her groggy demeanor, "I'm sorry for being so rude last night." Judy looked at her curiously. Perhaps it was too early in the morning for that grin to take form.

"Oh," Judy replied, "that's okay. Maybe we shouldn't have

such serious discussions anymore. You know? We can just talk about the usual."

Anna nodded, but said nothing. She wiped the sleep from her eyes and poured milk over her dry cereal. She went to the silverware drawer and fished out a spoon. "Do you have any coffee?"

"No," Judy replied after swallowing her mouthful of food, "my parents don't drink coffee. It's the whole caffeine thing. They say it's too much like illegal drugs because you can get just as hooked on it. I mean, I don't feel the same, but you know how it is." Judy noticed that she had been rambling. She hoped it did not seem too suspicious. The baby in her uterus still sat on her mind.

"Some parents," Anna said with a yawn. Her eyes were barely open. Anna had never liked mornings. She had been awake for half an hour before coming downstairs, but could not get back to sleep. She gave up and joined her friends in the kitchen for breakfast. "By the way, I spoke with Josh yesterday."

Judy choked on her cereal in shock. "What?" she said in a startled way. "What did he say? Did he mention me at all?"

Anna thought for a moment, rolling her eyes to the ceiling, summoning her memory of the conversation. "No, not really. Why? Did you like him? I mean I can see why." She giggled and said, "I can get a hold of him or exchange numbers if you like."

Judy breathed heavily. She wanted to decline the offer, but thought she should at least talk to Josh about the situation. "Can you tell me where he lives? It might be more special if I go to him in person."

"Look at you," Sandra said playfully.

Linda winked, "you got a thing for him?"

Judy said with a face as stolid as stone, "maybe I do."

The girls had all left before noon and Judy showered immediately and dressed herself in pastels. She was now walking to Josh's house. Apparently he lived a mere fifteen-minute walk away from her. She had been thinking of what exactly she wanted to say all morning. She at last reached his street, her heart pounded rapidly. She said over and over again in her mind what she wanted to say to him, visualizing what would happen. She had to apologize for giving herself over and spoiling their plans of virginity until marriage. She had to discuss what she wanted to do with the child. She wanted his support. Deep within, she felt, she knew she still liked him. Thinking about him made her smile.

Judy was extremely nervous when she reached Josh's door. Her hands trembled as she poked the doorbell. The bells resounded inside. She could hear footsteps within as someone came to answer. Through the glass framed in the door, she saw a blurred silhouette approach. The door clicked as the dark figure inside unlocked it. The door opened and before Judy stood a young, fat boy with messy hair and freckles. She was disappointed, as she hoped Josh would be the one to answer. "Um," Judy started, "is Josh here?"

"Just a minute," the boy said. He turned his head and screamed out loud, "Josh! There's some chick at the door for you!"

The scream hurt Judy's ears. She also felt a slight sting of offense being called a "chick" by this repulsive little cretin. He was probably in the seventh or eighth grade. A subtle scowl came to her face as she looked at the boy. Josh came and the boy left. It startled Judy to see him again. Josh jumped when he saw her. "Judy," he said nervously.

She smiled bashfully and said, "surprised?"

The two sat on the stone benches in Josh's backyard. They helped to accent the pond, flowers and shrubbery that decorated the household's yard. The two sat close, though on separate benches. Judy told him she had to talk to him about something important back at the door, though he had been reluctant. Finally, he consented to speak with her in private.

At first, they sat in silence, as Judy thought about what exactly to say. It was odd that she had repeated in her mind what to say on her way here, but her mind blanked upon seeing her beau. Josh sat staring at her intently, studying her, trying to guess what she was going to say. Inside, he knew what the conversation would be about, but had to wait for her to initiate it.

"Look," Judy said at last, "I want to talk to you about what happened after that party."

Josh quickly said defensively, "I'm sorry. I couldn't help it. I thought you were so beautiful. Whatever you do, just don't..."

She interrupted him, "I feel really bad about it. You know? And just yesterday I found out I'm..." Judy stopped. It was too hard to say the rest. Josh developed an instant facial tic. His eyes squinted as though awaiting a swift blow to his face. "Well, Josh, I'm pregnant."

He jumped up and threw his head back, then grabbed the sides of his skull. He let out a big scream. It rose above the fences, rooftops and trees. It rolled out in all directions and ascended to the heavens. It frightened Judy. He looked down at her with seething eyes. "I swear to God if you tell anyone I did that to you, I'll fucking kill you."

"Did what?" Judy said confused and scared. "Got me pregnant? You know I agreed to... Unless... you mean..."

Before she could finish Josh said, "wait, what did you think happened?"

Judy's eyes were wide and her face was frozen in concern. "I thought I lost control after all that alcohol. I thought I did something I shouldn't have."

"Oh," Josh said, a sudden change in his emotions instantly showed. "Well, what I meant was it could look bad that we both did that. You know, like at church and stuff? By doing that to you, I meant getting you pregnant. That's all." He looked at her, his eyes saying he hoped she believed him.

It became so clear to Judy. She was horrified. She had to ask him for confirmation. "No, I didn't, did I? I didn't agree to have sex with you, I mean. Josh, did you rape me?" He looked away from her. "You did! You raped me!"

Josh's lips curled to an angry frown. His face grew red. "Yes," he hissed angrily, "I did. There. Are you happy now? I raped you."

"I can't believe you," Judy said quietly. She jumped off the bench and ran away sobbing. Josh remained seated and watched her leave. Judy ran all the way home. Small droplets of tears filled her eyes, until she made it home. Then she cried with a deluge of salty tears, allowing them to flood down her face, rivaling the destructive force of nature. She had lost her virginity through rape. She was crushed. Judy had always dreamt of finding the perfect man to whom she could give the right of passage. How could this happen to her? How could she have been raped and impregnated by this violator? How could God let this happen to her? She dedicated her life to God and this happened. She felt sick. She ran to the bathroom and promptly vomited.

She lay sprawled on the sofa, tears pouring continuously out her eyes. She turned the television on, but barely paid attention to it. Her eyes remained fixed on the floor as guilt, resent and shameful thoughts raced through her mind. She was confused. Likewise she felt betrayed. A Christian man had done this to her and God let it happen. At the slumber party the previous night it crossed her mind and settled in as a final decision. Judy's meeting with Josh confirmed it. Looking at the portrait of her forgiving Savior with his sad eyes inspired her to her decision about the child. She first wanted to speak with Josh, but now thought otherwise. She was going to have an abortion.

The news came on and Judy glimpsed at the screen. The local celebrities that were the station's newscasters sat at their desk in the studio. Behind them, a backdrop of the city's skyline with the station's logo hovering in the sky helped to add flair to the set. A short melody sounded and letters scrolled across the screen to remind viewers what channel they were watching and add to the sensationalism of televised news. They announced the stories of the program in mere seconds, letting the local audience know what to expect. At first it appeared to be an ordinary day in America. A major retailer was robbed and violent crime continued to trek to the suburbs. As usual, the area's residents were shocked it happened there. People were conned by their fellow man and many were put to death on the streets. Scenes of police caution tape flashed on the screen with almost every story. State government issues were to be covered and a shocking incident in a public school were in store for the audience on today's grisly episode of life captured on film.

"Thanks for joining us this afternoon, I'm Kate Winslow," the blonde newscaster stated. She had a smile with brightly shining teeth, haloed by her lips painted ruby. Her face was colored in designer cosmetics, which highlighted her natural features and masked her true age. "All these stories, plus your local weather and sports. But first, a followup on Thursday's event. Local officials met with experts today to investigate the explosion at the mosque. We've got Gary Fuller on the scene with more."

The news caught Judy's attention. She had been so caught up in her personal problem that she had heard nothing of this news. For this moment, she forgot about the events in her life as she stared in horror at the television screen. The broadcast showed images of the ruins. The mosque had been reduced to ashes and only a charred skeleton of the building stood in its place. Through the ghastly images of authorities at the scene and closeups of the devastation, Judy heard Kate say, "explosion," "possible hate crime," "no survivors" and "likely arson." It was chilling to think this happened in her own city.

Kate turned the attention from herself to the reporter

in the field. Gary Fuller stood there stolid and without expression. He wore a blue dress shirt. His short, blonde hair waved in the breeze. His eyes squinted in the sunlight. There were blurred figures behind him. They were from various departments of law enforcement and government agencies. The man spoke, but Judy could hardly listen, captivated by the images broadcast into her living room. The pregnancy, rape and deaths of so many innocent people beset her. She could barely think and it became hard to concentrate on any one thing. She had been told by others that Muslims were not as good as Christians, and others still dismissed them as evil, yet she learned in school that God and Allah were the same, but the practices of the religions were different. In the end, Judy saw the big picture. She had always just blocked the thought and never sought to contemplate it. Now it seemed to be put into perspective. These were human beings and this was a tragic loss of human life. It did not seem to matter what their religion was. Suddenly, an epiphany came to Judy. Her problem was inconsequential in relation to this. She found herself questioning God all day. Was that so wrong? She had always been taught to just accept the strange workings of God and understand he has a plan, be it her unplanned pregnancy or the death of so many innocent people. She was raised strictly Christian and felt uncomfortable asking such things. She tried to stop, but it was hard. It seemed more and more like He did not exist, or had a twisted sense of humor.

Judy sped along the freeway. She was free to use the family's vehicles at any time, as she had her parents' trust. They took the high-priced German import they drive to the weekend retreat. On a subconscious level they had to flaunt their affluent ability and wealth to the other members of the church with marital issues. Judy now drove the other car, which was a behemoth on the streets. The family chose a sports utility vehicle, though they had a mere three people in the house. Like its European counterpart, it served its purpose of getting from one point to another. It was also to show their sense of conformity, while the German automobile was to set their status above the rest.

It mattered little to Judy now. She wanted any form of transport. She was on a mission. After a search through the phonebook and a map search on the internet she was on her way. Traffic was moderate and Judy breezed through the cars. Normally she was a safe driver, but today she was nervous, impatient and determined. "Move it," she screamed at a car moving only slightly over the speed limit. She honked her horn and swerved over to the next lane, nearly hitting an approaching car. There was a screech as they hit their brakes. The car honked at Judy. Her heart pounded. She was more nervous because of the traffic and she was moving into a part of town with which she was not familiar. The neighborhoods around the freeway passed her quickly and she did not notice the deteriorating buildings in these neglected parts.

Judy found her exit and pulled off the freeway. She pulled up behind the cars waiting for the light to signal them to the street. She swore she was supposed to turn left, but looked at the directions she scribbled down on a piece of paper. It was confirmed. She had to go left. Now she had to go roughly six miles to her destination. The light turned green and the off-ramp emptied as cars turned onto the road. Judy's heart beat faster as she neared her goal. Christian choir music played on the vehicular CD player, but Judy paid no attention. She awaited her intersection and drove more slowly now, fearing she would pass it. The road seemed to be endless and traffic was noticeably heavier on the street than the freeway. From her high-vantage point in this massive SUV she saw the traffic light ahead, though it was too far to see which street it was. She thought she would drive forever. Judy still loved God and throughout her journey she begged for forgiveness for doubting his existence and begged for more in advance of her inevitable future sin.

It felt as though her heart exploded when she reached

Third Street, her intersection to watch for, as she needed to be in a block of businesses just after the light. She caught glimpse of the place's name positioned over the entrance. The wheels made a loud screech as she turned sharply into the parking lot. An oncoming car barely missed her. Judy parked the car abruptly, jolting the vehicle. Loose objects in the back fell forward. Judy turned the engine off and sighed. She looked up at the sign and read it with a shudder: Planned Parenthood.

She sighed again. For so long she had been taught to hate these people. Members of the congregation had dubbed these people "baby killers" and aids to sexual promiscuity. Now she found herself at their mercy. Of course, she made this decision before her discussion with Josh that morning, provided he would not help her with the child. She was inspired by the forgiving gaze of her Lord on canvas. If she were to get an abortion, murder or not, she would be forgiven. Despite the manipulation of theological logic that had led to this moment, the uncertain nag of guilt tugged at Judy's mind and heart. She had to go through with this. Her eyes still fixed on the sign, Judy opened the door of the mighty SUV.

She jumped out and closed the door. Keys in hand she pushed the alarm button. There was a click, the doors locked and the headlights flashed twice. The car seemed safe now in this neighborhood. The ambience gave Judy a shiver. Planned Parenthood shared this lot with a tattoo parlor, bartending academy, Middle Eastern imported sundries and a small pizza parlor. It was like being at the drugstore again. It was hard to believe that was just yesterday morning. Judy wondered if they were open. It was hard to tell from this distance. She looked all around her just to make sure no one she recognized was nearby. She took a couple steps slowly forward. She leaned a little to the left to try to peer in the clinic. Judy held herself tightly with her arms to provide comfort.

"What you looking for?" a deep voice behind her asked.

Judy screamed as the tension snapped. She spun around

and pulled her arms up over her chest, as though to keep her heart inside. She looked at the man who spoke to her. He was middle-aged, well dressed and of an average build. He had thinning black hair that looked like a slashed-and-burned prairie. The skin on his face was somewhat weathered and he had small facial features, including his eyes, nose and mouth.

"I'm sorry," he said apologetically, "I didn't mean to frighten you."

"I'm not looking for anything," she said nervously.

"Oh, I doubt that," the man said. "Pardon me for being so bold, but it seems to me like you were looking at that Planned Parenthood over there."

"No," Judy exclaimed. She was frightened. Twice she had protested one of those places. She had heard stories about some Christians who only wanted to protect their pro-life opinions and slaughtered the doctors. Perhaps they did it to the mother too. Judy feared for her life.

"I'm sorry," the man said closing his eyes and putting up one hand, "I'm just observant. The way I see it, you're pregnant and need an abortion, but you're scared to death someone will find out."

Judy was shocked. "How did you, I mean, why do you think that?"

The man chuckled. "For starters, the size of that cross on your neck." He pointed at the golden giant and Judy grasped it. "Second, the way you keep looking around afraid someone you know will drive by and see you go in. I bet you don't even live in this part of town. Am I right?"

Judy looked to the ground. "Yeah, you're right."

"Also," the man said, "you're moving so slow. You're trying to build up the nerve to do it. Well, let me tell you that going in there will be a big mistake." Judy turned around and walked to the SUV, saying nothing. "Wait," the man said. Judy looked at him sadly. He smiled with a friendly and welcoming grin.

"You didn't let me finish. Why don't you let me take you out for a late lunch?"

Somehow, the stranger lured Judy to a nearby restaurant. It was the 24-hour kind that sold breakfast at all hours. The place was filled with morning scents, though it was mid-afternoon. There was the sweet aroma of hot pancakes with the heavy smell of frying bacon. Coffee and hot grease aromas drifted throughout the place. Patrons feasted upon plates of scrambled eggs, hash browns and sausage. A waitress came to the table at which Judy and the stranger sat. She looked worn and miserable, loathing her job and state of her life. She wore a yellow dress with a white apron. Her eyes were only half-open and her mouth drooped in a despondent frown. She had a look of perpetual sadness. She poured a second cup of coffee for the stranger without asking first, dribbled a little on the table and left without saying a word. The stranger opened a small, white packet of sugar and poured in a capsule of cream into the hot beverage, the mixed it with the fork, as the waitress neglected to leave a spoon at the table. Judy had nothing. A glass of water sat before her, but she drank none of it. Condensation formed on the glass and dribbled down, leaving a halo of water around the base of the glass. Judy just frowned with her head hanging limply and waited for the man to discuss his business.

The man took a sip of the steaming coffee and sat the mug down. He smacked his lips and folded his arms on the table, leaned forward and looked at Judy. "Enough small talk," he said smiling, "it's time we get to why I brought you here." Judy raised her head and looked at the man. He spoke again, lowering the volume of his voice, "I know you were hesitating back there for a reason. You need an abortion and you are afraid. As I mentioned before, I have a feeling you don't want it getting out."

"No," Judy said, "I don't. I was hoping if I went there it would be safe. I don't want anyone to find out about this. If it got out in my church or school, I would be ruined."

"Well," he said smiling devilishly, "I'm willing to make you an offer."

"What's that?" Judy asked curiously.

"I can give you an abortion with the utmost confidentiality."

"What do you mean? How do I know that? How can you do that?"

"Well, first of all I'll let you pick where the procedure shall be done. Second, there needs to be no names involved. I don't know your name and don't want to know, nor will I give you mine. I have my own equipment and I can give you a safe and discrete abortion. All I ask is for a little price."

It was certainly tempting. Judy was so afraid that this would be made public that she did not want to go through with it, though in time the pregnancy would be obvious. It was a definite rock and a hard place scenario. Though she was raped, she partook in the sin at the party. She began to realize that it was not the moral obligation, as prescribed by her religion, to carry the child to term, but her fear was to be ostracized by the church and her fellow Christians. She wondered if some would be accepting and realize her stress over this conundrum. She had been told for years that this was murder and that abortion should be condemned. However, things became far different now that she found herself in this predicament. Perhaps this stranger was her only way out of this awful mess. It would be between her, the man and God and no one else would ever know.

"Okay," Judy said. "I'll do it. What's the price?"

The man smiled and said, "$1,000."

"What?" Judy shrieked. Other people in the restaurant turned their heads and looked at the two. Judy suddenly became aware of this and quieted her voice. "Are you crazy? Do you know how much that is?"

"Fine," the man said. "Take the alternative route then." He was getting up and digging for his wallet in his back pocket.

"Boy, you'd hate for that to get out to your friends and family wouldn't..."

Judy thrust her arm across the table and grabbed his arm. "No, wait," she said. "When and where can we do this?"

"That depends on you. Anywhere and anytime you like of course. I'm versatile."

"How about tonight at my place?"

"Sounds good. Why don't you write down your address, and maybe a little map too. I'll be there whenever you want."

"Okay. How about midnight tonight?" Judy searched for a pen. The man pulled one out of his shirt pocket, along with a small pad of paper. He handed it to her, smiling.

"Sounds good to me," he said. "By the way, have the money ready in cash."

Later that night, Judy paced back and forth. She had ten hundred-dollar bills sitting on the table. It was easy for her to come up with the money. Though she had never worked at any job, she had plenty, with a special thanks to her affluent family. This past birthday her grandparents gave her a card with $500 inside. Her grandmother's handwriting read a cursive message inside, "Happy Birthday Judy, we love you very much. Grandma and Grandpa." It made her feel somewhat guilty to spend part of her bill with the gift that bore an attached sentimental message. The other half came from monetary gifts from holidays and birthdays of the past.

Judy looked at the clock on the oven. It was seven minutes until midnight. The house was eerily silent. Her heart pounded as the clock ticked away another minute. It was quite suspenseful. Small beads of sweat formed on her brow. Judy felt dizzy. She felt nauseated. She did not want to go through with this. By tomorrow morning this whole fiasco would be over at last. She wanted the man to arrive. She just wanted the nightmare to end. She wanted the baby out of her. Judy's mind swung like a pendulum. She was so anxious she was about to explode in a manic outburst of tension and emotion. She chewed on her nails. She looked at the clock again. It was now two minutes until midnight.

She huffed and scowled. She was annoyed. She had been ready for hours and wished she asked the man to come earlier. Then she thought a nosy neighbor might spy a strange car before her house, thus she requested him to come to this sleepy community at such a late hour. Regardless, she thought he could at least come somewhat early. She walked away from the kitchen to the darkened living room. She pulled back the curtain slightly and peered out to the moonlit streets. The sky was cloudless and the moon was almost full. The moon's light blocked all the weak stars from shining to Earth. Suddenly a pair of headlights came down her street. Judy's heart skipped a beat and a pulse of terror surged through her body. She froze and watched the car. It was moving slowly, but passed her house and continued around the corner. Judy growled angrily and stormed back to the kitchen.

It was now after midnight. This man never came. Judy regretted that she could not get his name. Likewise he did not know hers. Of course it would be better this way, as he recommended earlier. Judy sat down and drummed her fingers. She stood up several seconds later and continued pacing. She tugged at her hair and rubbed her hand down her face. It was unbearable. She debated going to bed, assuming he would never show, but there was no way she could get to sleep at this point. She would only lie awake in bed wondering.

Her anxiety preyed on her like wolves. It feasted on her mind. Grim fantasies quickly became comforting hopes. Once the child was purged from her womb she could continue her life as normal. No one from the Christian Club or church would ever know. It would be between her and God. If only people were more sympathetic to the issue. She would be looked down upon for carrying a child out of wedlock and she would be loathed and excommunicated for the abortion. She knew she could give the infant to a foster home, but the pregnancy alone would be the source of shame and embarrassment on top of physical stress to her body. She realized at this point how many times these same thoughts came to her head. Soon it would be over.

She paced like a frustrated tiger in a cage and broke her path when she stopped to check the clock in the kitchen. In the darkness of the room, the digital numbers glowed powerfully in turquoise. It was now nearly 12:30 and her shining grace had yet to arrive. She groaned in annoyance. She returned to the living room and plopped into the large chair, sinking into its soft cushion. She stood up again seconds later and looked out the window. The man still had not arrived. Judy began to walk in a great circle around the room and gradually spiraled inward, making her turns tighter. Her path was as a trek into a vortex, slowly sinking into an abysmal beyond.

Before completing her spiral she heard the faint purr of a motor outside her house. She froze as the engine stopped. Moments later the thud of a car door resounded. Judy's heart leapt to her throat and a weight settled in her stomach. Her knees shook violently. It was the most frightened she had ever been. She wanted to check through the window, but her legs would not cooperate. A surge of blood filled her head, burning her face and bringing a dull sting to her brain. A silhouette approached the door and the doorbell chimed. Judy stood there in the empty, dark room, motionless and watching.

She stood without moving, lost in fear. The room spun about her in her frenzy of horror. This was the moment she had been waiting for all day. Her legs no longer quivered, nor did any part of her body tremble. She had become still. It was fitting for the tense atmosphere, which had lingered about her throughout the day. The shadow beyond the door appeared in the narrow panes of glass with its figure. It too remained frozen in a menacing pose. Judy stared at its unseen eyes knowing the figure behind the door was for her. It was for her baby. The final doubts and fear flooded her head, testing levees of necessity and future disaster. She needed the abortion and only these three would ever have to know, she reminded herself. The trinity of God, this savior and herself would be bound in secrecy.

The bell rang again and Judy broke from her statuesque mode. She walked to the door and stopped, taking in a deep breath and huffing it out in a distressed sigh. She unlocked the door and flung it open. The stranger stood there looking like a macabre surgeon at a late-night house call. The air bore a crisp chill in the autumnal night. He dressed accordingly, wearing a black jacket and matching slacks. His hands were warmed with thin, leather gloves and he carried a handbag full of his instruments. His face was darkened, though Judy could faintly see his stolid face. Perhaps it was a mental projection, remembering his every feature from the restaurant earlier today.

"Sorry I'm late," he said grimly. "Are you ready?"

Judy was partially hidden by the ajar door, but replied, "yes, I think so."

"Do you have the money in cash?"

"Yes. Please, won't you come in?"

The man stepped into the house, but walked no farther. Before he could speak, Judy turned on the lights in the hall. He smiled to show his appreciation and continued inward, following Judy. "Where should we do this?" she asked. "Is the floor okay?"

The man looked around. "Oh no. I need something higher, like a table, but not a bed. This tends to make a mess." Judy gulped and felt uneasy. "How about there?" he asked pointing to the island in the kitchen. "That's perfect. Plus, it would be easier to clean afterward with the tiles on the floor and all." Judy nodded a bit. "Are you sure you want to go through with this? I mean it's not too late to..."

"Yes," Judy interrupted, "I must."

"Good, good. Now, let me see the money first."

Judy walked to the table. "Right here," she said, showing him the thousand dollars in cash. The man inspected the bills, picked one up and rubbed his fingers together with a crisp note of legal tender between them. He felt its power and his financial gain in his hands and there were nine more just like it on the table. He carefully set the bill on the pile and fanned them out, counting to ten. She was true to her word and all the money was there.

"Okay," he said turning back to Judy. "Get up there. Let's get started."

Judy jumped up and sat on the island as the man washed his hands at the sink. She always feared doctors, as there was always the chance something was so horribly wrong she would need sharp instruments put in her body. She knew an abortion would include having the baby removed, but was ignorant of the actual process. She tapped her fingers nervously on the counter and a numbness came over her head. Now was the time. It would all be over soon and this horror would end. The man turned off the faucet and dried his hand on a dish towel hanging over the sink. He pulled two latex gloves from a box in his open bag and pulled them down on his hands. They snapped against his wrists as he let go of the rim. He turned and looked at Judy with his hands away from his body and his fingers curled.

"What are you doing?" he said with a snide tone.

"I'm waiting for you," she said in response, sounding as though he had asked a stupid question.

"I mean you're still wearing your jeans. I need to get in there."

Judy's eyes widened. She was unsure as to how this procedure worked. "I need to take them off?"

"Yeah," the man said as though she were an utter moron, "I need to get into the womb. That's where your child is."

She felt uncomfortable and hesitated, but soon relented. The only way to finish this situation was to go along with what he requested. She unbuttoned her jeans, unzipped the zipper and pulled her jeans off. She took a deep breath and removed her underwear. It was humiliating. Never had she felt such shame, though the man seemed to care less.

"Okay," he said nonchalantly, "now get up there and lie down on your back." Judy followed his instructions, but tried not to make eye contact with him. Her legs dangled off the edge of the counter. She heard metal clinking together as he removed his tools. "Now put your feet up on the counter," he said. She could not see him, but rather, only the bright lights on the ceiling. The man forced her legs apart and she jumped, clamping them together. "Whoa," he said in surprise. "I just need to see better. Just try to relax and keep your legs apart. I can't see with them so close." Her legs shook and slowly spread wide. "Calm down," he ordered her.

It was extremely uncomfortable. Not only was the embarrassment nearly too much to bear, but being in this position hurt her hips. She did not look at the man, nor did she see what he was using on her. She pivoted her head side to side in anticipation. Her arms were folded across her stomach and she winced while waiting for the man to start. Suddenly she felt the prod in her loins. She gasped as the cold metal was inserted inside of her. She squeezed her hands together from the discomfort, trying hard to keep her legs positioned apart.

After several minutes, there was an intense pain. She felt it throughout her pelvis. It was so intense she could not tell what the man was doing exactly. She bit her lip to prevent a full-blown cry of pain, but sobbed quietly. Judy dug her fingernails into the flesh on her arms in the manner a raptor clasps a rodent in its talons. It was unbearable. She wanted to ask the man how much longer this would be, but she could barely speak. Meanwhile, the stranger diligently performed the abortion on Judy. He carefully used the tools on her to finish his job.

It seemed to be an eternity, as a seeming hell was purged

from her womb. At long last the pain gave way to a satisfying tingle inside. "There we go," the man said. "I call this operation a success." Judy huffed a loud breath of released tension. It felt as though she had not breathed throughout the entire procedure. She rolled her head to look at the man who leaned over to make eye contact with her. "Oh, there's no need to cry. Everything went just fine. You might be a little sore for awhile, so try to take it easy." Judy was relieved to have it all over.

She tried to thank him, but could not speak. She still felt a sharp pain inside her, but it would most likely subside within a couple days she figured. She felt relieved. "I hate to be so crude," the man said standing up, "but body disposal is not what I do. You'll have to get rid of that on your own." He bowed his head slightly, pointing to something with his eyes. He pulled his blood-soaked gloves off and dropped them in the trash, then turned to the sink to scour his hands with hot water and soap.

Judy rolled her head to the other side to see a plastic bag from a grocery store. It was weighted with a reddish figure inside, which was extremely blurred through the opaque plastic. Judy tried to sit up, but still felt the intense pain inside of her. She grunted and froze, poised on her elbows. The man was rinsing his instruments off and giving them a quick clean with dishwashing soap. He packed the tools back into his bad, as Judy lay in agonizing pain. He glimpsed over his shoulder and asked, "you gonna be okay?"

Judy choked as she breathed. She summoned strength to reply, "yeah. Just give me a minute."

He closed his medical bag and said, "if you say so." He looked at his watch and then at Judy lying shamefully on the kitchen island. "It's late and we're done here. I'll show myself out. You've got quite a mess to clean up." He walked to the table and collected his payment. "Can't forget this." He walked over to the counter and picked up his bag, then walked to Judy and hovered over her head. He looked straight down at her and smiled. "Don't worry, you'll be fine." He stroked her hair and continued, "it'll be sore for a little bit, but it'll pass. And the best part for you is that no one ever has to know about this." He left her there. Judy heard him walking down the hall and then the opening and closing of the door as he left.

Judy could only lie supine, staring at the ceiling, lost in thought. At last it was finished. She knew God had forgiven her as there are sins for worse offenses. Her only lingering fear now was the pain within, though the man gave his assurance that all was well. She remembered having her wisdom teeth removed and the soreness that stuck with her for so long after. Pain surely was just a part of surgery. She could feel the uncomfortable stickiness and itching of blood drying on her bare thighs. She did not even want to think of the mess at her other end. She was so tired now, yet would have to clean the mess tonight. The hardest part now was getting up.

Painfully, Judy sat up. She dropped down from the island. The shock of the landing hurt her sore insides. She fell to her knees, her right hand still gripping the counter's edge. She wheezed and stood up slowly. She saw the massive mess on the counter and groaned at the thought of cleaning it. She grabbed some paper towels and dampened them in the sink. She set to work, mopping up the small pools of blood atop the dried veneer. She had to scrub hard to get it completely clean. She fetched the bleach under the sink and poured a small puddle on the counter. The pungent smell burned Judy's nose. She continued to clean, then moved to the floor to scrub the blotches that dripped from the ledge. Finally, the island was clean and all evidence of the abortion was erased. All, that is, except for the fetus in the bag.

Judy poked her finger in and pulled the bag back slowly so that she could see her child that was not to be. She saw only a quick peek. It glistened under the fluorescent light and was a bloody shade of red, coated in slime. Judy only made out some vague human features, one a seeming arm in prenatal development. She cringed and looked away. It made her nauseated and sad. It was such a hard choice to make, but she felt inside that it was the right decision and was glad that only she had any say.

She picked up the grocery bag by its handles and took it outside to the garden. In the wee hours of the morning, by the pale light of the moon, she buried the child in the garden. She dug a shallow hole in the soil in the shade of the lilies. She held the bag upside down and shook it. The fetal glob fell into its grave by the flowers. Judy piled the moist dirt on top of the child and patted it down. This was her garden and her parents would never find the dirty little secret. At last, it was all over.

Judy had taken a hot shower to wash away the blood and dirtiness she had accumulated. Now she lay in bed. She was not proud of the choice she made, but she was thankful for the option. The child surely would have ruined her. She was even more glad for the stranger. This would be a secret lost in time and it was well worth the high cost. Despite the pain she felt relieved, as the burden of motherhood was lifted. The fatigue had finally settled in and for the first time in awhile, she would be able to sleep in peace. Her bed had never been more comfortable and her eyelids grew heavy. She closed her eyes and drifted to sleep.

Judy awoke feeling well-rested though the pain in her loins remained. She lay on her pillow, not wanting to get up. She wanted to sleep the whole Sunday away. Then it hit her. It was Sunday and she had church. She sprang upright and looked at the clock. It was just past 10:30. She had already missed the service, at least half of it anyway. She dropped back into bed and whined. She never missed church and felt of all days, this would be the most important for her to attend. Perhaps God would not mind just one day. "Good morning," a man's voice said from the corner.

Judy jumped up again and gasped. With the blinds tightly closed she could not see who exactly it was. Her eyes adjusted from sleep and she could make out the figure sitting on the recliner she had in her room. "Quite a mess you've got in here. I remember your room being so much cleaner." In all the chaos of the weekend, Judy had forgotten to pick up the blankets from the slumber party Friday night. She squinted trying to see the man and tried to recognize the voice. It was definitely not the man from last night. Who could it be? It hit her that she forgot to lock the front door after the man left, which allowed this uninvited guest in over the night. Then she knew exactly who it was.

"Josh?" she asked the image.

"Yeah," he replied, "it's me." He stood up and approached her. Judy became intensely scared. "I wanted to talk to you, but not at church, so I came over early this morning." He sat down on her bed. "I hope you don't mind."

Judy began to tremble, "what's to talk about?"

"Look," he began, "I'm sorry about the way I reacted yesterday. I know I was totally out of line yelling at you and all. But the way you talked to me yesterday, it seemed almost like there was more for you to say." Judy looked at him blankly before realizing that she never had the chance to reveal this boy was the father of a deceased child. She wanted to tell him that she was going to abort it, but he was unaware. He put a hand on her leg comfortingly and reassured her, "whatever it is, you can tell me. I prepared myself for the worst-case scenario."

Judy just stared at him while contemplating. She tried to decide if she should tell him about last night. Perhaps, she thought, it would be best to take this opportunity to get him out of her life and leave any issue of the pregnancy out of it. "You got me pregnant, you asshole," she said sternly, "what else is there to say?" Just before saying that, she wanted to tell him she would deal with the baby without his input. Josh looked at her in her eyes, like a wolf, hoping to weaken her with his predatory stare. He said nothing, but became gorgonized at the foot of her bed, like a statue, erected a memorial to sexual appetites and consequences thereof.

Judy tried to stay strong looking right back at him in deadlock. Despite reiterating the first half of the issue in a bold way, she could not yet muster the courage to finish the truth of the matter, but merely awaited for him to recover enough from the shock of her outburst. "So," he said, then paused, "I'm the father? I'm a father? There's nothing I can do about that then?" He looked her in the eye, his expression without flinch or twitch. Only an emotionless gaze, still as stone, stayed upon his face. Perhaps hearing this yesterday was not enough and hearing it again in these words settled in the truth.

"Yes," Judy said after a moment of silence, "you are."

Josh sighed and put his face in his hands. He rubbed his eyes and looked at her again. "I was afraid of this. I thought you told me that yesterday because you wanted me to stay with you." He leaned toward her and stretched his arm out to her. Judy grew more frightened and did not move. "Well," he began, "there's only one thing we can do about that then."

"You mean," Judy said, testing the waters, "getting an abortion?"

Josh recoiled like a vampire from deadly daylight. "Hell no," he said disgustedly, "I meant I'll help you raise it. I mean it might look bad on us that it's out of marriage and all, but it is my child and I'll help to support it."

Judy felt offended by his remark. "Excuse me," she said, "your child? I'd be the one to carry it. I'd have a lot more of the responsibility on top of having more high-profile shame than you. I think I should at least have more say in it than you." Angrily, Judy crossed her arms and glared at Josh.

"Quit being stupid," Josh snapped at her. "The decision has to be agreed on by both of us. I want to be a part of this child's life and you *will* let me be a part of it."

His argument for mutuality only angered Judy more. "What's wrong with abortion anyway?"

"Come on," Josh said, "do you really need an explanation?" Judy nodded her head. Josh grunted. "It's murder. Everyone knows that. The man should have just as much say in it as the woman and if they don't agree on abortion, it shouldn't happen. I mean, that shouldn't even be an option. Besides, we're both good, faithful Christians. We can't do that now, can we?"

"Good Christians?" Judy shrieked. "You? I can't believe I'm hearing this. You raped me you sick bastard. How can you call yourself a good Christian?"

Josh snorted, "acting stupid again." At that instant, Judy's hand moved quickly across his face and a loud slap of palm-on-cheek filled the room. Josh's jaw dropped and he put his hand on his reddening cheek. "You slapped me." Judy said nothing, but stared at him with fiery eyes. Josh stood up and walked to the door. He flung it open hard and it hit the wall, leaving a chip. "Bitch," he said furiously as he left. From her bed, Judy heard him stomp down the stairs and slam the front door on his way out. Despite this angry confrontation, Judy felt pleased.

She jumped out of bed, but fell to her knees as the crippling pain burst out in her abdomen. She grabbed her stomach and winced. She put a hand on the bookshelf to pull herself up. Judy staggered out of her room and walked down the stairs in agony. She stumbled and gripped the banister so that she would not tumble to the bottom. Luckily, she made it to the bottom without injury. Judy supported herself with the wall. The pain made her feel faint. At last she reached the living room and collapsed on the sofa.

She panted. Was this a punishment from God? Judy thought not, but rather a poor choice in her abortion doctor. It was so painful. Her parents would be home later today, perhaps they could take her to a doctor. Then again, that might not be wise. Somehow, passing it off as a stomachache would not work with a doctor, thought Judy. The man did say it would be sore, though this was horrible.

As she lay on the couch, Judy's mind drifted. She was glad it was over, though guilt gnawed at her conscience. It was great that she managed to confront Josh and assert herself, though along with guilt, she felt that perhaps her choice was too impulsive. Regardless, the church had an ugly air of superficiality within and out of its consecrated walls. There would naturally be much prattle about her and her family in their absence. She wished her church were more sympathetic toward women on this issue.

Lying on the couch with local programming on the television, Judy felt tired still. The pain was numbing and she felt a doped feeling of peace. She smiled. Perhaps, she thought, God loved her still and felt pity, thus he granted her respite from the soreness. It was nice to feel loved. Judy knew this unseen deity loved her, as she had been told by family, friends and preachers since her childhood. Judy was uncertain how long she slept the night before, but she felt tired now, and more peaceful than she had ever in her life. Life entwined with a soothing dream. Her body felt comforted, like cuddling with a lover before a fire on an icy winter night. As the arts and crafts program played on, showing viewers how to make floral wreaths, Judy closed her eyes and quietly slipped away.

Several hours later, after the sun sank from the sky, Judy's parents arrived home. They laughed and commented on their great weekend, feeling their marriage had significantly strengthened. Before opening the door to their home, they kissed and looked into each other's eyes. The man put his hand on his wife's back and led her into their abode. They giggled together, giddy from regaining matrimonial bliss, having rediscovered why they first fell in love many years ago. The two darted for each other's lips and kissed again. The born-again honeymooners moved deeper into the house, the bride flicked on the lights. They moved to the den, where the sound of the television was leading them to their daughter.

"Hello," the mother exclaimed cheerfully. "We just had the greatest weekend." There was no response. "Judy?" the mother enquired. Still no answer. "Are you there?"

The father noticed his daughter's hair, gently draped over the sofa's armrest. "Oh," he said softly, "she's there. I see her. She's just sleeping. We should let her be and get to bed." He winked at his wife and gave her a swift swat on the buttocks.

She poked her tongue out and then smiled. "Let me just say good night then," she said as she walked over to her daughter. The mother leaned over the sofa to see her perfect angel lying there. Judy's eyes were closed and one hand was under her head. The mother smiled and cooed. She stroked her daughter's hair, her fingertips glided across Judy's cold skin. The smile quickly faded and concern broke out on her face. She noticed the air conditioner was not on and Judy's skin was as cold as death. She placed her hand on Judy's jugular, searching for a pulse, yet there was none. Her arm darted back like a frightened animal. Her face wrinkled and turned red. Within seconds, her eyes and cheeks grew wet with salty water, like that of the abysmal ocean.

The parents stood together, comforting each other as their daughter's corpse was taken away. Neighbors peeked out the windows to witness the scene as an ambulance sat before their house, flashing red lights in the street. Days later, friends and family of Judy gathered at their church for her funeral. After all had left, the mother and father stayed graveside, watching Judy's casket from the catafalque to the cold earth below. Across the cemetery, a sea of black gathered around another grave. The lot was a virtual city, as tombs and gravestones, adorned with flowers, reached from the soil to the sky, each housing the residents who have gone.

Shortly after, the parents learned more. Their daughter's death was a result of internal bleeding in the uterus. It was revealed that the most likely cause of this was a black market abortion. The mother was overwhelmed by grief, but logic still came through. She knew her daughter well enough to discern that she became pregnant and would have been ashamed. They searched the city for the murderer, but it was apparent this procedure was bought on the street. To save face, the parents kept this incident a secret, always claiming that the death was too painful to discuss rather than divulging the cause. The cause of death never was revealed to anyone. Secretly, the parents resented their only daughter for being with child and more still, choosing to not carry it to term. Josh knew of her passing, yet never revealed that he had fathered the child. An obituary was placed in the paper, yet the stranger never saw it and never was caught, living freely without retribution. And thus, the tragic story of Judy ended, having died a mother to an unborn child, who was never discovered, lying eternally beneath the lilies in the garden.

Andy

As Judy prepared herself for her visitor that Saturday night, other areas of the city teemed with life. The masses crawled from their homes and ventured to different pockets of the city, each area competing for consumer cash. Having just finished exhausting weeks at work or school, the crowds gathered at the city's watering holes for entertainment. The people sought different goals. Some wanted merely a drink with friends, seeing a Saturday night out as a leisurely time to socialize. Some sought a significant other, as society insists every citizen should have, though many in this population would settle for a tryst, perhaps with breakfast the next morning attached to one night of fun. Others still sought refuge from home life. While the spouse tended to responsibilities, the other would sit alone in a bar drowning away misery. Alcohol has been a long time medication for sorrow.

Many others still abandoned the bar scene. Families chose other places, with parents reconciling the freedom of their youth for their ungrateful offspring. Throughout the area, this part of the population clogged the malls of the sprawling suburbs and crammed into megaplexes to see the latest, wholesome, predictable feature from the recycled waste of Hollywood. Despite having seen the same story before, they laughed and cried with the actors on the silver screen. Some filled the seats of this stop of a touring concert, others relaxed and laughed at comedians performing on stage. Whatever the venue, the people took full advantage of the sanctuary of Saturday night uninhibited, knowing that their day to rest and recover on Sunday would follow a night out on the town.

Deep within the city was a lively place called Flamingos. It was a bar and restaurant, offering live entertainment on weekend nights. It was open late and always drew a large crowd. Bright neon lights on the outside promulgated its festive atmosphere. Televisions clung to the walls and displayed music videos, scenes from movies and clips from television programs with the volume at a decent level to provide background noise and keep spirits high. Artificial palm trees and ferns gave Flamingos an indoor tropical appeal while posters of entertainers advertised venues on other nights at the place. The bar and dining area had glossy black tables, chrome chairs with black cushions and a white, tiled floor. The bar itself had matching colors with a black counter, chrome stools and white shelves boasting an impressive collection of liquor. Separated from the dining area by the entrance, the stage area was decorated similarly, but lights on strings clung to the red-curtained wall on stage. The floor of this stage area was carpeted red, though the actual stage was wooden, polished and set at ground-level, not so much as an inch above the carpet. The stage area had the same style of furniture as the dining and bar area and likewise, offered drinks for patrons to have while watching the show.

The night was still young and many patrons had yet to arrive. The show started at nine and it was only eight now. Soon people would pour into Flamingos and keep the waiters bustling and the liquor flowing. Slowly the stage area was growing in patrons, though more than half the seats were vacant. The chatter of people awaiting the show mixed with the background noise from the suspended televisions. Eight young women filled a table celebrating one's upcoming wedding. They squealed with delight and sipped sweet cocktails. A party of five sat at a circular table, while an adjacent table for six hosted a birthday party. From one table, a thin trail of blue smoke arose from a cigarette at a table for four, though it seated only one.

Andy Baker sat here. He awaited his friend, who, as usual, was late. If his friend said to meet at eight, it often meant eight-thirty at the earliest. It was an annoyance, but Andy loved his friends and treasured the bond and connection he had with them. He took one final puff of his cigarette and put it out in the glass ashtray. A glass of a tasty, green margarita sat before him. He drank a mouthful through the straw and then stirred the drink and pondered. He was not depressed, but often bad memories came to mind.

He thought of his time out of state at school. He hated it and considered his time there traumatic. There was a horrendous story there, with episodes of drug abuse, heartache, loneliness, self-mutilation and the occasional suicide attempt. He thought of that less and less as time went by, but there were times it returned to haunt him, so much in fact, that it overshadowed all other thoughts and consumed him from the inside. A couple conversations with his mother recurred as well, playing over again in his head. She once told him that if he married she would refuse to attend his wedding. Soon after he expressed interest in volunteering to help children in need, though she called him a pervert and advised he stay away from anyone's child. Tonight was hardly a night to sulk and dwell on such thoughts. He took a large gulp of his tangy margarita and checked his watch. He had been lost in thought for a mere ten minutes. Mike, his friend, had yet to show.

Andy was quite bored at this point. He hunched over his glass with his lips on the straw. He sipped the drink and chewed on the straw's end between drinks. He was a young man, only 22 and in his senior year at the university. He was handsome, with short, light brown hair and deep, dark eyes, the sort a person could fall into and never return. He was not a tall man, standing at a couple inches under six feet. He was slender and had well-defined features. Despite his attractive appearance, he felt his looks were inferior to so many others. He thought himself to be less of a god and more of a troll. He leaned over his drink with his back slightly curved, his shoulders shrugged and his arms crossed on the table, but close to his body as though he were guarding himself. In this pose, Andy looked much like a vulture. As he sat lost in thought he slurped his drink until the bubbling sound came from the bottom. He finished his drink rather quickly and unknowingly.

The waiter scurried over to his table. "Were you thirsty?" he asked. Andy looked at him and just smiled. "Can I get you another?"

"Yes, please," Andy said politely. The waiter took the glass and took it to the bar. It was often hard for Andy to be sociable, as he was quite shy. Within minutes, the waiter brought another drink to the table and scribbled into his pad to keep track of Andy's tab.

As the minutes passed and the stage area grew more crowded, Andy began to feel uncomfortable as he still sat alone. However, no one seemed to noticed him there, though he was the sole occupant at a table for four. Most any social setting he was in made him feel like a fly on the wall. He loved his friends and always felt more relaxed in these settings when they were around. He lit another cigarette and the plumes of smoke blended into the haze of the stage area, mixing with the smoke of dozens of burning cigarettes. The background prattle outweighed the music and the room became warmer as the body heat of the audience filled the air. The show would start in ten minutes. Andy kept glancing at the door to see if Mike and his friends had finally came. Finally, at long last, Mike entered the restaurant with two girls, Kim and Danielle. They were good friends of Mike, but quasi friends of Andy. They were both nice people and good conversation, yet Andy lacked the initiative to get to know them better.

Mike was taller and a bit heavier than Andy. He was just over six feet tall and had an average build. His hair was blonde and his eyes were blue. He was far less reserved than Andy and could strike up a conversation more easily. Unlike his friend, he felt far more comfortable in social settings and was not as afraid of people.

Mike spotted Andy and walked to the table. He had to squeeze through the crowds, as the seats filled to the maximum capacity and others in the audience had to stand. Andy felt himself to be lucky that the waiter had not asked him to forfeit his table, considering Mike had come so late. Mike sat down across from Andy and the two girls sat at the other seats. "Hey," Mike said in his usual friendly tone, "how's it going?"

"You're late," Andy said, "again. I'm starting to wonder if you have any concept of time."

"Sorry," Mike said annoyed, "first I had to pick up Kim and then..."

"Okay, okay," Andy said interrupting, unwilling to hear his excuse this time. "Like I said before though, I should say six o'clock next time and you'd be here right at eight. That or I'll bring a crossword puzzle."

"Come on," Mike said, "I'm not that bad. I'm only a little late."

"Sure, by nearly an hour. Shit, I'm on my third margarita."

"So I'll catch up then." Mike pulled out a twenty-dollar bill and looked around. "Where's the waiter?"

The waiter came to the table and Mike bought a dirty martini. The girls both bought strawberry daiquiris. Andy felt more relaxed now and the rest of the crowd seemingly became painted figures on the wall and the four at the table virtually became the only people in the room. Mike sipped his martini.

"Those are so disgusting," Andy said grimacing, "I don't see how you can drink those. It's just vodka and olive juice."

"They're good," Mike replied.

"Don't you remember? You had me try some of yours. It tasted like vinegar and salt with alcohol."

"Yeah, whatever." Mike took another drink of the dirty martini. "All you drink are those damn margaritas." Mike stared at Andy and swished his drink. "So anyway, I have a friend I think you might like."

"Mike," Andy said with an expression of annoyance, "please, you know I don't want that anyway."

"I'm just saying," Mike said in his defense, "I mean, how long's it been since you've seen someone?"

Andy looked at him sternly, brought his drink close to his mouth and replied, "not long enough." In truth, Andy had been hurt in the past. He was a sensitive man and the insensitivity of others, in and out of relationships exacerbated his outlook. It was hard to trust anyone enough again to give them his heart. It can only be broken so many times before it becomes irreparable. The lack of family support did not help matters either. He could not talk to anyone in his family about his job or school, much less something as personal as relationships. For several years now it became harder and harder to identify with his family. More and more even trivial matters became uncomfortable to discuss. He had been raised Baptist, though over the experiences he had in life, it was impossible to keep faith in something claimed to be an "all-loving" God. Ergo, he became the nonbeliever in this family.

Then, suddenly, the televisions ceased playing their random images and simultaneously showed the Flamingos name and logo. Appropriately it was a pink flamingo wading in shallow water beneath a palm tree. Loud music resounded throughout the room. It was a tune reminiscent of an upbeat musical on Broadway. The chatter dwindled and the crowd cheered. Mike, who had his back to the stage, sat sideways on the chair so that he could turn his head and watch the show and twist it 180 degrees to talk to Andy. Andy was excited, this was his favorite live show in town and he was a regular at Flamingos on Saturday night.

The announcer in the booth spoke loudly on the

microphone with the music still playing in the background. "Hello everyone and welcome to the Saturday Night Cabaret here at Flamingos. As always I'm your host Bryan. We have three lovely ladies here to entertain you tonight." Bryan paused for a moment, allowing the music to play without his overriding voice. "Of course the show wouldn't be complete without your Saturday night leading lady. The always fabulous, always beautiful, your hostess, Coco." The audience clapped and whistled. "Joining her, all the way from the south side of town is the versatile, and often sick and twisted styling of Miss Nikita Lamb." This performer did not receive a nearly as welcoming response as Coco. "And finishing our trio of divas this evening is that lovely Latina princess coming straight from the west side, Mimi Jimenez." There was another muted reaction from the audience for this secondary performer. "And now, without further ado, the moment you've all been waiting for, I give you Coco's Saturday Night Cabaret."

The audience cheered loudly and the theatrical introduction gave way to a song. The ladies walked out seductively. Coco wore a sparkling, gold dress that clung to her body. Her hair doubled the size of her head, rising up several inches and flowing back down the sides of her head. It was parted with a seeming gorge just slightly to the left of the crown of her head. She walked to the stage on glittery-gold, open-toe high heels. Her skin was smooth and blemish free. She walked and presented herself with confidence and proudly boasted through body language that she was a beautiful, black woman.

Following Coco was Nikita Lamb, who was slender and a few inches shorter than Coco, not considering the mountain of hair on Coco's head. Nikita walked into the room wearing a tight-fitting, white dress. The end of the dress was halfway down her thighs. Her head was crowned with a mound of blonde curls. She wore glossy white boots that came up to just under her knee. This was not her show though. She was merely a guest under Coco's name. Behind her was Mimi Jimenez, who had yet another vibrant hairstyle. Hers was large and black with large loops of curls. She was taller than the other two, standing well over six feet. She wore a shiny purple gown with black shoes. Like Nikita, she was here in Coco's renowned shadow. The audience could see all the vibrant culture and beauty of Mexico in her face. All three women had an obscene amount of cosmetics plastered on their faces.

The ladies stood on the stage and faced their adoring audience, who cheered and applauded the entertainers. The women performed, singing "It's In His Kiss" and danced on stage with graceful, feminine gestures. They gazed upon the audience with passionate eyes. However, the women did not sing the lyrics of the song, but rather they mouthed the words, passing the voices of the singers as their own. Andy watched them perform. He was captivated by their elaborate costumes and exaggerated appearances of womanhood. He smiled and sipped his margarita without taking his eyes off the stage. How he loved drag shows.

The audience cheered and laughed throughout the show. All three drag queens lip-synched songs with interludes, in which they would jeer the audience or each other. Coco was now performing, but had changed her wardrobe. While the other two performed their routines on stage, Coco rushed backstage to put on a new costume for her second act. Nikita and Mimi performed respectively, one at a time, and now Coco danced, wearing a black ensemble that looked like a sequined cocktail dress and a set of four-inch black pumps. Her hair changed to a brownish-black veil of tight braids. Coco moved through the audience off-stage and collected tips from her fans. The song neared its end and she rushed back to the stage, as quickly as she could wearing heels. She stuffed the bills in her hand into her artificial cleavage and grabbed the microphone from the announcer.

"Hey," she screamed into it, "thank you all so much for joining us here tonight at the Saturday Night Cabaret right

here at Flamingos. As always, I'm your talented hostess Coco."
The audience cheered and applauded. "Let's see who we've got
in the audience tonight." She walked off the stage, back into the
crowd with the microphone in her hand. Andy's heart skipped
a beat. Although he was quite inebriated, he feared she would
put him on the spot, a traumatic experience for someone as
shy as he. He knew it was part of the show and nothing had
ever happened to him before, but he always feared it would.
He tried to calm himself in repeating a makeshift mantra in
his mind. There were a lot of people in here tonight. Odds
were she would pick on someone else.

Coco walked to the table that seated the several young
women at the bachelorette party. "Oh my," Coco said with
a hint of predatory intent in her voice, "what's at this table?"
The girls giggled and one hid her face. Another screamed
something barely audible over the din of the audience's chatter.
"What? A bachelorette party?" Coco sneered and said, "girl,
you're messed up. You'd rather see men in dresses over men
who take it off? If I were you I'd rather see the strippers." The
future bride laughed hysterically. "So what's the boy's name?"
The girl said something inaudible over the background noise.
"Brad?" Coco said. "Was your first date behind a dumpster?
Don't laugh. A girl's gotta eat. How much did he pay you?"
The girl blushed and her friends laughed and teased her.
"Congratulations though sweetheart. Ooh! Look what we've
got over here." Coco tripped over something and stumbled.
She giggled a little and said, "ooh, there goes my leg again.
Old football injury."

Nikita poked her head out from backstage. "Football
injury? Coco, stretching your leg while doing the whole team
in one night does not count as a football injury?"

"You hush," Coco said with a hiss. Nikita ducked back
into the dressing room. Coco moved toward Andy and his
heart raced. She stopped at another table and hovered over
a large girl. "Damn," Coco said sounding surprised, "you are

stacked. Look at that." Coco pointed down at her. The girl's face reddened in embarrassment. "Stand up girl. Come with me." Coco pulled the girl to the stage and presented her to the audience. "Look at these," Coco said, poking one of the girl's breasts. "Are they real?" The girl nodded and chuckled. "The boys must love you. And the girls too. What do all y'all lesbians think?" There were a few whistles over the laughter and the girl laughed but said something to Coco muted by the audience's reaction. "What do you mean you're straight?" Coco said exaggerating disgust. "Eww, you go sit down." The girl laughed more and returned to her seat.

"We have such a lovely audience tonight." Coco said gliding back out to the floor. "But oh, look right here," Andy watched her, horrified as she dashed to his table. She stopped at his and Mike's end of the table. Both looked up at her, but she locked eyes with Andy. She sat down on his knee and Andy just looked at her in fear, knowing all eyes were upon him. He was hardly afraid of Coco, as he had complimented her on the show a few times before. He was, however, afraid of the attention brought to him. At this very moment he felt the searing gaze of countless eyes staring in his direction, though he dared not take his eyes out of their fixation on Coco, thinking it would be better to not see people staring back at him.

"Hello," she said flirtatiously, "what's your name?"

"Andy," he said abruptly.

"Is this your boyfriend?" she pointed to Mike.

"No."

"Do you have a boyfriend?"

"No."

"What?" she shrieked jumping up, nearly making Andy fall out of his chair. She grabbed his arm and yanked him out of his seat. "Oh no, no, no, no," Coco said as she pulled him to the stage. She twirled Andy toward the audience, but he could only make out some figures through the bright lights pointing toward the stage. Coco put her arm around his shoulder and said, "Andy, I have a job for you." Quickly she pulled her arm off him, grabbed the cash from her chest and flung it into the air. It fluttered to the stage floor divergently. "Pick it up for me, would you sweetie?" Andy was not humiliated by this, but felt judged by everyone in the room, feeling they were subjected to seeing his ugly face and repulsive body instead of the song and dance numbers from the performers. At least, to him his appearance was unpleasing to the eye. He bent over to pick up the bills and the audience began to laugh. He wondered if he had sat in something or if his pants had split. He whipped his head around to see Coco making an exaggerated expression of lust, as though he was the most beautiful creature she had ever seen.

After collecting the money he walked up to her and she put her hand out to receive it. Instead, Andy pulled the elastic fabric from her chest, stretching it back far. He dropped the money in and let the material snap Coco's chest. She seemed surprised and let out a light scream. She put her arm around his shoulder again. "What a bitch," she said smiling. "I like that." The audience laughed again. "Come on now," Coco said more enthusiastically, "wouldn't you guys out there just love to...you aren't straight like old brick house over there are you?" She looked at her last victim in the audience and sneered. Andy shook his head. "Good," Coco said, "wouldn't you guys out there just love to have this adorable little guy as your boyfriend?"

After that remark, to Andy, it seemed the world and time itself had stopped. Some people said he was attractive, but only in response to him saying he was not. In truth, whether with friends or alone, no one ever seemed to talk to Andy or even give him a furtive glance across a crowded room. Now, in front of this crowd he would get a poll from the audience of the Saturday Night Cabaret at Flamingos. It was not as though he would pursue any of them, but for his own deflated ego, it would be nice and likewise, flattering to hear that he was in some way desirable. Otherwise, if people out there remained silent it would be a strike against his already low self-esteem. This moment should not take so long, Andy thought. The words from Coco's mouth traveled as waves through the air, reaching the ears of the audience. Each person's ears worked the same, capturing the sound and processing it, recognizing it as a language, deciphering its meaning and at last, understanding it and reacting to it. The process was so complex, yet happened so quickly. This was all relativity Andy thought. Understanding her words and connecting their meaning to his image, which stood before them would take no time. The audience was silent, thus his verdict. Andy looked down to the floor. It was a consequence with going to a drag show.

Arising from the audience came whistles and howls. Shocked, Andy's head snapped upward. Perhaps some out there pitied him and sensed his humiliation. Coco thanked him and sent him back to his seat, then announced her next number. Andy sat back down as quickly as possible. He felt hot and his body leaked small beads of nervous sweat. Mike sat there grinning. "See," Mike said, "told you all the guys like you."

"What the hell are you talking about?" Andy responded. "You saw how long it took for them to do anything. That was all sympathy."

"Whatever," Mike said with annoyance in his voice. "It was like half a second between when she said that and they wanted you. I'm sorry that they can't cat call at warp speed, princess."

"Look," Andy said, "I just..."

"Drop it," Mike hissed. "We're here to have fun, not listen to your bitter, ice-queen pity parties." Mike never intentionally tried to hurt Andy's feelings, but on some matters he was quite direct. Sometimes hurting his feelings was a byproduct of his point. A couple years ago, when Mike first met Andy, he saw a depressed young man with no friends, confidence or self-esteem. Mike befriended him and buttressed Andy with a greater support system and helped him out of the rut he was in at that time. Mike always wondered why Andy felt so bad and after trust increased between the good friends, he found out that Andy had been through a lot in the process of self-discovery.

Andy came from a conservative family. He had known he was gay for several years, but concealed it as best as he could. His parents were both devoutly Baptist and staunch Republicans. Both factors were unkind to his sexuality. Naturally, he was raised as a Baptist too and feared the messages the church announced about gay and lesbian people. It referred to them as horrible people, brainwashing the congregation to loathe gays and lesbians as people who intentionally defy God by choosing an alternate lifestyle. In his early teenage years, when he first knew he was gay, he fought it in every way he could. He tried to force himself to become aroused by females and prayed to God constantly to make him a heterosexual. Eventually he came to accept that he could not change this about himself, but would have to suppress it to make his family happy. Of course, with the church dubbing him as an aberration and occasional headlines of anti-gay harassment, including mauling and death, Andy felt his best option was to bury the secret and pose as a heterosexual. Naturally, as his life played out, he grew to accept and respect who he was, finding the closet to be a sad and lonely place, so full of others too frightened to come out, but likewise, so empty. One secret he did keep was a regretful experience. In high school, there was an openly gay boy that Andy admired for his courage, but resented for his own cowardice. To prevent his peers from thinking he was gay, Andy called the poor boy words the homophobic bandwagon used quite liberally. Eventually, he came to realize that his life was for him to live, not his parents, the church, classmates or anyone else.

Andy left Flamingos quite drunk. Mike was right behind

him with the two girls he brought along. "Hey," Mike said, "I'm going to take Danielle home, but Kim and I are going to hit up the club to dance off the booze and sober up. You care to join us?"

"You like that lesbian dance club, don't you?" Andy asked. "At least, I think you're going there, right?"

"Yeah," Mike said.

"Are you sure you aren't really a lesbian?"

"Okay, honey, you're drunk." Mike gave him a peck on the forehead. "Anyway, are you down?"

"Actually, I'm going to sleep. I think I had too much to drink tonight."

"When do you ever not drink that much? Be careful. You live way out in the boondocks. Don't crash or get pulled over or anything."

Andy was silent for a moment and at last replied, "good night, Mike. Have a good time at the club." The two gave each other a parting hug and went their separate ways. Andy was unaware how poor his motor skills were at the moment. It seemed now, in the outside air, that the alcohol flowing through his blood was taking a greater effect. He shifted from left to right, walking and curving like a sidewinder on the scorching desert sands. Likewise, a dizzying sensation rolled like waves through his head. Andy felt a bit sick. A slight feeling of nausea sat in his stomach, made worse by the spinning in his head. He stumbled to his car and placed one hand on it as he leaned forward. He searched for his keys in his pocket with his free hand. It all felt like a jumble of metal in his hands. It was hard to distinguish the car keys from the house keys and loose change. He grabbed everything in his pocket and pulled it out to sort it.

He twisted around and leaned his side against the car so that he could stable himself while searching for the key to get him to bed. Andy took the car key out of the pile and shoved everything back into his pocket. He attempted to unlock the door, but missed the slot twice. On his third try the key entered the lock and he unlocked the door and entered the all-powerful driver's seat. He was much more successful getting the key into the ignition. He turned the key and the motor sounded as it came to life, like a sleeping beast, woken up to hunt. Andy pulled the lever back and put his car in reverse. He pulled backward and turned the steering wheel, pointing the car away from the parking space and toward the street. The car lurched forward with its drunk driver at the wheel. Andy stopped at the street and scanned for any oncoming traffic and more importantly, patrolling police cars. Seeing none, he pulled out onto the street.

He drove south, toward the freeway leading to his house in the distant, sleepy suburbs. Andy did his best to keep the car in his lane. In times before he had taken city streets because of less traffic. The roads were more or less derelict this time of night. The signs were a blur of green and white, until Andy's eyes could focus on them well enough to read. His knuckles whitened as he held the steering wheel tightly. He was quite nervous and feared tonight would be the night he would be caught driving under Bacchus' influence.

The little demons of that god played in Andy's body. An exorcism to expunge the hedonistic possession was almost needed to drive, but unwanted by the driver. Alcohol had been an important part of his life since he came of age. He drank nearly each night, showing his faith and devotion to Dionysus and the divine pleasures thereof. The playful spirits pulled up memories and thoughts, each bobbing up for short intervals, then quickly diving back into his subconscious. Was it a curse or blessing to be gay in America? It was considered to be a place of equality, but it was anything but that. It shall be better to remain single the rest of his life. Why had Christians, who did not know him, hate him? He had so many friends that loved him, despite being gay. It was not a fault at all, yet some people could not understand. Then the thought of his mother came. How he loved her, though simultaneously, hated her for her cold heart. He could not concentrate on any one topic, nor could he contemplate one with deep thought. At last he arrived home. He entered, trying not to wake anyone and passed out on the couch.

A warm hand stroked his head and Andy slowly opened his eyes. The morning light was blinding. "Good morning, sweetie," said a familiar voice. He looked up and saw Melanie looking down upon him smiling. "Don't you have work today?"

Andy jumped up. "Oh," he exclaimed, "I'm late. I need to run."

Melanie put her hand on his arm and said, "relax. It's seven-thirty now. I thought you said you had to be in at ten today, so I thought I'd get you up." Melanie stood up and walked to the kitchen. "I made you some coffee, but what did you want for breakfast?"

"Nothing for me, thanks," Andy said, "I'm not really hungry." Actually, he felt quite sick at the moment. He resisted the urge to throw up.

"You must've had a wild night last night." Melanie walked out of the kitchen with two mugs of coffee. She gave Andy the mug with the rainbow flag design. Melanie was a beautiful woman, despite being just over 50. She had a beautiful face with short, black hair, a delicate and small frame, and striking blue eyes. "So," she began again, "meet anyone last night?"

Andy knew he had told her his thoughts about dating again, but felt he was in no place to get argumentative. After all, Melanie and Tina allowed him to stay with them until things blew over at home. "No," Andy said, "guess no one was into me. By the way, where's Tina?"

"You know she doesn't like to get her ass out of bed before ten," Melanie said. Tina was Melanie's partner. The two had met at the same time Andy was a toddler and had been monogamously coupled for two decades. Andy first met Tina two years ago at the Foundation for Human Rights, a political action group full of hope and dedication to protecting and gaining rights over the full spectrum of the gay community. The government classified the lesbian, gay, bisexual, transgender and questioning people as different from human beings, known in this sense as heterosexuals, and thrust conservative, hateful and bigoted legislation and civil action upon them.

After leaving the painful relationship behind him, Andy left his out of state university and started anew in his hometown. Shortly after returning he released the burden of skeletons in the closet by revealing them, and thus himself. He came out en masse, telling his mother and his oldest friend, a heterosexual male. From others' stories he swore the friend would take it the hardest. However, his mother did not take kindly to the news and the two drifted further apart, though he and his friend grew closer. Feeling lost, Andy researched groups throughout the city via the phonebook. He wanted to find common ground through experience and increase his support network. He wanted to meet people who did not judge him for this one aspect of his life. He wanted people who could understand. He found the Foundation for Human Rights and began volunteer work, meeting new people, including Mike, Melanie and Tina. He found Tina's strong personality and pride in herself attractive and she felt as though he were a son of hers, often referring to him as her baby boy. Four days ago, a spat between Andy and his mother flared into a loud battle of screaming and unbridled anger, forcing him to seek refuge at Melanie and Tina's apartment.

Soon Andy showered and dressed for work. He felt a bit nauseated from last night's drinks. The tequila sat sickeningly in his stomach. His job was only minutes away from his house, but was easily a half hour commute from this shelter. Somehow, his job at the mall did not seem important enough for this travel time. He lived in the distant suburbs and felt the isolation that came with it. He preferred the central city and if he could immediately afford it, would move here right away. Tina and Melanie lived in an apartment in the predominantly gay and lesbian neighborhood on the fringe of downtown. In the past, they attempted to live in a suburban setting, however, the two were pressured out by their neighbors. Unaware of the demographics before moving to the house, Tina and Melanie found themselves in a diverse neighborhood, full of Protestants, Baptists, Catholics, Anglicans, Presbyterians and even the exotic Mormon family two doors down. Originally the couple felt it would be good for them to live with a bench on their front porch and greet the neighbors in passing, inviting them in for coffee, extending an invitation to an open house in the crime-free hinterlands of the city.

Unfortunately the couple found life in this serene setting to be anything but the American Dream. The neighbors welcomed them upon moving to the neighborhood, but the two unabashedly admitted to being a couple. Their welcome wagon, fouled by hatred, spoke out to the neighborhood, spreading instant disgust and utter rancor like the Black Death. People who did not know the couple branded them as being sick and refused to make conversation or even eye contact. Parents demanded their children avoid the house, assuming the lesbian couple would violate them and rumors amongst the youth spread as to what wonders and curiosities must lie within the forbidden house's walls. After several months, Tina and Melanie developed a worse reputation, as they tended to fight back, throwing insults back at the philistines. One morning they found in blue letters spray painted on their garage, "Dykes." It felt bad to leave the neighborhood, almost like giving up without a fight, letting these hateful people win the battle. For personal safety and comfort they moved to the gay neighborhood and found a more ideal setting around downtown than in the isolated, alienated suburbs.

Andy drove down the street and onto the freeway. The morning sun glared in his eyes, piercing through his sunglasses. He hated this job. Customers were always so rude and constantly complained, projecting their own misery onto him over the smallest frustration. They argued over a price they swore was a dollar less. In a life of being walked over and losing time after time, a victory of saving a handful of change made them feel powerful to belittle the clerks. Often their frugality came with aspersions. Andy hated it and longed for a better job. However, he needed money while in school.

Andy raced up the freeway. It was a waste of a beautiful Sunday. He just spent over eight hours toiling like an ass in a millstone, waiting to drop dead. The customers were annoying as usual and made his day miserable, on top of his hangover. At least it was all over. The saving grace of his job was his coworkers. He had a large network of friends at this job and conversations with them made the work day much more tolerable. Andy may have been shy around other gay men, but he was quite charming and made friends easily with others. Many were understanding and he could be open with them and tell people an amusing anecdote from when he went to a bar or club, or why he was not dating a girl without wearing a mask of lies and having to quickly change the subject.

Andy opened the door to Tina and Melanie's apartment. A heavy smell of Italian seasonings greeted his nose as he walked into the apartment. Garlic, oregano, basil, tomatoes and other distinct scents mixed in the air, pleasuring his sense of smell and tantalizing his empty stomach. He turned toward the kitchen and watched Tina clumsily work with the food. A steaming pot of spaghetti boiled on the stove with the tomato sauce simmering next to it. Tina was finishing slicing up a carrot for the salad. A bottle of red wine sat on the counter. Tina had not noticed that Andy arrived. "You cooked?" Andy asked, surprised. Typically it was Melanie who made the food.

"Hey, boy," Tina said, "I'm getting pretty good at this cooking thing." Tina never used to cook, but within the past several months she took a liking to it and experimented often, though with tried and tested recipes, still skittish to create her own culinary concoctions. She wanted to test her skills in making baked goods, soups, salads, entrees and anything else to satisfy the cooking bug. In the past, Melanie had always cooked and if she could not for any reason, Tina settled for fast food, pizza from a nearby restaurant or a simple sandwich. "Hope you're hungry," Tina said. "I'm making us some spaghetti."

"Oh," Andy said, "that's okay." In truth, Andy's stomach was on the verge of eating itself. He had only coffee that morning and had no money for lunch at work. His survival instinct urged him to take the food, but simultaneously, he suppressed his appetite with guilt. Tina and Melanie did not have much money, but they tried to feed him constantly, feeling he was too skinny. On top of that, he felt bad that they gave up their privacy and space so that he had a place to sleep after the fight with his mother.

"Come on boy. You got to eat."

Andy relented, but agreed to it. He went to the bathroom to change out of his work clothes. When he stepped out, he saw Tina allotting the dinner to three sets of dishes. Melanie dug through the drawers, making a large racket. "Where in the hell is that goddamn corkscrew?" she snarled. She looked up at Andy and smiled. "Hi sweetie. Want some wine with your meal?"

"You know me," Andy said sheepishly.

"Okay," she said reaching up for the wine glasses, "I'll get you some as soon as I find that fucking corkscrew. You want any wine babe?"

"Nah," Tina said, "that shit gives me heartburn." Melanie took down two glasses and looked at Tina. The two gave each other a quick kiss on the lips. Tina took the plates to the living room while Melanie, who at long last found the elusive corkscrew, poured the wine and helped Tina with serving the dinner. Within a minute the three sat with the television on and watched programs while feasting. However, at Tina's, the television was like background music, as the conversation carried on, often drowning out the program. At times it was a good thing. Andy, who detested sports, could sit through a baseball game with Tina, finding her commentary and passion for the game amusing. She would stand up and scream, shout obscenities, insult the players and all around, make for a better show than televised sports.

"So how was work today?" Melanie asked.

"Same old, same old," Andy said casually. "Glad to be back here though. The mall was basically holding auditions for porn though."

Tina laughed, "what happened?"

"Like every other straight couple was making out and groping each other. Maybe someone put an aphrodisiac in the water." Andy shook his head. "Anyway, it pisses me off that they say we rub it in their faces when they do stuff like that."

"I know, right," Tina said. "They can't have gay marriage crumbling their perfect little world, but they can do that shit in front of everyone and it's okay. Before long they'll have separate places for us queers in restaurants. They'll have to ask 'hetero-sectional or non' when you walk in. Unbelievable, these people." Andy always loved Tina's hyperboles, though deep down feared there could be truth in her words.

"You know," Andy said, "they're probably just scared we'll do better, given the divorce rate."

"Aye," Tina said, preparing for a political tangent, "they call us sexual deviants and more than half of them can't even stand to be with each other. They think we're all about fucking everything that walks and can't settle down and be faithful." She put her fork down and began speaking loudly. "Right, look at how many of these heterosexual relationships involve cheating. I know it happens to gays and lesbians every damn day and all, but still, they can't say shit. There are cheaters and shit on their side too." She paused and Andy was about to reply, but Tina continued. "So you know the whole anti-gay marriage thing, they say, is to protect marriage from the courts and its good name being dirtied up. They say that or marriage is traditionally between a man and a woman. But it's all bull shit. They fucked up the institution of marriage long ago." Andy opened his mouth to speak, but Tina spoke more. "Like you said, look at their divorce rate, and how many of them probably end from someone's affair. Plus, those Mormons marry like seven women, don't they? They think it's the man's right to pick and choose his pussy for the night."

Andy laughed at the way she put things. She made excellent points and was an intelligent woman, though put her words in profane and vulgar ways. People thought it to be strange that he spent so much time with her, given that she was 50, more than twice his age. Tina and Melanie were both dear friends of his and made him laugh, in addition to sharing wisdom of experience. He met both through the Foundation for Human Rights and fell in love with Tina after seeing her confidence, strength and determination. He had an instant respect for her after their first meeting and appreciated the influence she had on his life. She was an integral part of his life and helped him regain his self-respect, confidence and courage. She taught him how to use homophobia as a source of empowerment.

"Anymore," Andy began, "it seems people can't mind their own business. Especially those Christian groups."

"Uh huh," Tina said in accordance. Melanie sat watching the television and eating her dinner. She seemed uninterested in their conversation.

Andy took a sip of his wine. "Every time some big civil rights case or something that regards someone's personal life and decisions makes the news, there's always that Christian group who feels they have to step in and control other people."

"Oh, hell yeah," Tina said. "Don't you know? No one's capable of making their own decisions, so the church takes that liberty. These people make me sick. They really do. I mean, if they think their religion is all about loving one another and that we're all God's children, then why do they have to fill their lives with such hatred?" She leaned forward and said angrily, "it's because they're miserable, hateful people who have so much spite in their black hearts that they have to try to ruin life for the rest of us."

Of course, Tina was merely preaching to the choir. Andy agreed with her on all of these points. Earlier this year, he volunteered for the Foundation for Human Rights at the Gay Pride Festival. There was an extravagant and colorful parade through a major street and people, gay, lesbian, straight and from all walks of life gathered to watch. Drag queens, political groups, men and women of all sorts marched, some wore next to nothing, others donned casual clothes, some dressed alike and others still bore colorful costumes. The colors of the rainbow appeared in all sorts of ways. They waved as flags, floated as balloons, sparkled in glitter and flashed in lights. Residents of the high-rise condominiums flanking the thoroughfare watched from their balconies. It was a parade to celebrate life and accepting diversity. The parade ended further down the road and the festival began.

Andy met Mike there and they made small talk before their shift at the Foundation for Human Rights booth at the festival. It was not long before a raucous came barreling toward the people, who innocently enjoyed a festive day. It was a vehement mob of Christian protestors. Andy stood, watching in disgust and disbelief as they approached chanting and carrying signs and Bibles. Andy's eyes darted from one hateful sign to the next. "God hates fags," was written in huge, black letters. Another read, "God made Adam and Eve, not Adam and Steve." The most sickening sign, however bore words of praise around the picture of Fred Phelps, the pious villain, who celebrated the murder of Matthew Shepard. In turn, these protestors celebrated his cruel intolerance. Andy was used to seeing and hearing discrimination against gays and lesbians, as many uttered, "that's gay" in modern parlance, referring to something they did not like. Regarding these protestors, he was far more disturbed by their age. Many were around his age, despite having thought the younger generations were more tolerant, though there was a considerable number of middle-aged and senior detractors. Some made it a family event and brought their small children along to join them in the mob scene. The youth of the group watched attentively as their parents slandered the revelers, learning at a tender age how to hate people.

One young man approached Mike and Andy and waved a Bible at them. "God hates you! Faggots and dykes can't enter the Kingdom of Heaven," he screamed. "Please, to save your eternal souls, come with us. We can set you straight. We can make you normal."

There was a glottal hack immediately after that. Mike spat on the protestor. It splattered in the young man's face and he cringed as though it were acidic poison. A young woman rushed to his side. "Are you okay?" she asked.

"That filthy pervert just spit on me," the man screamed.

"Oh my God," the girl said nearly panicking. "Quick, let's get that washed off. Who knows what diseases he might have. Hurry, let's go. Let's get a doctor and get you tested. He probably has AIDS." The girl walked him away from Mike, who smiled in triumph. The protestors watched leerily, now afraid of what might happen to them. They did not understand gay people and could only fear the worst.

"Good job," Andy said.

"He was an asshole," Mike said.

Just then, a middle-aged woman approached them, followed by a Christian crony. "Young man," the woman said calmly, "that was uncalled for. You could get him sick."

"With what?" Mike said. "A cold? I feel fine thank you."

"I meant AIDS. You people carry that."

"Fuck off, bitch," Andy said angrily.

"Excuse me," the lady said, startled. "I don't care for that sort of language being spoken to me. There are children around."

"And we don't care for you coming here to call us perverts," Mike retorted.

"Look what you're teaching your children," Andy said.

"We just came to save as many of you as possible," the lady said. She spoke in a euphoric tone. Her state of mind and expressions seemed to be drug-induced, no doubt high off the myth of Christ's grace. Her friend stood by her side. The silent woman stared at them through half-opened eyes, her jaw hanging, leaving her mouth slightly open. Her limp, blonde bangs touched her eyebrows, covering what Andy swore was a cicatrice from her lobotomy.

"We want you to know," she uttered in a quiet monotone, "that Jesus loves you very much."

"Oh yeah?" Andy replied, "first thing, that sign says otherwise." Andy pointed to the "God hates fags" sign. "Second, how could he love me? He's dead."

The woman who first spoke smiled. "He lives in the hearts of people. He spreads his loving words through us."

"You call this love?" Andy asked. "It seems Jesus is a sadistic, sick man if he wants to spread his love like this. If he's all-loving, then he'd accept us for what we are."

"But he does," she so stubbornly replied, "he just doesn't like the choices you made."

"Choice?" Mike asked furiously, "I didn't choose to be this way, just as you didn't choose your heterosexuality. Also, did Jesus tell you this personally?"

"The Bible tells us," she replied.

"Jesus didn't write the Bible," Mike said. "Ordinary men with their usual prejudices wrote it."

The woman stared blankly. Religion had brainwashed them beyond repair. They could no longer judge people based on merit and character or true human value, nor could they decide anything without consulting the Bible or clergy. They could not see Mike and Andy or all the on-lookers for being fellow human beings, but only as demonized animals, for the Bible told them so.

Breaking from this memory, Andy asked Tina, "so, is anything going on tomorrow at the FHR?" He often shortened the Foundation for Human Rights as FHR for the sake of brevity.

"Oh yeah," Tina said enthusiastically, "didn't I tell you about the protest?"

"No."

"Those fucking assholes from FCF are having some big rally and we're teaming up with a few other groups to protest them. Just their way of spreading hatred and making the country better for heterosexual Christians." The FCF, or Fundamental Center for Families, was a nationwide organization that sought to augment women's rights, annihilate gay rights and promote Christianity and Christian thinking in public institutions. It was a sworn enemy to the gay community and promised the demise of social progress through lobbying city and state legislation.

"What exactly is their rally for?" Andy asked.

"Same old shit, you know. Dehumanize the queers, limit women's choices, rub Christianity in our faces a bit more."

"Don't they do that enough? I mean, they accuse our one day of Pride as rubbing it in their faces, but they don't have to recognize it. Though Christmas and Easter are forced on us, as well as them having churches everywhere." Andy gestured with his hands to emphasize his point. "They can't complain about rainbow stickers or flags on anything. They wear those crosses around their necks. They put those Jesus fish on their cars. They can't say we're too open and flaunting about it either. I always see those damn church crowds on Sunday. They're everywhere. They have no right to say we rub it in their faces."

"Oh of course they do," Tina said. "They want a monopoly on marriage and society. They think it's their right to get in our faces and lives and tell us what morality is. These Christians, let me tell you, I think it'd be more moral to let us make our own decisions without using their usual, hateful ways." She waved her fork in small circles in the air. "You know, the way they tell everyone it's okay to condemn and hate queers it's no wonder there are so many hate crimes against us. What's worse is that the government backs them and says it's okay by them to hate us too."

Truly, Andy thought, whatever governmental properties religion had once served, it was now obsolete given the scientific and societal progress made in the world. At one time, perhaps, religion maintained order in society with the promise of damnation for those who defied its doctrine. Presently, nations worldwide had a strong enough structure and legal system to maintain order without religion. Religion may have been a common foundation to meet people with a temple, church or synagogue as a cornerstone for social gatherings and law, but over time the basis became perverted, allowing religious thinking to overcome logic, truth and reason. Now religious power used its fundamentals to dominate politics and provide backing to otherwise unjustifiable hatred.

It seemed silly that people nationwide hated him without having met him. It seemed even more asinine that he could talk to these people and they could adore him, but revealing that he was gay would transform their charmed impression to absolute rancor. The issues regarding the LGBTQ community were at best, ludicrous. It was a terrible notion that he and others like him had to fight for protection from the overly intolerant. The criminals spawned from the church found brutal means to express their insecurities. Not long ago, in this very city, Andy read an article about a middle-aged gay couple, whose skulls were bashed in with hammers. It was one of countless grisly murders that happened in America day in, day out.

Certainly, the church did produce a wealth of murderers, though it sent thieves out into the public as well. All across the country they infiltrated city halls, legislative buildings and courthouses to further demonize and slander the spectrum, thus stealing their civil rights and lowering them all on the scale of humanity. Somehow, being denied the right to marry, adopt children, have any say at a partner's passing and a large number of other rights denied did not seem in the least to promote morality, but rather to call a group of people inferior and to tell fellow countrymen and women they were unwelcome in America, the so-called land of equality and freedom.

Understanding seemed so simple. All it required was listening. In his retail position, Andy saw hundreds of strangers each day. Looking at them he could not tell what happened in their private lives, nor did he care to know. He was content with his own life with no desire to pry, much less to interfere, with those of others. He could see any random stranger, obviously not knowing them, not knowing whether or not they were married, yet realizing that if they were, it did not affect his life in any way. People often asked if he had a girlfriend, a question attributed to assumed heterosexuality. He took offense to that as heterosexuals took offense to being thought of by anyone as gay. Fortunately at work and at school he could be open, as his job would not fire anyone based upon sexual orientation, and they even provided benefits to same-sex couples. Likewise, his university welcomed the diversity of the student body and protected all its students. It also offered its faculty rights the government denied. How sad that educational centers and corporations would offer such things to their people, though the democracy in which Andy lived denied them.

Andy sat in class the next day, unhappy it was Monday. Perhaps that was a general, public affliction. He managed to cram five classes into three days, though usually worked all of the other four in the week. He had to reconcile responsibility and recreation and would go out with friends despite having work or school the next morning. Monday was not overly exhausting. He had a literary survey class from nine to ten-thirty, which was split between today and Wednesday. Then at eleven-thirty he had a critical theory class, which lasted an exhausting three straight hours. He presently sat in this class. Although the subject interested him, Andy could not help but doodle in his notebook or follow his mind as it drifted from his concentration on the professor to some other fancy. Soon, the professor dismissed them temporarily for a fifteen minute break.

Andy dashed outside with the stampede of students, while others went to discuss something with the professor. As he hurried down the stairs, Andy dug in his pocket for his pack of cigarettes, then pulled them out and promptly poked one in his mouth while still in the building. He fumbled for his lighter as he scurried out the door and then quickly lit his cigarette and inhaled deeply. It was surprising how the first breath of tobacco after so long was so satisfying. Andy reached into his pocket again, this time for his cell phone. It was missing. He worried a little that he lost it, but then remembered he was in such a hurry to get out the door this morning that he left it at Tina's apartment.

Andy stretched a little before entering the classroom and then went to take his seat. After a few minutes, Professor Janet Stein resumed her class. "Okay, well it looks like most of you are back from break now, so let's continue. We discussed feminism and feminist issues and how they pertain to literary theory, so now I would like to discuss the other portion of your readings from last week. So let me say some details on queer theory and then you tell me what you think." This week they were discussing one of the newer theories in literary criticism, with readings from Judith Butler and Eve Sedgwick. Andy found them both interesting and was happy that the school was introducing them to the entire class.

Sometimes the debates in class were reason enough to attend this class regularly, although it was the usual class crowd: the intellectuals, the ones who felt they had to say something regardless of poignancy, the ones who liked to argue for the sake of arguing, the ones who felt so vehement about their stance they would defend it to the end, the jokers and in Andy's case, the silent. Several times before, debates had to be cut short by Professor Stein. It never ceased to amaze Andy that something so trivial could cause such a commotion. Despite his semesters of silence, he was fully prepared to jump into today's argument. The professor had previously criticized him for always being so silent in class. She encouraged him to speak more. Today, he would emerge as a new warrior on the battleground.

"Well that should pretty much cover things," Professor Stein said, "so is there anything you'd like to add or bring up in this discussion?" She looked around, but everyone was silent. "Surely someone wants to say something about queer theory."

Andy panicked. He would have no problem discussing this and arguing it in class, but he had trouble initiating the debate, preferring instead to compliment someone's argument or be impugned by their words. It was unbelievable. Not one person wanted to discuss the matter at hand, though a couple male pigs went head-to-head with a militant feminist just prior to the break while discussing feminist theory. If only he were not too shy to initiate the discussion. Then he thought, all it would take was to open his mouth and comment on the readings. He could feel the words rise in his throat and onto his tongue, but his jaw clenched shut, keeping him quiet. He told himself to just say it. If he did, others would follow suit. Perhaps they were all uncomfortable talking about this and if he were to say something, they could have a formal class discussion.

"Well," the professor said, "if you really have nothing to say about the subject then I want to fill you in on the American Indian readings for next week. We'll be looking at theories regarding American Indian folklore and modern writers in your book and in your supplement packet."

Andy wanted so badly to take charge of this and discuss the writings of Butler and Sedgwick. It seemed to him that a topic like "the performance of gender" would cause controversy and a wide-scale debate in class. What was man? What was woman? Was the performance of being man inherently homophobic? Was the reconciliation of manhood to compassion and understanding of gay men a defiance of manhood? And what of the drag queens the class read about? The exaggeration and performance of men as women was an interesting topic. The essays mentioned it. Andy gave the class discussion much thought over the week, though it would not happen now. He had no problems going to protests or taking on anti-gay adversaries with support. If only he had the courage of Leslie Feinberg to address such issues, or that of John Waters to relax and have fun with subjects such as these. What is man? What is woman?

Professor Stein promptly dismissed the class after giving them several minutes of lecture time on next week's readings. Andy regretted not starting a discussion. Perhaps it just was not meant to be. He threw his backpack over his shoulders and began to leave. He looked back at Professor Stein who was talking to a student with a couple more queued after him. Temptation beckoned him to get her to bring the topic up next week, as she had for other students before this. He stood there watching, then turned his head and walked out the door.

Andy drove away from the university having finished the day's schedule, constantly asking himself, "what if?" He felt bad and knew he needed to change. Despite having come so far in life, he still had so much further to go. He had the determination and courage to help the gay community, though not on his own. He was too reliant on others and thus, could not lead. Here in the theater of cultural war Andy showed his support and had hours upon hours of volunteer work behind him, though it was always for someone else. He was not afraid to be cast into the spotlight as a gay man. Deep down inside, he was afraid of the ignorant, intolerant people out there. It was one thing to be gay. It was another to be gay and in direct opposition of the conservative hegemony. Despite it all, Andy wanted to be stronger. He wanted to change. It hit him. He changed his course from the apartment toward change on the horizon.

He pulled into the small office complex where the Foundation for Human Rights called home. There were many social services in the building, such as a child psychologist, a small youth center and a center to help curb alcoholism. Andy had an idea for a long time, yet never took it to the right people. He loved his city and wanted to help it and the gay community within it to grow and blossom. They had a gay district, but he had a vision for something far greater and not concentrated on the bar scene. He had an idea for something the city was lacking and something that could ultimately unite everyone. Under the increasing anti-gay sentiment and rifts between people, the gay population of his city could stand together and not allow such imperialist thought to sweep them under the rug. America was their nation too and despite the strong message that gays, lesbians and others in the spectrum were not welcome. Andy wanted to show that they too could fight for what was theirs.

"A community center?" asked Julia. Julia Pike was the executive director for the Foundation for Human Rights. She was in her forties, though Andy was unsure of her precise age. She had been a successful director, managing the organization well. Under her leadership, they were able to defeat a postcard to Congress supporting a ban on same-sex marriage. She was quoted in the local paper as saying the supporters "were not seeking the moral good of the country. These are mean-spirited attacks on human beings." Also she saw in the anti-discrimination law and hate crime protection status. It was not enough in society today as there was more work to do.

"Sure," Andy replied, "we don't have one and it would be a great way to bring people together."

"How so?" Julia asked. She always stood cautious of something, needing much convincing in order to support it.

"Well, look at all the social clubs. They're held in places all over. An LGBTQ community center would be a great central place. Not only that, it would provide an alternative to the bar scene. We would reach out to people not into the bar scene and youth who can't go to those places. People can go somewhere to feel accepted without going to get drunk."

"Andy," Julia began, looking down at her desk, "it's a fine idea and all, but this has been brought up before. I mean it's a nice notion and all, but it's just something we really can't do right now." She looked up at him. "Something like that is way too expensive. I'm sorry."

"FHR can help support it. It could help unite our community."

"But FHR can't fund it all on our own."

"We need sponsors. The Gay and Lesbian Chamber of Commerce, social groups, FHR and other groups could help to fund it. We could raise money to buy the property. I've seen a lot of places that put up money just for charitable things like this."

"I can't just say yes though Andy. It'd have to be presented to the board. Plus, we need someone dedicated enough to make sure those funds are acquired." She sat silently for a short while. Neither spoke. At last she continued. "How about you come to the next board meeting and present it. I'll tell you this though, you can't go in like this. They'll want something in writing, plus you'll have to go out and see if you can find sponsors." Andy looked disenchanted. Julia cared about him and saw promise in the youth. Young activists like him were the future hope of gay and lesbians. "Tell you what Andy. Do the work, come to the meeting next Wednesday and I'll back you up all the way."

His eyes brightened and he smiled. "You really mean it?"

"One hundred per cent."

He rushed over to her and hugged her. "Thank you," he whispered. She patted him on the back.

"What are you ladies doing in here?" said a voice at the office door.

The two split and saw the tall figure of Ms. Geraldine Reeves. Geraldine was six-foot four and had large hands and a masculine appearance, though her hair was long with a faded brown color. She was nearly 60. Geraldine was born intersexed and allied herself with the gay community. Eventually, the time came for her to choose a gender and she underwent surgery to become female, though her body still bore many masculine traits. Growing up between two genders made life difficult. In years long ago she remembered the American government condoned treatments for gays, lesbians and people like her. Their only crime was being different. In years long ago, castrations, institutionalization, shock therapy and lobotomies were approved to rid America of its "sub-humans" in proper Nazi fashion.

Julia began, "Geraldine, Andy was just telling me about his plans to make a community center here."

"How lovely," Geraldine replied. "I would love to help you out. Will there be a place for people like me? We sort of have a club for it now."

"Of course," Andy said cheerfully. "It should be for everyone. Gay, lesbian, bisexual, transgender, straight...anyone. Your organization could simply move in after it's finished."

"Wonderful then," Geraldine exclaimed. "People will have a place to go at last. On the whole, I'm used to it, but people still stare and it does bother me at times."

"By the way," Andy said to Julia, "is there anything you need help with today?"

She thought for a moment. "No," she said at last, "nothing I can think of. Unless of course you want to write something up for us. They thought up some Day of Truth bull shit, which is to encourage children to protest us in schools."

Andy shook his head. "Sickening," he said. "Is it because of the Day of Silence?"

"That it is," Julia said. "Parents can get a T-shirt for their children to wear to school to say they hate us."

"Figures," Andy said angrily, "and the Day of Silence is only to show our problems that they created. But they find the need to attack us for it?"

"That's why we need people like you. I mean, the youth will have to take over in the future and if too many stay silent and apathetic, they will win in their little cultural war. It starts small, like denying us rights they have, but soon enough..." Julia left her words hanging ominously in the office.

Andy replied, "I think their problem is ignorance and stubbornness. No matter how many times I told my mom it wasn't a choice she still believe it was because people in her church said it was."

Andy left the office thinking about that. No matter what actual gays and lesbians have said, the opposition still called it a choice. What was worse was that his own mother believed the opposing side over her own son. She feared Andy would miraculously make his brother gay, as though he had some Midas Touch. He had even heard it referred to as a disease, yet with no explanation as to how it was contracted. After coming out to his mother, Andy cried for two straight hours in the privacy of his bedroom. He shook with fear and was afraid to face her afterward. However, she initially seemed to accept it, claiming she still loved him. Though resent had a noticeable presence in their life at home. Over the following months she criticized him and from the social standpoint, she took the side directly against him. Regardless, she was a self-called good mother. The thought that his own mother could do that and call herself a good mother bothered Andy. So many others worldwide had their own stories. Some were equal to his in sadness, some were more fortunate and sadly, many were worse.

Andy stepped out of his car and walked to Tina's apartment. He came in view of her door and saw Melanie run out. He was curious. She was yelling out to him and running for him. Now he was quite concerned. "Andy," she said excitedly, "are you feeling okay?"

"Yeah," he said. "Actually I feel better than okay. Why?"

"Something big happened. You have to come up right away." She led him to the door, oddly escorting him to their place, holding his arm tightly. She put her hand on the knob and said, "prepare to be surprised." She opened the door and Andy walked in feeling giddy. He could not see it immediately, but believed there was a great surprise in store for him here. The said something was deeper in the apartment, though he saw Tina looking at and talking to someone. She turned to him.

"Hey boy. Good to see you," Tina exclaimed. "Come on in." Andy approached her curiously, knowing something hid just around the corner. The suspense was maddening. He smiled like a child seeing gifts at a birthday party and walked in with hopes and excitement rising quickly to glorious highs. He cleared the entryway and got full view of the apartment and his surprise on the couch.

He stopped, frozen. He looked at the couch and saw what this wonderful secret was. The anticipation burst upon seeing it. There was a moment of emotional weightlessness within as his excitement fell into pure horror. The smile on his face melted. The cheer in his eyes relented to pain. The raised posture wilted like a dying flower. There on the couch sat his mother.

Days ago all the fury of hellfire blazed out her eyes. Today, the flames had been extinguished by resolute tears. The wrathful look of a dragon disappeared, revealing the softer side of his cold mother. Even the extra-sensory feel of her spiteful aura became one of seeking peace. Despite the look in her face, Andy knew all too well that appearances were almost always deceiving. She stood up quickly. "You," she said. At that, the chronicles of Andy's gay life scrolled by.

With great courage, he came out to his mother, but later faced the ill fate for his bravery. It was his demise in family life. His understanding friends, gay or straight, supported him. He had many good times with them. Now, the peace and tranquility he detected in his mother snapped to utter hostility. She moved toward him like a charging bull and he felt the imminent pain quickly approaching. To protect his body, his mind drifted elsewhere. He was to be murdered with the rage of the assailant of Danny Overstreet, the motive being only to "waste some faggots." Surely he would be treated medically as Tyra Hunter, denied life by difference. And yet, it would be in the fashion of Gwen Araujo, killed amongst friends. It would be a copycat killing of contempt. Andy awaited the worst as his bloodthirsty mother approached.

She grabbed him with both arms and embraced him tightly. Andy stood there blankly, unsure of what to do. His arms hung limply at his sides. It took a bit to put everything together. Perhaps his mother did actually come here to make amends. Perhaps she was ready to understand him. However, he questioned how she found him. She never knew where Tina and Melanie lived, nor did she have any means to contact them. That aside, it felt good to be hugged by his mother and after breaking from the shock of the situation, he hugged her in return. What did it matter if she was willing to love her own son?

"We had quite a chat waiting for you to get here," Tina said.

"How did you know where to find me?" Andy asked breaking away from his mother's arms.

"Did you forget something this morning," Melanie asked, jiggling his cell phone in her hand.

"I felt bad and missed you," his mother said, wiping tears from her eyes. "I finally tried to call and she answered. We talked for a little bit and then I agreed to come over and meet with you." She looked at Tina and Melanie, who stood side by side, hand in hand. "I'm sorry," his mother said, her bottom lip quivering. "You are my son and I do love you. It's been hard for me, hearing about homosexuality as I have since before you were born." Andy loathed the term "homosexual," but remained silent, awaiting his mother to finish. "Well you have wonderful friends, Andy. They invited me over and we've been talking about this for an hour and a half now. I'm ready to accept this and work on changing. I'm sorry I had been so blind and hurt you before. You're more important to me though, so I'm willing to accept it." A tear rolled down her face. His mother was a proud woman and realizing her years of ignorance through conservative rhetoric and doctrine made her reject her own son.

"Of course," Tina said, "we could only do so much. We got your mother to agree to go to a PFLAG meeting, so she'll be able to talk to others and get the support she needs."

"Mom?" Andy said inquisitively.

"It's true," she answered. "I'm willing to educate myself better on this subject. It broke my heart to have my own son out of my life." The two hugged each other again. They thanked Tina and Melanie for mediating this and helping to resolve it. They left the couple's home. However, they did not return home. Their home was marked by tension, rejection and anger. They left for the future and for a better understanding of each other as mother and child.

In times to come Andy could leave his mark on the gay community and the city. Within a couple years, on account of his leadership an old building, slated for demolition for its futility became the city's center for social programs and organizations to help gays, lesbians, bisexuals, transgenders and anyone curious or questioning, unsure of themselves, needing guidance, someone to talk to, information and support. It became a place for everyone to find a place to belong. Andy pushed that they name it after Tina, his friend and a long-time activist.

After befriending others from the PFLAG meetings, Andy's mother grew more accepting of her own son and the many others she did not know that faced similar problems with an unloving family. Eventually the two could discuss the topic openly and without shame. His mother saw that it was just a part of life. Though personally she wanted to see his wedding with a bride glowing at the altar with grandchildren to come, it was only her desire and not her son's happiness. In the end, that was what mattered most. It was most important for her to stand back and let him live life that would be best for him, rather than suffering through a bad marriage between himself and a woman to make her happy. Why should he have to lie and be miserable in wedlock for what she wanted? It was not her life to live, not anyone's but Andy's. She grew to accept that children, at some point in life, stray from parental expectations.

As for Andy, he would become a success in activism and an outspoken leader. Like his mother, Andy changed as well. His disbelief and utter fear of relationships and falling in love fell through when a persistent suitor proved himself to be reliable and faithful. Although on the whole Andy's accomplishments helped the gay community, his name was not widely known. He became an unsung hero to the public, though in political circles his name was quite popular. He was a hero to progressives and a wretched antagonist to conservatives. Regardless, it did not matter to him. He was helping people. That was all that mattered to him. Andy became a great combatant in this cultural war and made tremendous progress on putting the humanity into the gay community, rather than being labeled with words. He fought an unending battle to bring courage and equality to others here, courage to be themselves and the equality they were denied, in the land of the free and the home of the brave.

Pearl

The morning sun had always been subjective. Those high on life welcomed the first rays of the day. Others saw it as ringing in the work day and graveyard shift knew it as the end. Hungover people thought of it as a blinding curse. Flowers opened to it and vampires closed it off. It was a major part to the innumerable citizens of the planet in the plant and animal kingdoms. After the early beauty of sunrise came the full power of the great star. It was morning near the end of rush hour and downtown came to life.

The city's skyline, like all cities, had an architectural aesthetic from a distance. However, more of an American standard, being in downtown was a different world. There were mid to high-rise buildings making up the densely clustered area. The variety of styles, sizes and features displayed each building's history and character. The old and weathered stood with the aged and charming. Fountains and statues memorializing some person, group or cause shared the downtown space with the towering office buildings dedicated to the living workforce. Each showed a unique part of local and American history. Some pre-Depression buildings were claimed historical, while others rotted, still awaiting a prospective tycoon to renovate the space or a developer to demolish it. They increased in size and changed in appearance up until World War II. Cold War era buildings came with bomb shelters, in case the Russians became hostile with their nuclear arsenal. As the late 20th Century progressed, greater works of concrete, steel and glass rose above the outward growing cityscape.

Now skyscrapers, forever stuck in their foundation, reached for the nomadic clouds, seemingly to be free like their prisoners of work inside. Old-time glamour neighbored post-modern towers of all functions. The urban core was a mix of restaurant and retail space at the street level, capped by high-rise condominiums, offices and major hotels. Like many places, the city tried measure after measure to improve downtown and decrease the exodus of money and residents to the suburbs. At times it was seemingly quixotic, as progress was slow and light-density infrastructure bound downtown, confining it to several city blocks and hindering the urban renaissance.

The downtown workforce continued to pour in, bringing life to this district. Cars honked and engines roared as people chatted outside over cigarettes and coffee before beginning their day. Various city sounds made the streets a noisy place with the generic urban noises. Rising above the din, on the twenty-first floor of one of downtown's high-rise hotels, a woman named Pearl dressed herself and made herself up in peace.

Pearl was in her mid-50s. She had a rosy glow to her creamy skin. She had short, curly hair with a golden color, despite becoming paler over time. Her skin had definitely changed with time, though the pangs of growing older had been kinder to her than others. She had beautiful, blue eyes, the color of Bahamian waters. She wore round glasses with a golden frame and earrings with a single pearl at her lobes. She wore a long pastel pink skirt and an off-white blouse. She put on a light-blue blazer and glossy white shoes. Pearl spritzed on some perfume and checked her stockings again to ensure there was not a run in either of them.

Pearl walked to the window and opened the curtains, exposing the sprawling cityscape. It was beautiful. From this vantage point she saw several of the office buildings before her as well as the smaller infrastructure amidst various trees beyond downtown. Only a few clouds glided lazily across the sky. She heard there was a chance of rain today. The skies did not suggest such a forecast. It was a beautiful Monday morning. Just then she broke from her trance and looked at the digital alarm clock by the bed. It was nine-fifteen. "Oh my," she said walking away from the window. She had somewhere to be at ten-thirty and had to rush. She grabbed her briefcase and the room key and promptly left.

Pearl watched the elevator doors anxiously. The elevator quickly descended to the bottom floor. She looked at the floor counter, watching it drop. She was a bit hungry and remembered there was a small café next door to where she had to be. The elevator stopped and the brass doors opened. She walked quickly through the lobby. The doorman greeted her warmly as she exited the hotel. She smiled and returned his greeting with, "good morning." Outside was a small line of taxis, patiently awaiting a fare. Pearl opened the door to the first one, poked her head in and said, "Words of Wisdom Bookstore, please." The driver glanced over his shoulder at her. "Do you know where it is?"

"Yeah," he replied in a gruff voice, "I know where it is. Hop in."

Pearl quickly got into the car and closed the door. Pearl noticed a strong cigar smell in the car, but could not determine if it was from the driver or the previous passenger. It hardly mattered. She enjoyed the sweet smell of cigar smoke. The driver turned on the meter and stomped on the accelerator. The cab rocketed forward. After several minutes of whipping through downtown like being in the backseat of a stuntman's car, Pearl paid the man and left him a $20 tip. He thanked her happily, offered to pick her up, though she declined and he drove away. Pearl looked at her watch. It was only nine-thirty-nine and she did not need that long to prepare, so she stopped into the café for some breakfast. She did regret not arriving earlier, as a line was already forming before the store, though it did not open until ten.

She sat inside with a cup of coffee, sweetened with vanilla, cream and sugar and had a lemon-poppyseed muffin sitting on a plate. She skimmed through her notes and double-checked to make sure everything would go flawlessly. She pulled out her book titled *In Jesus' Name We Prey* written by Pearl Bryant. The night before she confirmed the delivery of her latest book reached Words of Wisdom for her book signing today. She picked a piece off her muffin, popped it in her mouth and continued skimming her notes.

Pearl was a controversial author, though popular and successful nonetheless. She wrote about the evils of religion in times in the past and likewise, the present. *In Jesus' Name We Prey* was her third book and her current promotional tour was her second. Of course, she toured the usual New York, Los Angeles and Chicago, as well as other cities her publisher set in between. She always brought a crowd and quite often, a heckler or two. A self-proclaimed heretical atheist, her take on branching off into a new sect of being godless, she called her writing a calling, but on no one's will but her own. Perhaps though, it was a calling in life that a suffering society needed a voice of logic and reason.

Fast becoming a prospective author for the critical canon, as she had written theoretically about the effects of religion in literature and popular culture, Pearl took great pride in her writing and wrote theory alongside her greater works. Critics from the church and a list of other religions and religious-affiliated political organizations called her a heathen and a demon who came to dismantle the church and morality of religious teachings, or as she called it, dogma. In an interview she smiled to that response and said she was only one of those two. She argued that simply living life seemingly constituted being a sin and one outstanding factor in one's life reserved a special level of Hell. Pearl did more than justify the ways of God to man, but questioned the ways of man to God, or rather the fear of chaos without spiritual beliefs as well as twisting rhetorical words for centuries to condone oppression and persecution.

Many institutions thought of her works as vile and evil as the Urilia Texts. Pearl was pleased her work got such attention. When several religious organizations launched a boycott against her books, temptation of satisfying curiosity lured members of the religious flocks to her books like sweet apples of knowledge. Some found enlightenment in atheism, others became offended and angered by her words. The sales from the church's free publicity were a boon to Pearl and the once-skeptical publisher and a slap in the face to the religious groups and publishers who doubted talented Pearl.

Pearl called them her Pantheon of Critics, as many religions jumped on a bandwagon. She joked that if all it took to get these religious fanatics to stop hating and killing each other, setting aside their differences to focus on this shared interest, then she would aim for world peace, targeting the Vatican, Mecca and Jerusalem in her next book. She argued religion's detrimental effect on individuals and society. Her harsh criticism and revealing essays brought scorn on her works. Although she often collected and detailed examples taken from day to day life and from the news, she also pointed out facts buried in history and religious denial.

In truth, many great massacres throughout the history of civilization were committed in God's name, or at least, as she wrote, some god's name. Her latest book bridged the centuries between the Roman Empire and post-September 11th America in *Chapter Three: Burning Bridges*. She wrote how Christians crossed this bridge of time without paying the toll. That is to say, they went from being an oppressed minority under Nero and Caesar, to being a dominant and over-dominating world religion. The secret churches centuries ago rose up, into government offices, taking power of many powerful world nations. Christianity had long forgotten its oppressed roots and today, in the seat of power, forged a history and global society of blood, discrimination and unprecedented cruelty.

Pearl focused heavily on Christianity, as it infected most of America and her audience was mostly American, though she had a smaller cult following in West Europe, namely Great Britain and France. She said religions spread like disease and plague the world with biased thought. Based on religious values, many people had instant hatred for certain groups of people or ideas. She supported this argument with tensions between Israel and Palestine, increased hate crimes against Muslims and animosity toward Islam in America, numerous European nations and select others worldwide. Regardless, her disgust in this area was not the religion. Casting the religious identity aside, these were human beings dying and being treated as anything but human beings.

Although it might seem from her defense of Muslims that she was a supporter of Islam and decried the hateful zeitgeist, she spoke out against Allah as well. She stated that Christianity and Islam have been in a centuries-old war. It was her belief that the Crusades were anything but over. Of course, she acknowledged the oil companies had a healthy thirst for Middle Eastern oil and cared less about how much blood in the land of Islam was spilled to satisfy it. Beyond that, she believed there was the on-going conquest for the Holy Land. In the end, it seemed to her that the Christ versus Mohammed battle was no more than a kindergarten spat in a sandbox, as the Christians wanted the Holy Land because the Muslims had it. Likewise, there was no shock in the news anymore when a suicide bomber took away the lives of innocent people in Jerusalem. The Muslims wanted something someone else had. In this regard, religious wars were so childish.

These were two religions to beware of, she thought, because not only are they volatile, they are spreading across the globe in a cross-cultural, religious type of Manifest Destiny which knows no bounds. She discussed the case of Asia. The continent was quickly becoming an economic god with a third of the world's consumers and the financial power exploding across Asia. Not only had the occidental nations taken strides to increase business with Asia, even in the early stages of globalization with Marco Polo, but the world's religions sought to overtake their beliefs. Islam had appeared in China and overtaken Indonesia. Other nations that missionaries invaded had a growing number of Christians. After Europeans conquered the Americas in the name of God, they destroyed the traditional way of life for countless, indigenous people. The ideas spread to the African continent and helped to ravish the natives and culture there. Catholic missionaries forced the Africans into their beliefs and an earlier Saharan conquest took the desert nations of North Africa in the name of Allah.

On a smaller scale, the attempt to convert others still ensued. Churches set up missions to this day and the warriors of God sought to find more lost sheep for the flock. Marquees displayed clever slogans to bring in passers-by, people went to public places to lure people to church and what Pearl considered the worst example, they went door to door. It was all rude and an invasion of personal space. Truly it was no different than the colonialism of other cultures.

Pearl also decried the monetary hypocrisy of religion. In *Chapter Eight: God Loves Money*, she questioned the materialism of spirituality. It was not enough that they based their lives upon and believed in something, with the freedom to go to a house of worship, but corporations cashed in on the devout's need to boast it. They wore crosses of silver, gold and platinum, some bejeweled to show how much they loved God. Perhaps someone with a diamond-studded cross on a necklace loved God more than someone who bought a simple gold-colored pendant. Similarly the consumer spending power adorned their homes with religious paraphernalia, creating the home version of church with little shrines. They offered the mobile versions with the all-too familiar Jesus fish and dashboard figurines. She also wrote about the religious fashion statements with Jesus printed on a T-shirt with a phrase to show much they loved their Lord. Pearl wrote over twenty pages on the subject, but said in a nutshell, this is no more than consumer tithing to a capitalist simoniac.

Pearl dug in her purse and pulled out her cell phone. She looked at a paper with a lot of phone numbers and names on it. She found Words of Wisdom and dialed the number. She promulgated her arrival and apologized for not coming sooner, then requested to be let in through a back entrance to get past the mob lined up before the store. The manager happily obliged and got Pearl in through the stockroom's door behind the building, out of sight from the immense crowd. A short, stocky woman in her thirties opened the back door.

"I truly am sorry for not coming sooner," Pearl said sincerely.

"Don't worry about it," the manager replied sympathetically. "We're just now opening the store and the presentation's at ten-thirty. I do want to thank you personally for coming. I'm happy to have you here."

"Truth be told," Pearl said, "I'd rather come to an independent bookstore like yours than a major chain. It's been my experience that workers in these smaller stores are so much more knowledgeable and familiar with the merchandise." The manager beamed and took her to a desk to let her further prepare.

Pearl skimmed through her notes once more. Her heart beat faster. She personally did not care for book readings, but it was part of the deal with the publisher. She had to admit that they were good for public relations and sales. Still, it made her nervous to speak in front of a large group of people. Luckily she could conceal her stage fright fairly well and was able to speak to the audience. She heard someone approaching and before she could turn around she heard, "we're ready for you Ms. Bryant."

She stood behind a large, cardboard sign the publisher put out for the book reading. It had Pearl's profile shot at the bottom, a print of the book's cover at the top and script introducing her and the book in between. Pearl's heart beat faster being this close to speaking and she held the book close to her chest. She listened to the manager speak into the microphone. Pearl wanted to see the size of the crowd now. It looked quite large earlier, but now it could easily have changed in number. Most likely it increased. She peeked through the crack between the wall and the sign, but could only see a sliver of one section. From what she saw there were no empty seats, as the ones she could see were full and there was a group standing behind them, leading her to believe all seats in the house were taken. She cringed at that and gave herself a pep talk under her breath, calming herself before the big speech.

"And now," the manager said excitedly, "Words of Wisdom Bookstore is proud to present Ms. Pearl Bryant." She took a deep breath and thrust herself into view and walked to the podium without delay. The audience clapped. She was indeed correct. The audience was large. Pearl did the math quickly in her head before speaking. They were seated in two sections with an aisle down the middle. There were eight rows, each with five chairs in it. Each seat was filled. That was eighty people, plus the large group standing behind them. Pearl smiled and sat the book down on the podium.

"Hello," she said, "I thank you for coming." Pearl spent roughly twenty minutes speaking to the audience before opening her book. She introduced and acquainted herself with the crowd. Her voice trembled somewhat and her hands shook nervously. Her legs trembled lightly, but this was unseen to the audience, as they were hidden by the podium. She brushed over her repertoire, describing in brief her other books, then gave a cursory overview of her latest work along with an introduction to it and her reasoning for writing it. *In Jesus' Name We Prey* was merely the latest book detailing the horrors and irrational nature of religion around the world. She dubbed it an obsolete institution as science and government arose to give humanity answers to the unknown, legal justice and public order. "Now," Pearl said, "I'd like to read some excerpts from my book." She opened the book and said, "this part is from the chapter *Dr. Jekyll and Mr. Christ*, which should make sense after I read this. That is, the title should make sense." She fidgeted with the bookmark nervously, unseen to the public, hidden by the podium. Pearl began reading, not making unnecessary, unnerving eye contact with her large audience.

"I feel I must devote an entire chapter to the utter hypocrisy of religion. It's appalling. Here you have something preaching its peace, understanding compassion and enlightenment, but it blatantly disregards human life, dignity, diversity and rights of individuals." Pearl glanced up at the audience, who listened intently. By this point, she began to calm down and could deliver her speech without as much fear. She continued this passage. "Christians boast that their religion accepts anyone and everyone, and that their God is all-loving. Well, anyone and everyone (minus Christians, of course) can plainly see the error in this logic." Pearl licked her lips and felt a bit of discomfort. The coffee she had earlier had worked its way through her. She feared she would have to interrupt this reading with a bathroom break. She tried to focus on finishing this passage. "First, the Bible is claimed to be the proof of God's love and existence, though the same could be said about ancient Greek myths, but I'll discuss that later. In truth, the Bible is just a book. People invented their own bias and prejudice and called it the Word of God." The need to urinate became more intense and Pearl hobbled a little. "Second, just look at noted Bible stories and tell me how God loves all his children. In Noah's Ark, God just got fed up with his children and had them all, with very few exceptions, killed with the flood. Sodom and

Gomorrah is a strong basis for Christian hatred of gays today and when someone lives a different lifestyle, God's answer is to destroy them. God often sends his word down to Earth through prophets and tells them who to hate and kill and the Bible details this." She took a deep breath knowing she would not be able to continue much more. "It is not God's hatred, but man's hatred attributed to God." She smiled and looked up at the audience, then over at the manager. She would have to take a quick bathroom break. It was quite embarrassing. She motioned the manager to her and whispered in her ear.

"Oh," the manager said quietly. Pearl walked off the stage, hurrying toward the bathroom and the manager stepped up to the microphone. "I'm sorry ladies and gentlemen. Ms. Bryant must…well, it seems we have misplaced something and she must get it before the next section of the reading continues. We thank you for your patience." After a few minutes Pearl returned smiling and feeling relieved. She apologized and continued reading the passage.

As Pearl read, the audience listened with interest. Pearl continued on with this passage, saying that Christianity is in itself, hypocrisy. The Bible was a book and nothing more, though so many heeded the spiteful, mythical words within its text, regardless of the message. It said to love one another, but also to punish sinners with death. The Bible outlined who to hate for centuries and raised peculiar questions most Christians never knew were in the texts. Isaiah detailed dining on feces and Proverbs considered no woman to have virtue. Pearl stated that now Christians pick and choose from the Bible. It was okay to hate abortion doctors and gays, as the Bible condemns them and so many others, but it was fine to drink, have sex with anonymous partners as long as it was a heterosexual and indulge in pork, shellfish, all of which the Bible forbids. It was blatant hypocrisy.

The Bible did not promote love and it did not promote understanding. It stated that there was grace and eternal paradise only for a select few. Life should be treasured and appreciated, for in reality, it is short. Christianity, conversely, is quite morbid, as its symbol of the cross refers to the death of Christ and the sheep of the flock look forward to the day they die, so that they can go to a place not proven to exist. Surely there could be no worse way to look at life than to await the day of death. Despite pleas and personal stories from people such as women who aborted a child or a lesbian couple who wanted to marry, Christians believed that single, insidious book over fellow human beings. That, Pearl argued, was exactly why Christianity was not a compassionate philosophy and a small part of the whole of Christian hypocrisy.

"Well now," Pearl said looking into the audience, "that concludes the reading segment of today's presentation. I would love to hear from you now. Any questions? Comments?" A man in the audience quickly raised his hand. Pearl's eyes darted to the motion, "yes, sir?"

The man stood up and began, "first, I love your work and wouldn't have missed this for the world. However, you never mentioned it in previous books and I have yet to read this one, but I was curious about your stance on religion in the long term." Pearl was confused by his question. It was poorly worded. She looked at him trying to interpret the meaning by reading him. Before succumbing to misunderstanding and asking him for clarity, the man spoke again. "What I mean is, what do you think will ultimately happen to the world because of religion?"

"Ah," Pearl said, "that's an excellent question and I'm glad you asked it. It definitely is something I should address in writing. The ultimate consequence is apparent in today's news and social structure: chaos and armageddon. Call that an extreme, but it's a valid argument. Religion has such a horrendous hold on societies, both local and global." She shrugged. "A lot of world problems are linked to religion. No, I cannot blame all the societal or world problems on religion, like say a stock market crash, cataclysmic natural disaster or global warming, but the way we as human beings treat each other has a basis in religion." She began moving her arms as she spoke. "Look at tensions between the West and Middle East. A lot of that is deeply rooted in the rivalry between Christianity and Islam. On the whole, Christians have been completely intolerant of and not willing to understand Muslims and vice versa. And that's a drop in the bucket when you look at the global scale." She sighed and shook her head. "We all know of violent outbreaks around the world. Hate crimes happen all the time in America to people of various faiths. Europe has seen religious intolerance happen over and over again. Christians went after pagans and alleged witches centuries ago and concerned Europeans go after Muslims today. Violent clashes happen in Israel because of religion and India has its share of tension with so many faiths sharing so little room." She leaned forward austerely. "Religious propaganda encourages oppression and discrimination to others and those in power carry it out as the law of the land. Religious zealots like these can't see past faith or what have you, and just see people as people. They are steering our world to a horrible future, one with a likely, horrible end." Pearl stopped and paused for a few seconds, then continued, "if something like religion continues to cause problems amongst people and they refuse to cast aside differences and share the world with each other, then they will ultimately destroy each other and others will be caught in the line of fire." She waited for the man's reply.

"Thank you," he said smiling and promptly sat down. Pearl scanned the audience again, looking for the next question. However, the next eager speaker jumped up out her chair. She was a middle-aged woman with an angry look about her. She had short, black hair and looked like a generic soccer mom with three children, an obscenely large vehicle and a Republican household in the suburban extremities.

The eyesore of a golden cross hanging around her flabby neck twinkled in the store's lights.

"How dare you write and say crap like that," she said furiously. She stood with her hands on her waist and glared at Pearl menacingly. "Christians believe in loving one another and encourage peace and compassion, no matter what you say. God loves everyone, even a cruel, hateful person like you."

Pearl smiled and thought: there is always one in every crowd. It mattered little. These were her favorite people in the audience. The larger audience disappeared and she felt more at ease dealing with just one person, even if the person is a philistine. "Well ma'am, I'd like to ask you a question if you don't mind. Do you support same-sex marriage?" Pearl asked this question of Christian conservatives, as it helped her to prove her point easily.

"Of course not," she retorted snidely, "they are sexual deviants and something like that would give marriage a bad name and break apart our society."

"First," Pearl began, "no it wouldn't. Gays and lesbians throughout the country are in relationships and there has yet to be an apocalypse. Marriage would allow them to be treated as equals. However, rather than debate this topic, listen to what you just said. If you think that way about human beings who happen to be different than you, then you can't possibly love them. Dare I ask how you feel about about abortion doctors, Muslims and pagans? It sounds like you hate them actually."

"I do not," she said defensively, "I feel they just shouldn't have the right to marry."

"Part of loving someone is allowing them to do what is best for them. If you feel that people you don't know should be denied a simple right to express love and commitment, then you absolutely do not love them."

"People like that have strayed from God and his love and purposefully reject His word."

"People like that? Listen to yourself speak, woman. And what, exactly, is his word?"

"Someone who researches the Bible just to insult people like you should know."

"I hope you aren't trying to say, or should I say, preach, the 'love of God' to me."

"That's exactly what I'm doing."

"The Bible can't prove that. It's just a book. The Koran can't prove anything either. Nor can the Torah. Whatever your religion is, its holy text cannot, under any circumstance, prove the god's actual existence."

"I don't need the Bible for that."

"Then why read it?"

"Because it tells of the love of God."

"Were you even listening to our conversation?"

"The Bible helps spread the word of God to others."

"No, the Bible can't prove there is a god at all. It can't spread something that doesn't exist. The Bible infects and encourages people to join an overgrown elitist cult. The Bible can't spread the word of God, but people read it and feel they must do what they think it says. Go to a book discussion group and see how many people read the same material in different ways."

"The Bible does spread His love and it's up to the person to accept God into their heart. I can feel His love. That's how I know God exists. I know of His love from the Bible, but I can feel it inside of me."

"Ma'am, there are casinos all over Vegas that make millions on the same logic."

"Excuse me?"

"Feeling it. One guy may drop $1,000 on the roulette wheel because he feels the ball will land on sixteen. Another may lose a fortune at blackjack because he feels his twenty won't be beat by the dealer. It's the same principle." She pointed a finger at the woman. "God is just a hunch. In this case, you're gambling that if you spend your time devoted to

God, you'll be in a paradise when you die." Pearl smirked. "You're promised it outweighs earthly pleasures. However, it's not proven to exist and it is nothing more than a hunch. So, you can gamble by telling yourself, or rather, having people tell you to live your life a certain way, missing out on so much and feeling certain things toward people for something you hope will pay off well in the end."

At that, the heckler's face reddened in fury. Her blood boiled inside. She realized that she had been defeated. She said nothing as she grabbed her purse and stormed out the building. The audience turned their heads and watched her leave. There was a murmur resounding from them. Pearl always loved these conflicts. She smiled and said, "so, are there any more questions? Or, in the last case, accusations?"

Pearl sat at the foot of the bed in her hotel room. The evening news played on the television as she scribbled the local headline into a notebook. They were covering the incident at the mosque again, saying there was a breaking discovery about the cause of the fire. She figured it would be a perfect example for her next book. There was a knock on the door and Pearl looked up, facing the entrance to her room. She set the notebook down and walked to the door. She unlocked all three locks on the door and twisted the knob.

"Room service," the young man at the door said.

"Ah," Pearl said, "thank you." She paid and tipped the server and he left her with her meal. After the book reading, Pearl went shopping for a few hours, considering there was little to see in this city. Her last meal was a little after noon. She had some mediocre teriyaki chicken at the mall food court. She was amused walking around in public. She was certainly a well-known author, yet unlike the big stars of music, television and film, she could live her life in peace. The paparazzi never bothered her and she was not chased and swarmed in public places. She had the benefit of fame without the marauding fan base that comes with it. She wondered if other authors had the same sort of fame: recognition without loss of privacy.

It was a question she always wanted to know. The people of America seemed too interested in private lives. Film and television stars were idolized and seemingly lived sad lives. Pearl would hate for her life to be scrutinized and made public. It was a strange phenomenon. Perhaps the biggest difference between her and the stars was that the public knew her by her words while they knew stars by face, thus she could go undetected in public. It was possible that on the whole, people just considered movies and television more important than reading. In any case, these people were made into gods.

Pearl paused and pondered that notion. Then she scribbled the idea into her notebook. It would be a great topic for her next book, already about to be written. Pearl sat the notebook aside and turned toward her dinner. It was a turkey sandwich on wheat bread with a variety of vegetables and condiments and a slice of provolone. A glass of chilled chardonnay accompanied the overpriced meal. She finished her dinner and went to bathe in a hot bath and relax. She lay in the steaming water with the glass of white wine perched upon the edge of the tub. Pearl dipped a washcloth into the water, folded it and put it over her eyes. She had a flight the next day at mid-morning, bound for Phoenix. The following day she had another book reading. She was nearing the end of her tour and wanted a rest from the road. She took a sip of the wine and sighed.

Pearl's book became a best-seller for several weeks and only a year and a half later, her next book hit shelves and caused another uproar amongst the religious. Ironically, these very people still contributed to more than half her sales. Pearl could not understand it, nor did she care to do so. They paid to be offended and put money in her pocket and the publisher's profit. Pearl was often cited by civil rights groups and advocates for the separation of church and state. Sadly, Pearl exercised her freedom of press to a dogmatic governing body. She inspired many to take action against the looming theocracy facing America and angered many to encourage its arrival. Pearl became a voice in the counterculture against the Christian hegemony, though politicians ignored what she and her readers as constituents had to say.

II

After days of research, investigation and toil, officials confirmed the circumstances of the tragedy at the mosque. Evidence showed that it was intentional. The explosion happened because someone created it. The media set up camp in front of the crime laboratory awaiting the results. Now the news would stay on television for days, perhaps weeks. They invited guests, both relevant and obscure, to look into the incident. Despite the overwhelming evidence, it was unclear why someone did this. All the authorities and public had to work with was speculation.

Many theories arose immediately following the release of this information. Some suspected it to be a terrorist attack against Muslims. Believers of this story claimed that one angry person wanted to retaliate against fundamentalists who waged a war against America and its allies, thus showed that they will fight Allah. Others claimed it was a mass murder form of hate crime. One conspiracy theory quickly arose that a Muslim fundamentalist did it just to stir anger and tension in the Islamic world, giving rise to renewed hatred of the West. Whatever the reason, the people in the mosque that fateful Thursday night had died. It was a tragic loss of human life.

Tensions were already rising before the release of information as some were quick to blame the explosion on an individual. Protests and demonstrations were already scheduled and more came under planning after the news reported the blast to be intentional. Throughout the city tensions grew thick, promising a catalyst for the rest of the nation. People

111

reverted from civil conduct to bestial behavior as groups began to choose sides and lines were drawn. The local police prepared for the worst and the national guard was put on alert before more blood was spilled.

Min-yeong

As Pearl rested in her hotel that Monday evening, the locals went about their business elsewhere. Somewhat distanced from the high-rises of downtown, a large area of clustered neighborhoods bustled in two worlds: one the locals left and one they lived in now. These ethnic areas made a hybrid between the motherland and the American city. One particular area was a group of several neighborhoods with heavy influences from Asia. The city had a Chinatown and Little Saigon, home to Hmong people and other refugees from the atrocious Vietnam War. There was also a relatively small Japanese neighborhood and its neighbor, a little Korea. All these neighborhoods had apartments, townhouses and commercial areas with a heavy influence of one of the home nations. Although largely populated by their influential groups, many immigrants or American-born people lived elsewhere, but came to these centers for specialty shopping or socializing.

The small-scale Korea was a smaller ethnic neighborhood in comparison to others. Two major roads crossed in the middle of the neighborhood and the local Koreans called this intersection *Sijang*. It was the commercial area serving the community and all four corners had buildings two to three stories tall. The area offered Korean restaurants, shops selling foods and goods from Korea, a travel agency and many other services, with business conducted mainly in Korean. Just behind the services on the southeast corner was a church with a tall, blue steeple. On the northeast side, behind the shops was a Buddhist temple.

Sitting on the bottom floor of one building was a restaurant named *Gimchi Cheonguk*, though that was the name written in Korean. The anglophonic "Kimchi Heaven" was written beneath the *hangeul* script. The restaurant was named after the quintessential Korean dish of spicy, pickled cabbage. It was quite crowded tonight. Yang Min-yeong scrambled in the kitchen to keep up with the orders. It was her restaurant and only she and her sister-in-law worked in it, though often she called on her daughters for help. Min-yeong worked quickly in the kitchen and kept her customers happy with surprisingly fast service, despite the restaurant's small staff and often large crowds.

"Cheong-ha," she yelled out from the kitchen. Her daughter ran to the counter to help her mother. Min-yeong put a large tray on the counter and her daughter picked it up to take to Table Eight. It was quite heavy for such a little girl and she struggled with it. Cheong-ha was quite small, as she was only twelve, but she was always at her mother's side at the restaurant, willing to help in any possible way.

She set the tray down on the table and unloaded the food onto the table. "Here you are," she said happily, "*kalguksu* for you and *bibimbap* for you." Cheong-ha placed the variety of side dishes down with the meal. She was hungry and eyed the customers' food. The *kalguksu* had a generous helping of noodles and the broth in which they swam smelled heavenly. The garlic smell made her stomach rumble and the sight of slivers of vegetables and egg nestled with the noodles tempted her to sample the man's food. The *bibimbap* was equally inviting with fresh vegetables, rice, chili paste and the fried egg crowning the dish. She set down the *gimchi, dotorimuk*, bean sprouts and pickled daikon. She smiled and asked, "anything else I can get you?"

"Uh," the man said looking at one of the side dishes with an air of slight disgust, "no thanks. But what is that?" He pointed to the brown cubes of gelatinous *dotorimuk*, coated with chili.

Cheong-ha decided against saying the Korean word and stated simply, "acorn jelly." The man said nothing and she left the table.

Min-yeong called Cheong-ha into the kitchen. Her daughter wearily dragged herself back there. She had come to the restaurant immediately after school and had not eaten since lunch. The hunger dizzied her. Min-yeong spoke to her in Korean, "*you look so tired. Here, I made you some* tteokpokki *and* songpyeon." Min-yeong set down the bowl of *tteokpokki* and a plate of *songpyeon* and placed a pair of chopsticks alongside it. Min-yeong made an excellent dish of *tteokpokki*. She made her own rice cakes for the dish and put just the right amount of carrots, onions and garlic in the mix. She then added a hearty portion of chili paste and then dusted the concoction with chili powder. Her *songpyeon* was beyond compare, using her same rice cake recipe, though adding toasted sesame seeds, cinnamon and honey in the middle to make the classic Korean cookie.

Cheong-ha smiled and replied in Korean, "*thanks mom.*" She bit into a sweet morsel of *songpyeon*, tasting the rich flavor of toasted sesame seeds blended with the sweet cinnamon and honey. She ate the food quickly, alternating between the spicy and sweet dishes. She still had patrons to serve, though it was hard to pull herself from eating.

Cheong-ha gobbled her food and quickly ran to pick up the next order. She took it to a table of three Korean men. They had already gone through two bottles of *soju* and had ordered a third. They were all nearing drunkenness, but Cheong-ha was bringing them their dinner. One man ordered a bowl of fiery *gimchi jjigae*. Min-yeong always made this spicy cabbage stew hotter than usual. It seemed to glow red with the excess of chili she used. The man who ordered it was telling a joke in Korean to the other two men and he laughed a bit as he told it. Cheong-ha set the bowl of stew before him along with a silver bowl of steamed rice. She gave the other man his meal of *bulgogi*, the beef still sizzling on the plate. She set the deep bowl of *naengmyeon* before the third man and cut the long, thin noodles with a pair of kitchen shears. This man ordered it with chili paste, but Cheong-ha brought him a small bottle of spicy mustard for his cold noodles. She set the third bottle of *soju* on the table and left. The men focused on the Korean joke and paid no attention to Cheong-ha, but noticed she had brought them food. They opened the bottle of rice liquor and poured each other shots before eating. Cheong-ha returned to the kitchen to eat more of her dinner. Before she could pick up her chopsticks, Min-yeong called out her name and asked her to take another order out.

After the restaurant closed, the two cleaned it and began the short walk home to their nearby apartment. Min-yeong spoke to her daughter, *"thank you for your help today. Your sister has to study for school and your aunt won't be back until tomorrow."*

"That's okay," Cheong-ha replied. She thought about and quietly lamented her father. He passed away four years ago and life had been difficult ever since. He died of lung cancer. The family restaurant had been founded and named by him and after it grew in popularity, his sister immigrated from South Korea to help. Tragically he died three years after she arrived.

Cheong-ha looked at her mother. Min-yeong was middle-aged, but appeared younger. She was beautiful. Her hair was short and jet black. She was thin and small, but a strong woman regardless. However, after her husband's death, her deep, black eyes froze in permanent sadness, acting as a window to the pain that sat inside.

The mother and child reached the apartment and entered, both exhausted. Min-yeong ran the restaurant all alone until her daughter arrived after school. Min-yeong rarely got any rest, as she worked in the restaurant seven days a week. She flicked on the lights and called out, "*annyeong?*" There was no answer. "Su-jin," she cried out. There was no reply. Min-yeong blurted out a flurry of curse words in Korean. Cheong-ha froze, feeling quite uncomfortable by her mother's angry display. Su-jin said she would be at home studying all night, but she was not here. Cheong-ha excused herself and went to bed. Min-yeong turned the lights off and sat in the recliner in the dark.

Min-yeong was born in the slums of war-torn Seoul in 1955. Her father survived the Korean War, though he committed suicide in 1959, after fathering two children. The horrors of war became too great mentally, burdening him, driving him to his own demise. From a young age she had to work hard. Her mother grew ill during the harsh Korean winter and died in 1969, shortly after she met the man who would become her husband. The two fell in love instantly, but grew tired of Korea's slow progress after the war. They saved enough money and made arrangements to ride on a cargo ship departing from Incheon, bound for Long Beach. Once in America they migrated further inland and rested in their current home city in 1973. They found life in America to be much harder than they originally imagined.

While in Korea, Min-yeong worked in a restaurant near the American military base in Seoul. It helped her to learn to cook and gain skills in English. With her culinary skills, they were able to open and operate a Korean restaurant in America. The restaurant became a success, though it became harder to manage after her husband's death. They had two girls, both born in America: Su-jin now eighteen and Cheong-ha now twelve, the elder an increasing burden. Min-yeong had only visited Korea once since leaving. She went just months after her husband's death shortly after the September 11th attacks, and was shocked to see the changes. She left a nation badly damaged by war and ravaged by poverty, but returned to a new world. South Korea had made great progress in her time away from the homeland.

Faintly, there was the sound of the door unlocking. It creaked open quietly. Su-jin entered the apartment, so as to not wake her mother. It was close to two in the morning on Tuesday and her mother would be furious if she were caught being out this late. It was a school day after all. Su-jin quietly closed the door and put one hand over the lock as she turned it, trying to muffle out the loud click it was known to make. It was quite quiet and Su-jin turned away, relieved. Min-yeong's voice arose ominously from the dark chamber. "*Where were you?*" she asked in Korean.

"Mom," she shrieked, startled, "I...I was...studying." Su-jin spoke in English through her fear.

"*Speak in Korean! Why were you out so late?*"

"Mom," Su-jin replied in English, "I'm sorry, but I have this huge project and I was just at..."

"*I said speak in Korean! You can speak English all you like outside this apartment, but when you speak to me you must speak only in Korean. I raised you to hold onto your roots better than that.*" Su-jin could not see her mother's expression, but could tell by the silhouette made with the backlighting from the lights outside that her mother removed her glasses and was wiping away tears. Min-yeong spoke again, "*I tried so hard to let you know of your ancestry. I wanted you to feel connected to Korea, even thousands of kilometers away. I wanted you to have a great future, so I pushed you all through school. What has happened to you? These days you've gone so far downhill. You never help at the restaurant anymore and don't try in school. You won't even speak to me in Korean.*" Min-yeong stopped and cried.

Su-jin hated these guilt trips, but relented. In Korean she replied, "*but mom, you didn't let me just be a kid. When I wanted to play, you made me practice the violin. When I wanted to see my friends, you made me study. When I wanted to relax, you made me work in that damn restaurant. So I'm sorry, mom, if I'm just now getting to live my life for myself.*"

Min-yeong stopped crying and looked at her daughter in utter shock, masked by darkness. "You want be America girl?" she said in English, much to Su-jin's surprise. She forgot how thick her mother's accent was when she spoke in English. "You want friend but no future? Why you me talking like that? Go. You no want my help. Why you staying? Go. I want you have good future and you no want." Min-yeong stood up and walked to her bedroom. "You know, our restaurant make money. You want eat? You want clothes? We no restaurant having, you no eat and you no have clothes." At that, she went to bed. She had an early day and it was late already. Su-jin stood in the dark as her mother slammed the bedroom door behind her. She huffed and crossed her arms, making an ugly face at her mother's bedroom.

Min-yeong slipped into her nightgown and crawled into bed. It was nearly two-thirty now. She unfastened her necklace. It was a small cross. Her late mother gave it to her. According to a family legend, it was given to her mother by her father, who received the cross as a gift from a grateful medic for his bravery saving the lives of wounded soldiers during the war. It was one of the few things she brought to America with her and one of the few subtle reminders of Korea and her national pride. She held it in her hand and stared at it for a few minutes. Her ancestors converted to Christianity when the missionaries invaded the Korean Peninsula many years ago. Min-yeong had been raised Christian, but retained her Korean traditions. Sometimes it was hard for American Christians to separate her Korean beliefs and practices infused with Christian teachings. She pondered how many Christians had faith in God and were blessed, yet her life had no shortage of pain, tragedy and misfortune. At that thought she set the cross down and looked at the photo she kept bedside. It was of her and her husband with Cheong-ha and Su-jin, both very young in the picture.

Min-yeong turned off the lamp and closed her eyes. Through the thin cracks of her closed eyelids, tears rolled out into crestfallen trails and dropped to the pillow like many fallen hopes and dreams.

Min-yeong yawned as she unlocked the restaurant door. She wanted to forget last night. She did not even bother to see if Su-jin stayed or not, as she felt angered by the situation even the next morning. She looked around the restaurant and sighed. She felt it would be a long day. She walked into the kitchen to get things prepared. It was just past ten now and the restaurant opened at eleven. Min-yeong went to set up the pots and pans and get the cash register ready to keep a roof over her head and food on the table.

The restaurant was fairly large. It could hold about thirty-five patrons. Rather than having them sit at short tables on the floor, as many restaurants in Korea did, she provided her diners with chairs and taller tables. There were a couple plants by the entrance. They were tall and green, like short trees. There were several large pictures adorned on the walls. This was the newest feature to the restaurant, as Min-yeong had them put in last year. One was a picture of a beautiful young woman dressed in an elegant, pink *hanbok*, the traditional wardrobe of Korea. It reminded Min-yeong of the smaller one she got for Cheong-ha when she was a small child. Another picture was of the Namdaemun in Seoul. Min-yeong remembered seeing it on her last visit. Once an elaborate entrance into the city with flanking walls that kept invaders out, now the Great South Gate had modern roads and buildings sprawling around it with a nearby market covering several city blocks. Likewise there was a picture of the Gyeongbokgung, the former royal palace in Seoul. Many naive customers thought it was beautiful and surprising that it withstood time for so long. Min-yeong never corrected them by saying the Japanese destroyed this palace during the period of occupation and what stood in Seoul now was a replica. She also featured pictures of the Dokdo Islands, a troupe of *samulnori* dancers, Seoul Tower atop Namsan and a scene at night with an endless tunnel of bright lights and signs running vertically on the buildings.

The various scenes from Korea gave the diners a glimpse into the nation's sights and heritage, but to Min-yeong it was a reminder of her culture and homeland. After her last visit to Korea she saw the tremendous progress of the country and since then, envied it. The Korea of the 21st Century was a much different world than that of the immediate post-Korean War era. Her homeland had been through so much over the centuries. Min-yeong carried with her the anti-Japanese sentiment passed down from her parents. Her grandfather was executed during the period of Japanese occupation in the early 20th Century. Despite having told her children this, neither Cheong-ha nor Su-jin had a mutual resentment. Both were born and raised in America and despite the American conflict with Japan in World War II, there was little rancor amongst the people throughout the country toward the Japanese. Immediately following Korea's independence from Japan, war gripped the peninsula and ushered in the tense rift between North and South Korea. The Seoul Min-yeong left was a third world slum. Now it was a bustling metropolis bearing ample culture, arts, entertainment and sophistication. Deep within, Min-yeong wished she only had the patience and faith in years past to stay and see from within Korea rise to an Asian powerhouse. On many occasions including today, she regretted so hastily leaving. In some ways the pictures on the walls were a mockery to her misfortune in life. Despite it all, the Seoul of today was an alien place, one different from the same city she left years ago.

Min-yeong gripped the cross around her neck and muttered a forced prayer to God in Korean. She walked into the kitchen and prepared the rice in the large rice cooker. She busily toiled in the kitchen, getting the restaurant ready for the lunch crowd. Her restaurant did surprisingly well at lunch, with workers flooding in from nearby office buildings and businesses. She began preparing several rolls of *gimbap*, as it was a popular food for a light lunch or quick snack. She dropped a mound of sticky rice onto a rectangular laver, and spread it. Then she placed a long stick of sweet, pickled daikon, strips of shredded carrots, a stem of ham and one of egg, matchstick-slices of cucumber and finally crab meat in it lengthwise. She rolled it and sliced it into thick circles. Many people equated it to sushi, but Min-yeong would always correct them on the name.

"*Annyeong?*" came a voice from the dining area.

Min-yeong looked up and saw the woman standing at the counter smiling. Min-yeong smiled and approached her. It was her late husband's sister, Hye-seon. She spoke to her in Korean, "*how was your trip?*"

"*It was nice,*" Hye-seon replied. "*Did everything go well at the restaurant?*"

"*Yes,*" Min-yeong replied, "*but next time you go out of town, take Su-jin with you.*" She turned around and walked to the refrigerator.

"*Why? What happened this time?*"

Min-yeong pulled out a canister containing *gimchi* from the refrigerator. "*She is always so disrespectful. She came home at two this morning, she is not doing well in school, she refuses to speak in Korean to me...*" Min-yeong sliced the head of pickled cabbage to prepare the *gimchi* for any form in which she would need it for the day, whether as a side dish or main ingredient. She cut it as a woodsman would take an axe to a tree, chopping in swift, hard blows, showing her anger. "*I swear she's ashamed to be Korean. She doesn't eat my cooking anymore, won't even try to speak Korean, she dresses like a whore like all the rest of the girls at that school.*" She sighed despondently. "*I just don't know what to do with her anymore.*"

Hye-seon shrugged her shoulders. "*She can still speak it, right?*"

"*Of course she can*," Min-yeong replied. "*She just stopped speaking it a couple years ago. When I speak to her she can understand it. When I'm very angry with her she will break down and speak it. She shouldn't have to be yelled at to speak it though.*"

"*Hey*," Hye-seon said with the intimation of a brilliant idea, "*why don't you send her to Korea?*"

Min-yeong stopped cutting and turned toward her sister-in-law. "*What? You mean like on vacation? To see her roots?*"

"*No. I mean send her there to live. She could stay with mother. She has only seen Su-jin once ever. Wasn't she just a little one when that happened? Well, I'm sure mother could whip her into shape. Su-jin could see and experience her homeland and after a few years there, lose those nasty habits she learned in America.*"

Min-yeong contemplated the notion. It was genius. Su-jin could speak Korean and could communicate with the people there. Her grandmother had only seen her once when she came from Korea to visit years ago. Even Cheong-ha was too young to remember that, though she was certainly not the problem child in this case. "*That*," Min-yeong said, "*is an excellent idea. Yes. I'll send her. I'll tell her tonight.*"

Throughout the day, the idea kept coming back to Min-yeong's mind. From that thought, other thoughts spawned. She knew America was full of rotten kids, though there were many good kids too. Cheong-ha was an excellent little girl, contrary to her older sister Su-jin. She wondered which parental mistake she made, or which terrible influence corrupted her oldest girl. There was one incident that Min-yeong recalled that happened over a decade ago that perhaps inflicted Su-jin and spread throughout her young mind, creating the girl she was today: rebellious against and ashamed of her Korean heritage.

When Su-jin was seven, her mother would bring her to church every Sunday. Min-yeong could understand only about half the sermon, but went in faith regardless. Rather than have Su-jin sit through the tedious religious lecture, Min-yeong sent her to Sunday school. Su-jin soon befriended a young girl named Suzie. The two became great friends and the mothers talked in passing off their daughters on play dates or at church. Soon autumn arrived and Su-jin pleaded with her mother to let Suzie celebrate *Chuseok* with them. Min-yeong was reluctant, but eventually agreed to let her daughter's best friend celebrate the holiday with them.

Chuseok was a holiday Min-yeong took seriously. It was the one Korean holiday for which she would close the restaurant. After leaving Korea she faithfully celebrated *Chuseok* every year, though it had been limited to her immediate family only. However, Min-yeong saw no harm in this blonde-haired, blue-eyed little girl celebrating this day with her friend. Su-jin explained it simply as "Korean Thanksgiving."

Suzie came to the apartment in a frilly white dress with little pink ribbons. She was surprised to see Su-jin's family dressed in colorful clothing. Su-jin and Min-yeong wore the same type of dress, but Min-yeong's was a brilliant red with floral decorations on the vest. Su-jin wore a less fancy outfit colored yellow with some colored stripes on the sleeves. She, unlike her mother, had a headdress wrapped around her head with a string of beads hanging loosely like garland. Suzie thought it to be amusing that both were small females with their frames, but they looked quite fat in these costumes. The father wore a simpler suit. It was a blue coat with blue pants. Suzie wished her mother saw it, but she had dropped her off and left.

Su-jin showed Suzie how to make *songpyeon*, the sweet rice cake dessert synonymous with *Chuseok*. They bowed humbly to the ground and the father spoke solemnly in Korean. Su-jin later explained their connection to ancestors. Min-yeong explained how *Chuseok* followed the lunar year. In honor, they made dishes for those who passed. It was a meal for the living and dead. Suzie excitedly told her mother all about the festivity, though her mother could not share the enthusiasm. These old Korean rituals seemed pagan and she felt her daughter's religious affiliation that she chose for her was threatened. Suzie was not to speak to Su-jin anymore and her mother likened the *Chuseok* celebration to devil worship.

It was a matter of time before Suzie's mother spread rumors like wildfire throughout the church. Suzie even turned against her former best friend and the Sunday school class ridiculed and ostracized her. Likewise, people gave Min-yeong hateful stares at church and people refused to speak to her. Both mother and child became pariahs. Though Min-yeong wanted to stay at the church in her everlasting devotion to God, Su-jin's pleas to leave the church alongside Min-yeong's uncomfortable feeling every Sunday forced them to abandon the church. Rather than finding another house of worship, Min-yeong decided that her love of God was understood. The Almighty could surely feel her love, thus she could practice freely in the comfort of her own home or even the restaurant.

Min-yeong looked upward in the kitchen with the slices of *galbi* in front of her. The next order was up, but her mind was elsewhere today. These slices of ribs could wait for a quick prayer. She finished and shouted out to Hye-seon to pick up the order. As she set the raw meat on the counter, Cheong-ha came through the front doors. "Did you need help, mom?" she asked as she walked toward the kitchen. Min-yeong thought it was strange and a bit alarming that Cheong-ha said that in English.

"No," Min-yeong said in English, "you go home."

Cheong-ha quickly replied in Korean, "*what's wrong mom? You almost never speak English and always want us to speak with you in Korean.*"

Min-yeong concealed a smile. She responded in Korean, "*nothing is wrong, Cheong-ha. If you see Su-jin at home, tell her I must talk to her and that she had better be there when I get home tonight. Also, tell her to bring her appetite. We're eating together this evening."*

Hye-seon stepped between the two and took the order of *galbi* to the table. Cheong-ha left feeling a bit anxious. Min-yeong watched as Hye-seon put the pieces of raw beef onto the grill over the hot coals in the middle of the table. It seemed so exotic to the table of Westerners, but to Min-yeong and Hye-seon, it was a small part of home. It was bringing a little piece of their homeland to the occidental palate.

After a long day at work, Min-yeong stood in her own kitchen and prepared a special meal for Su-jin and herself. Su-jin sat at the small table fretting. Her nervousness was highly evident. She wondered what her mother was going to say. The only words spoken to her this evening were to sit at the table and wait. Su-jin played with the chopsticks before her. With her index finger she pivoted one of the pair back and forth, making a faint clink each time one stainless-steel part of the pair touched the other.

Min-yeong set the table and placed several dishes between her seat and Su-jin's. Su-jin felt a bit queasy from her stressed nerves. If her mother was angry, she never feared or relented to show it. Her mother was strangely quiet and complacent. Su-jin eyed the foods her mother set on the table. There was a dish of *gimchi*, the very dish her mother used to pack in her lunches as a child and the children in elementary school would taunt her for it. There was also a dish of spicy tofu, one of silvery anchovies, two small bowls of a seaweed soup, one dish of the sweet daikon, and one of spicy cucumbers. Min-yeong returned with two hot bowls of *gamjatang*. Su-jin grew more curious as to why her mother was doing this, because she had forsaken most Korean food for the all-American hot dogs, hamburgers and apple pie, but she could never resist her mother's *gamjatang*. It was a fine soup of meat, potatoes, vegetables and spicy chilies. Min-yeong brought two small bowls of steamed rice to accompany the entree.

"*Let's eat,*" Min-yeong said before sitting down.

"So late?" Su-jin replied, once again violating her mother's rules. "It's getting close to midnight."

Min-yeong sighed and sat down, "*not in Seoul. It's a good time for dinner right now if you were in Seoul.*"

Su-jin rolled her eyes as she put a spoonful of the soup in her mouth, her stomach feeling better upon seeing her favorite Korean dish. She swallowed and said in defiant English, "don't be ridiculous mom. We're not in Seoul, we're in..." Merely saying those words triggered the realization. *Gamjatang* was Su-jin's favorite food and aside from special occasions, her mother only made it for her to break bad news. At this point, it was apparent why this meal was happening and why Cheong-ha gave her sister the austere warning from her mother. Still, Su-jin needed confirmation from her mother to verify the news. Horror overcame her face and Su-jin stared at her mother through wide eyes in silence, not breaking her stare. At long last, the young girl broke the silence, speaking to her mother in perfect Korean, "*what do you mean if I were in Seoul?*"

Min-yeong hid her smile behind a spoonful of the soup. Hearing her daughter at long last communicate in the native language was like hearing the most beautiful melody sung by enchanting songbirds. "*So, you really can speak Korean. That's good to know. And I thought maybe you just forgot.*"

"*Mother, what did you mean by that remark about Seoul?*"

Min-yeong looked at her with a serious expression. "*Su-jin, you are extremely disrespectful. You speak English to me and you know that in this house I want you to speak only in Korean. You stay out late with friends and you know I want you home by ten. You ignore your schoolwork and you know I want you to do well. Most importantly, you have forgotten where you came from.*"

Su-jin jumped up and shouted, "*I was born here. I am an American.*"

"*Sit, Su-jin.*" Her daughter scowled, but obeyed. "*You may be American by birth, but by blood you are Korean. You should take pride in your country."*

"*I do take pride, mother. I am an American. Don't even pull this shit with me. You left Korea, not me. How dare you tell me to take pride in that place when you decided to leave it long ago.*" She scowled fiercely at her mother.

Min-yeong, appalled, dropped her spoon in the soup and gawked at her daughter. "*You do realize the Korea I left was different than the one today, don't you? Your father and I wanted to start a family and the Korea we left together was no place for you or your sister. We came here to benefit you. Just because we left it doesn't mean we can't be proud of it.*"

"*Okay, then. That's what this whole meal is for?*" Su-jin felt a bit of relief. "*So you just wanted to tell me I'm a disrespectful idiot and that I should be proud of Korea.*"

"*Not exactly.*"

"*Then what?*" Su-jin whined and became more impatient with her mother.

Min-yeong calmly put a piece of the spicy cucumber in her mouth and masticated, staring across the table at her daughter. Looking at her, Min-yeong could not help but see this visual personality trait they both shared. When either Min-yeong or Su-jin were frightened, they always masked it with anger. Perhaps it was a subconscious attempt to scare away the opponent. In Su-jin, it had never been more obvious than now.

"*Hye-seon...your aunt and I have decided that it would be best if you were to stay with your grandmother in Korea.*"

Su-jin growled at her mother like an angry tiger. She bellowed in English, "the hell I will."

"*Su-jin,*" her mother shrieked, "*that is why you are going to Korea!*" She stared down her daughter with blazing ferocity burning from her fiery eyes. The power of her gaze seated Su-jin. "*You are a rude little girl who has taken everything her family has ever done for her for granted. We have not only meant, but*" *have done well for you and Cheong-ha. All these years we have made sacrifices for you and have only acted in your best interest. I am through with this disrespect you bring into our home. You are going to Korea."*

Quietly Su-jin muttered, retreating to the safety of her mother's language, *"what if I try harder?"*

Min-yeong sighed, *"Su-jin, I have threatened you in the past. Do you remember when I wouldn't let you leave the house, aside from school, for a month? Yeah, well that was after a couple threats of taking away a week of your privileges. Sure, you were good for a few days afterwards, but you let your guard down and became what you were again."*

Su-jin tried to retort, *"so you just took away my freedom like you want to do now. Isn't that why you left Korea in the first place?"*

"What are you? Stupid? I told you already that we left Korea to make a better life for you. The country your father and I left was poor and crippled by the war. We were never slaves. No evil dictator tried to threaten our lives if we were unhappy with his rule. In the country we left it was hard to make money. Korea's a free country, but the kids are better behaved. You need to get in touch with your roots and learn some discipline."

"Are you crazy? I can't just leave this all behind."

Min-yeong seethed at that remark. *"Leave all what behind?"*

"Oh...umm," Su-jin began, searching for a valid reason to stay. *"Like friends and...school. You just want me to give it all up like that?"*

"School? Su-jin, your school called me at work and said you were failing in all but one class. I think it was art. Anyway, why are you concerned about leaving school if you do so poorly in it?"

"Okay, fine," Su-jin said yieldingly. She caught herself at this and decided to revert to Korean rather than exacerbate this dire situation with her mother. *"You want to know the truth? Yes, I love art. I want to be a painter. I know you had some other future planned for me, but I'm sorry. This is what I love and what I want to be. Yes, I have a boyfriend too. I can't and won't leave him to go to Korea."*

Min-yeong grabbed the cross around her neck again. Su-jin came to realize it was her mother's gesture of comfort. It was, in a way, a symbolic prayer. She could be asking for guidance or strength or some other wish she needed to be granted. Whatever the desire, her mother never spoke while speaking to God. *"Su-jin, you know I would support you if art is what you love. Dreams should be a guiding light, as they can take you to a happy place. However, do not take that as a sign of my sympathy. I am angered by this boyfriend. This news tells me that he is the reason you do so badly in school and why you are out so late. Besides, why have you not told me about him before?"*

"Because I knew how you would react."

"I think it's wonderful my girl found love. I think it's horrible that she lost my trust concealing him."

"So, if we talk some more, maybe I can convince you to let me stay here...with you?"

Min-yeong sighed, *"you just don't get it. You are still rude to me and your sister. I am offended that you refuse to even acknowledge your Korean heritage. You are still going to Korea to stay with your grandmother. Now, eat your soup."* The two finished dinner in silence, not even looking at each until they finished. Su-jin walked quickly to her room and slammed the door. The noise made Min-yeong jump. She put a hand over her startled heart and gasped. She muttered and cleaned the dishes, then went to bed.

As tired as she was, Min-yeong could not sleep. She lay awake staring at the ceiling. Perhaps now Su-jin would respect her maternal status, obligation and authority. Min-yeong thought about the small cross around her neck. She clasped it often, though usually was unaware of the motor reaction. She wondered if God always listened. Again she felt as though she and her family had been neglected or forgotten by God. She knew it was wrong to question such things, but the thought often occurred. She sighed and let it go. Again, it crossed her mind. She had invested her entire life and faith into something that constantly bombarded her with suffering and misfortune. The only good she really got out of this life was her daughters and the success of her restaurant.

As she began to drift to sleep, she heard the front door slam. She sprang out of bed and ran to the front room. Her heart raced fearing her home had been invaded by a thief of the night, but quickly she realized a thief would have attacked her immediately. She flung open the front door and saw a car parked before the stairs to her apartment. It was running and a shadowy figure dropped a bulky package into the trunk. Min-yeong recognized the shape at the car. It was Su-jin, running away in the night.

"*Su-jin,*" she shrieked, "*what are you doing?*"

Su-jin responded callously in English, "fuck you, mom." She raised her middle finger at her mother, who watched helplessly from the banister as her oldest daughter prepared to leave her life. The car door slammed shut and the wheels screeched as the driver wheeled Su-jin away from the apartment complex. Min-yeong became limp. She slouched over the railing, supporting herself with her arms. A flood of tears poured from her eyes. Her daughter was now no longer a part of the family.

Min-yeong rolled over and her back slid down the railing as she witnessed yet another twisted act of fate befall her life. She pawed at her face, wiping away the steady flow of tears. After several minutes of crying over her loss, she grabbed the cross hanging from her neck. She held it tightly and clenched her teeth as her words to God sounded in her head. With one quick jerk, she snapped the cross from her neck, then pulled herself to her knees and promptly tossed it as far away from her as she could. The relic given to her by her mother sailed through the air and fell somewhere in the dark asphalt of the parking lot. Min-yeong returned to her apartment and caught glimpse of Cheong-ha's eye peeking at her through the crack of her ajar bedroom door.

"*Go to sleep*," she said, the melancholy sound of sadness lingering in her voice. The door closed quietly. Min-yeong went to her room and collapsed onto the bed, where she cried more until the tears relented to sleep.

Su-jin did not return the next morning, nor the one after that, nor at any time to come. In time, Su-jin became only a memory in the small family. The driver was her boyfriend. He was a young, artistic type, much like Su-jin. The two spent three years together, one lustful and happy, the consequent tense and miserable. Eventually Su-jin left his studio apartment for New York, hoping to take the art world by storm, though never quite made it. The rest of her days were spent in northern New Jersey working at a major grocery chain. At times she missed her mother and regretted her treatment of her, but out of utter shame and humiliation, never returned to her home city.

Min-yeong abandoned Christianity that night Su-jin left and never questioned faith again. It was apparent that no higher power could exist. The more she thought about the issue on her own, the more ludicrous religion, or any greater being seemed. It was a substitute for the unknown and for love. If there was a god, the deity would be of the sickest sort to plague humanity with such ills. Min-yeong toyed with the idea of returning to Korea, but the restaurant scene was entirely too competitive in Seoul. In America she could sell the food of her homeland and be a unique addition to the local dining culture. She did, however, take Cheong-ha to visit the motherland the following year. Unlike her older sister, Cheong-ha stood by her mother and later in life, took over the restaurant. Sometimes at night, Min-yeong would wonder about Su-jin, though in time, her daughter became all but forgotten. The vivid memory of her faded and later became just a feeling. It was the feeling that at one time and at one point, there was someone else there. Though like her mother's servitude in the name of Christ, Su-jin became a distant scourge of the past.

Cecelia

A ll around the towering structures of commerce and spread throughout the central city were large neighborhoods of older, smaller houses. Some communities became dilapidated and unjustly dubbed "ghettoes." Others appreciated in value as historic homes. Others still were more medial. They were in a transient state, uncertain of which way to go. One alternative option was to go down. This was the option facing a neighborhood bordering the high-rises, separated by a street. These houses confined the financial core from expansion. A corporation chose this city as a hub to expand its operations. With no room amongst the other skyscrapers to build, the developer chose this neighborhood. Of course, that would come with the cost of removing the people and small businesses. Feelings were mixed amongst the neighbors. Some had pride in their neighborhood, others had roots here. The rest wanted the money for their property and would gladly relocate. The gain of this building would mean the loss of an eclectic group of people, businesses and history.

That Tuesday morning, the day before Su-jin left Min-yeong, a young woman named Cecelia sipped strong, chicory coffee from a pale blue mug. She was in her late 20s, a homeowner and an entrepreneur. She had silky black skin and long, wavy hair that cascaded down the crown of her head, along the nape of her neck, over her shoulders and ending at her upper-back. Cecelia was a success story, though not quite a full rags-to-riches sort. Born in a bayou community in Terrebonne Parish of southern Louisiana, Cecelia Reeves left her small town home on account of the lack of work. She first tried Baton Rouge, but left after a few months. She grew tired of the unruly college parties seeping from Louisiana State University. The state's capital city lacked a certain something she desired, though she could not quite tell what it was. She then wandered to New Orleans, where the crowds of tourists and revelers were unbearable. The city was both beautiful and exciting, but a bit much for Cecelia.

Luckily, Cecelia was keen and learned fast. Though her time working in Baton Rouge and New Orleans was short, Cecelia learned business and leadership skills having worked closely with her former bosses. She moved to this city and fought hard for a small business loan. Her gamble paid off and she found herself in her current position. She bought a two-story house and converted the bottom floor into her store while she lived on the top. The store and Cecelia's creativity brought in plenty of money, allowing her to live comfortably. She lit a stick of incense and meditated before getting dressed.

Cecelia owned a shop named Divine Trail. It was a supply shop for the mystic. Her clientele included witches and new agers. The store had crystals, idols, incense, tarot cards, candles and various pieces by which to perform magic. She rarely used the backyard for her personal use, thus used it as a meeting ground for witches. On Wiccan holidays, followers of the God and Goddess gathered to celebrate their faith. The house's kitchen was not only for Cecelia's domestic use, but also served as a place to prepare food for The Sweet Apple, the store's small restaurant. She could only seat four people at a time, but could accommodate a dozen if the customers would sit outside.

Cecelia was indeed a witch. Her store hosted two fortunetellers available by appointment. By diversifying her business with retail, food, festivities and leasing a room to psychics, she made her living off the devout Wiccans and the curious. Each morning she uttered a litany to the divine forces ruling over the Earth. Being in close touch with other witches, she learned new rituals and spells to add to her ever-growing Book of Shadows.

Within the covers of the book, Cecelia wrote chants and words to the higher power. She included zodiacal and astrological maps to guide her through the influential maze of heavenly bodies. She diagramed the human body with references to chakras and special points. There was a section for alchemy, referencing the magic and capabilities of herbs, plants and the like. She expanded the medicinal chapter to the healing power of certain stones. The final chapter left many open pages for further expansion. It was the place for spells, all tried and tested by Cecelia either by experimentation or reference by other witches. Her grimoire was for no one's eyes but her own. It stayed a secret, though in good faith and compassion she offered spells to other witches on occasion. Not one spell dabbled in black magic, as Cecelia believed that would alter fate, a punishment karma would retribute threefold.

Witchcraft was not a newfound path upon which Cecelia came, but rather her family was raised with Wicca. While so many others in the Bible Belt flocked to churches, Cecelia, her parents and three siblings practiced witchcraft freely in their own home in the bayous of Terrebonne Parish. It was just a way of life for them and one none in her family would trade for any other faith or practice. Unlike the restraints of so many other religions, Cecelia's had one simple rule: to do as she pleases without harming anyone.

Faith aside, Cecelia had other matters now. The proposed office building would stand on her property. They offered her money for the land, but Cecelia had grown to love this space. She was advised to accept the offer and move her business to a location with more space. In truth, her store was a success, but not to the extent to own a massive space. Though she found an alternate space in the event the corporation won, part of her store's charm was the location. It was in an old house in the heart of the city. On top of the business, this was also her home. She had chosen a side and felt it was best to combat the corporation. This was a historic piece of the city, but more importantly these were people's homes and lives. Several small businesses flourished in this neighborhood. Many like Cecelia's ran out of old houses. Many of the business owners here objected to the development of this building and united as an organization to prevent the razing of their properties and construction of offices.

The house next door was run by a little German man. He made clocks by hand, which drew in customers for the artisan beauty and quality of his clocks. He was a close acquaintance of Cecelia. She had invited him over for coffee several times before. He once offered her a heavily discounted clock. Cecelia ventured over to see the timepiece and was amazed by his store. There were wristwatches, pocket watches, sundials, wall clocks, mantle clocks, grandfather clocks, all set in a plethora of materials. Oak, cherry, ebony and woods from distant forests formed frames. Brass, gold, platinum, silver and precious ores from deep mines glistened in the lighting. Standard and Roman numerals circled the clocks' faces. The time on each clock was set just imperfectly, maintaining a constant drone of slipping time, of seconds, minutes, hours slowly ticking away.

Next door on the other side of Cecelia's shop was a small coffee shop. It was independently run and a place Cecelia often visited. It had a magical appeal and drew in a unique array of people, standing as a major destination for the local underground scene. Its lack of affiliation with corporate coffee shops and setting in an area tenaciously holding onto the city's history brought in its colorful clientele. It was liberal and culturally revolutionary, standing as a landmark to the counterculture. It was popular with witches and pagans, meaning it brought business to Cecelia's shop and vice versa. Musicians, artists, writers, poets, hippies and the occasional vagabond frequented the shop. It was a place of inspiration.

On any given day one could see an artist busily sketching the next great masterpiece or a writer frantically scribbling ideas through words into a notebook. Twice a week they offered the floor to artists of song or word, allowing poets to speak and musicians to sing.

Also in the neighborhood was Margaret, an artist known only by that name. She owned a gallery and displayed her paintings hanging from the walls and situated on easels. She found inspiration where others saw nothing. There was beauty in what others could not see. She earned the respect like a Renaissance master in the arts community and many wealthy patrons of the arts hung her works in their homes. She had paintings of a whore smoking a cigarette, scenes of urban decay, poverty-stricken children, death and so many other depictions considered repulsive. Yet, Margaret was a wizard of bringing the beauty out of these subjects. Likewise she brought the ugliness out of physical beauty with dark shades and shadows on super models, melded in atrocious chiaroscuro, and the foul aura of skylines and churches.

The clockmaker, coffee brewers and painter were among those losing their properties. They felt close like a family. None were in the same business and there was no competition in this colorful neighborhood, except of course, the battle between corporation and small business. City officials and some business owners welcomed the proposal. Naturally, they faced no threat of demolition, but rather would benefit from its arrival. A coalition of residents and entrepreneurs including Cecelia formed a committee to protect their investments.

Cecelia, having showered and dressed, finished up her ritual of a morning blessing, lighting incense and reciting a short prayer to the God and Goddess. She had been working on a lengthy letter, which was one form of protest. She argued to keep the corporation from finding a home on her property. She had even researched the project and available space in the city in hopes to redirect their interests. Unfortunately the only available spots to accommodate the dimensions of this building were at the shortest distance two miles from downtown. Several others to be displaced were also in the process of writing their letters of protest. There was so much for her to say and the letter continuously grew. It had become several pages long, though after many arduous hours over the computer, she was at last nearing the end.

"Hello," a voice called at the stairwell. "Sissy? Are you there?" Sissy was Cecelia's nickname, originating in her childhood.

"Yeah, Autumn," she replied, not taking her eyes off the computer screen, "I'm here."

Autumn was the only other employee in the store. The two had become friends in New Orleans and felt as though fate had brought them together. They were kindred spirits and one could say, soul mates. They had an instant connection and became the closest of friends. They kept in touch after Cecelia moved away, as the formed bond remained unbroken. After a short time Autumn joined her friend here.

Autumn walked up the stairs and up to Cecelia. She tapped Cecelia's shoulder with her index finger. "How you been, baby? You still working on that thing?" Autumn had a deep voice, though still feminine. She was much larger than the slender Cecelia. She was proud of her round features and used her girth as a source of empowerment. Her skin was a bit darker than Cecelia's and her hair was much shorter. Though many of their physical traits contrasted the two were compatible in every way.

"Uh huh," responded Cecelia. "If I'm gonna keep this place I need to keep these assholes away from this block."

"Girl, you need to give those mother fuckers more than just some goddamn letter."

Cecelia still looked at the screen. "You know I want to. But they got something I don't: a whole team of lawyers."

"Well, you ready to do this?" Autumn stepped back toward the door.

"You know I am. I'm gonna tell those stupid sons of bitches they can't just..."

"No, not that," Autumn said. She held up her arm and pointed to her watch. "We open in ten minutes."

Cecelia's eyes opened wide and she leapt out of the chair. "Oh shit," she exclaimed, then ran past Autumn. "Come on, let's get down there." She could not have made it to the first floor faster if she had jumped. She dashed to the safe and fumbled with the knob. She got the door open and flung it wide to find it bare. "Oh my God," she screamed, clenching her fists and raising them to the sides of her head. "We been robbed!"

Autumn laughed behind her. "I already opened the register."

Cecelia flashed her friend an angry look. "I should break you for that." Autumn continued laughing, though she knew the stress was hardly funny. At times, it is important to find humor in a dire situation.

After nearly an hour of being open, a large woman came into the store, waddling quickly like a fat fowl. "Sissy, honey, I'm sorry I'm late."

"Hey there, Beverly," Cecelia said with a smile. She stood behind the register talking with Autumn. "You ain't late. You got five minutes still."

"I have so much to set up in that room though." Beverly was in her forties and one of the store's two psychics. She paid Cecelia $250 per month for the space, worked three days a week and charged $40 for half an hour plus tips. Beverly moved toward the back. Cecelia converted a parlor in the house into a room for the psychics. Beverly worked Mondays, Tuesdays and Saturdays, while Bernard, the other psychic, worked Wednesdays, Thursdays and Fridays. It was good money, attracted specific clients as well as newcomers and were by appointment only, though if there were an open space in the schedule either psychic would gladly squeeze in a walk-in.

Beverly rushed with her large bag of soothsaying tools and frantically ran, as though in a state of hysteria to the parlor. Cecelia and Autumn watched from behind the counter. Internally they were amused, though their expressions showed utter nonchalance. "Does that crazy bitch know her first appointment ain't for an hour?" Autumn said, shaking her head.

This Tuesday the store was not overwhelmingly busy, but there was a steady flow of customers. After the first hour, Beverly had a full schedule of people coming for a psychic reading. Though business was coming along and making Divine Trail a good profit, all was not well. The coalition against the looming menace threatening to displace homes and businesses had set a deadline for tomorrow to submit a letter of protest. Cecelia had been preoccupied with orders, keeping track of income and expenses, planning for the Samhain festival coming soon and all other manners of moving her store ahead in the business world that she had not been able to finish the letter and still had more to write by tonight. The whole issue festered in Cecelia's mind.

The chimes over the door rang as a woman walked into the store. She was young, had pallid skin, thick glasses and curly blond hair. She wore clothes with style and sophistication, yet also captured the rebelliousness and freedom of youth. She made a grand entrance with her head held high and her arms out to the side like an angel descending to Earth. "Why, hello Cecelia," she exclaimed in an aristocratic fashion.

"Hey there, Margaret," Cecelia replied with a cordial smile.

"I thought I'd come in and check a couple things." Margaret adjusted her glasses and approached the counter. "Number one, did you finish that letter?"

"Almost," Cecelia responded guiltily. She fidgeted her

fingers and looked away from Margaret. "But I promise I'll finish tonight. I'll have it in the mail for tomorrow."

"Good, good," Margaret said with a wide smile. "Also, I'd like to inform you that the city council is willing to hear us out. You absolutely must mark your calendar for that. Finally we can let them know we don't want those assholes taking our space." She grinned with hope.

"Oh," Cecelia said looking at Margaret again, intrigued. She grabbed a pen and looked for a piece of paper. She could never find anything behind the register when she needed it. She found a pad of sticky notes and poised the pen over it. "When is the meeting?"

Margaret put her arms on the counter and bent over, supporting herself on her elbows. "The twenty-fifth of this month at 1 PM. It'll be at City Hall. I guess we will meet in the foyer or just ask the front desk or something." She turned toward Autumn. "You coming Autumn?"

"Nah," she replied quickly, putting her hands up in the air. "If Sissy's going I need to stay and watch shop."

"That's good." Margaret turned her attention back toward Cecelia. "She can fill you in later. Speaking of watching shop... your *friends* are back again."

Cecelia leaned back in frustration. "Again?" she whined.

"Oh hell no," Autumn said angrily. She stomped away briskly, headed to the door. She flung it open, sounding the chimes and stepped out onto the front porch. Indeed, this small posse of three had returned. They were three young men from a church who protested Cecelia's shop. They were self-appointed messengers of God who came to dispel Cecelia's customers, promising them salvation and eternal paradise through repentance. They brought with them signs, decrying the nature of the shop, dismissing it as devil worship and a guaranteed path to Hell. This was now the seventh time they had come to protest and tried to expel Cecelia and her sanctuary for witches from the city.

Autumn put both hands on her hips and scowled fiercely at the young Christians. "What the hell are ya'll doing? I thought I told you not to come back here no more."

"You are pulling people away from the path to God," one of the men shouted, pointing his finger accusingly at her. They accused the witches of bringing members of their congregation into a path of evil, though neither Cecelia nor Autumn practiced black magic and likewise, condemned it.

"You mother fuckers got three seconds to get off our lawn before I snap your Christian asses in two." Autumn shrieked this angrily.

"You use your magic against us and are possessing people into leaving Jesus Christ," another one of the men shrieked, pointing at her.

Autumn stormed down the stairs and quickly moved toward the three men, singling out one who was presumably the ring leader. He raised his arms to protect his head from her hand. Autumn slapped at him wildly. "Get the fuck away right now!"

The protestors fled and Autumn shouted at them as they ran. Cecelia and Margaret stood at the window watching and laughing. Autumn walked back toward the shop staring into some other world while uttering a long string of obscenities under her breath. As she walked back into the store, she said, "tired of these people." She saw Cecelia and Margaret laughing hysterically, nearly to tears. Autumn grimaced. "What? Ya'll think this is funny?" Autumn shook her head and flashed a displeased look to the laughing women, then abruptly walked away from the counter.

Margaret spoke through chuckles, still recovering from the amusing scene, "oh my... I remember you tell...telling me about them before." Margaret laughed some more. "Do they... do they do this often?"

"No," Cecelia said, wiping her eyes having finished laughing, "just once in awhile. Guess they don't like us witches. They think I'm conjuring up demons from Hell or something. As a matter of fact, I think it's pretty damn funny. They actually think I'm going to churches and putting spells on people to make them come here. I swear... you know what? Any Christians, or I guess former Christians that come here do it on their own. Their religion don't work good enough so they come here."

"Well," Margaret said putting her hand on Cecelia's arm, "Cecelia you know I think you do a fabulous job. I just love your store and you're doing very well for yourself here."

"Thank you, Margaret."

"We're like family." Margaret gestured with her hands. "You, me, Hans next door, that whole coffee shop over there, Autumn...everyone." She looked at Cecelia warmly. "So if you have a problem, you just let your old friend here know. If those protestors come back I'll be out there with Autumn."

"That's very sweet of you Margaret, but I swear I'm about done with that letter." Cecelia knew Margaret was urging her to finish.

"Who said anything about that letter? I'm just letting you know. You want to get a cup of coffee?" Cecelia shook her head. "Not now of course, but after business hours?"

Cecelia sighed. "I don't think so. I need to get caught up tonight. Maybe tomorrow or whenever?"

"Sure darling," Margaret said putting her hand on Cecelia's shoulder. In her peripheral a golden object caught her eye. She turned to face it. "Oh my God," she said walking over to it in awe. It was a statue about a foot tall, painted primarily in gold, though black, blue and white added to the detail. It had the body of a slender man with a towel wrapped around the loins. It had the head of a predatory bird, but Margaret could not discern if it was an eagle, hawk or osprey. Her avian knowledge was quite limited. It stood on a black base with gilded hieroglyphics etched around the perimeter of the base.

Margaret bent over and supported herself with her hands on her knees. "Is this Egyptian?" she asked curiously.

"It sure is," Cecelia replied, not leaving the counter.

"Correct me if I'm wrong, but isn't this an ancient god?"

"That's right. It's Horus. And before you say anything it's a statue to help people concentrate. They can put a face on what they believe in."

Margaret stood there contemplating the notion. She was agnostic, though it would almost seem she worshiped a pantheon of great art theorists and critics. She followed the creed of catharsis and heeded philosophy of the aesthetics, taking to heart the platonic cave allegory. She was merely a vessel for the arts to transcend. Margaret pondered this notion staring at Horus. What was a god exactly? It meant different things to different people. It was not concrete and when one deeply contemplated the issue the mere idea of an extant god seemed too abstract for human understanding and wholly intangible. When coupled with societal, governmental and international problems religion caused the notion became silly. Staring at the piece rushed inspiration through Margaret's head as though an ancient-Egyptian muse in golden skin showed her scenes of horror dressed in beauty that must be captured on canvas. She closed her eyes and let the aesthetic essence flow freely, soon to transcend through the artistic process and be captured in oil-painted images.

"How much is this?" Margaret asked, standing upright.

"Thirty dollars," Cecelia replied.

"I'll give you a hundred for it." Margaret dug in her billfold for money.

Cecelia stared at her blankly. "A hundred dollars?"

"Cecelia baby, you have any idea what this magnificent piece is doing to me? I already thought of a painting." Margaret stared at the ceiling and painted the air with her hands. "Theology. I will attempt to capture the love and hate of religion. You will see the compassion and brutality of it.

I've somewhat started that one already and this would be an excellent addition to my work."

Cecelia said in ethical protest, "but Margaret, you want that for a hundred dollars for just one painting."

Margaret waved her arms wildly in front of her. "No, no, no, no. Think of the potential. I can make a series with this." She looked upward, thinking for a few seconds. "Picture this: What Would Horus Do?"

Cecelia shook her head. "Okay, if you insist. That'll be a hundred dollars."

Margaret exited quickly and waved her hand to Cecelia, who put the money in the cash register. Margaret always was a bit eccentric. Autumn pulled a box out of the backroom to stock the shelves. She was putting more tarot cards in the glass cabinet. Cecelia saw her doing so and the action triggered a mnemonic note. "Oh Autumn," Cecelia called out. Autumn looked at her, but said nothing. "Is there enough room for a new set, or could you make enough room for one?"

"New set?" Autumn asked. "We're carrying a new style?" She was intrigued and approached the counter. She had always loved looking through the new styles of tarot cards, reviewing each and every card in the deck.

"Well, sort of. See, I ordered more cards and they sent the box yesterday and threw in a free trial set. I guess they want to see how it sells. They only sent three decks. One is for a display and if we can sell the others we can order more."

"Let me see," Autumn said grinning like a child awaiting a surprise. Cecelia pulled the unwrapped box of cards out from under the counter and handed them to her friend. Autumn looked at them and jumped back upon reading the title. It read *Tarot of the Macabre*. She opened the box and looked through the cards. "Eww," Autumn said, dragging out her disgusted reaction, "these things are nasty."

Unfolding before her, Autumn saw the morbid pictures adorning each card. The first in the deck was The Fool. It was represented by an emaciated corpse. It was pallid with protruding ribs and gangrenous gouges. It had blackened eyes and no hair on its body. The ghoul was nude and carried a long, small coffin in its right arm, slung across its shoulder. It lumbered across a wasteland aimlessly. Another horrible image was The Lovers card. Two hideous beings, both androgynous embraced each other with lithe arms, holding one another with their serpentine limbs. One was colored blue, the other purple. They stood locked into a deep kiss. However, only the torsos and heads were remotely human. The two were conjoined at the loins into a long, twisting body knotted about below them, which ended with a thick stinger. It made the revolting pair two entities united by a scorpion tail-body in eternal fornication. Further in the deck was the grim Moon card. An eclipsed moon sat at the top center of the card. Below a sea of thick blood sat with a monstrous crab emerging from its sanguine shore. Flanking the terrible sea were two columns, one on each side, cast in skeletons. Skulls stared out with jaws agape, surveying the landscape with their hollow sockets. At the base of each pillar was a lycanthrope with bits of ragged flesh hanging from their mouths and glowing yellow eyes staring at the counterpart across the grisly sea of blood.

"You really think anyone will buy these?" Autumn said grimacing and flipping through the deck.

"Who knows?" Cecelia replied looking at the cards disgustedly. She had already glimpsed at them, but still found them unpleasing. "They're creepy. Why are you still looking at them?"

"Oh, I don't know," Autumn said, keeping her eyes on the cards while still looking at each one. "You know me. I always look through the entire deck." Autumn continued to look through the carnage and grim portrayals on each card. She had never seen a deck of tarot cards like this. She applauded their aesthetic beauty, as they were well drawn and unique, though decried their gore and dark imagery. She packed them back into their little box and set them on the counter. "They gave you these free?"

Cecelia put them back under the counter. "Yeah, I don't know why. Well, they gave me them free to sell, but they want to test it first. They gave me a little feedback form."

Autumn put one hand on the counter and the other on her hip and leaned forward. "You ain't gonna sell a damn one of those. And if you do, I'd hate to see who buys them." Autumn stood up and something out the window caught her eye. She walked to the door and looked out at the lawn. "Oh, those lousy mother fuckers." Cecelia looked too and saw the three Christian men lurching outside again.

"Here," Cecelia said clearly annoyed, "let me handle it this time."

"Sissy," Autumn said in protest, "you are way too skinny to…"

Cecelia looked at her sternly and said, "I've got it." She walked out the door and looked out at the protestors from the porch, staring with piercing eyes. "Can I help you?"

"Stop promoting Satan," one shouted angrily with his hands cupped around his mouth. "You're corrupting our people and destroying our values."

Cecelia approached them and said in an angry voice, "first of all, this store… my store, celebrates Wicca, not Satanism." She waved her arms furiously as she spoke. "We're about love, not black magic and hurting people. If you can't understand that, I'm sorry." She stuck out her index and middle finger, counting her next argument before the Christians. "Second, I am not corrupting your people. I run the best damn witch shop in town and word of mouth gets around. Your religion doesn't work for everyone, so if people decide they want a change and become Wiccan, then that's their choice. Deal with it. You can't make them stay in your church or believe what you think they should believe. Plus, you got a lot of damn nerve to say I'm corrupting people." She put her hands on her hips and glared at them as she now spoke. "You take advantage of people who can't think for themselves and tell them what they should believe. That includes pushing your religion into all our faces and telling us there are people we should hate."

One of the men tried to argue, but Cecelia silenced his rebuttal, holding her hand up, palm facing him. At that, Cecelia crossed her arms and spoke more calmly. "Wicca is most certainly not about that. And what was that last thing you said? Oh, that's right. Traditional values. Boy, don't you know your religion is basically stolen from Wicca? You just picked one god and took a bunch of men's words to say how you should live. Today you just twist that all ass backwards to hate people and get what you want. Hell, you even stole our holidays. Christmas and Easter were stolen from us." The men looked puzzled. "That's right. We give gifts at Yule, but you just said it's the birth of Jesus. You stole a lot of traditions from us for that holiday and Easter too." She shrugged her shoulders. "I hope you realize what a fool you are and get your ass off my property and don't come back." Cecelia turned her back to them and walked back to her store.

The men gazed at her furiously until one screamed out, "for God so loved the world, He..."

She spun around and showed her frustration with the men in her face. "That's it," Cecelia said throwing her arms down, "I'm going in to call the cops." She walked away from the men, who shouted at her from the lawn. They screamed the Bible's propaganda, irrelevant verses they had memorized and still accused her of devil worship. By the time Cecelia made it to the phone inside they had left.

"You know what Sissy," Autumn said standing uncomfortably, seeing her friend was distressed, "why don't you go have some tea or something, work on that paper of yours if you want and let me take over down here."

Cecelia looked at her with several seconds of trembling

and heavy breathing as she shook off the anger the men had caused her. "You sure?"

Autumn waved her hand, showing it was nothing. "Yeah," she replied, "I'm a big girl, as you can see. I can handle it."

Cecelia looked down and shook her head feeling guilty. "Okay, but only for a little bit."

Autumn grunted, "just get upstairs now."

Cecelia drank a cup of hot tea, had a corn cake and worked on her protest paper. She nearly finished when she realized the time seeing the clock on the bottom right of her computer screen. It was half-past four and her shop closed in a half hour. Like this morning, she scrambled downstairs realizing the paper was consuming her. She had been upstairs for hours, leaving Autumn downstairs alone the whole time. "Autumn," she cried running into the room, "I'm sorry, I..."

"Sorry," she snorted, "what for? Told you I could handle this all on my own."

"I know, but..."

"But nothing. I know you were working on that paper. So what are you sorry for? Protecting our jobs? Your home?"

Cecelia tried again to express her apologies, "no Autumn, I left you..."

"I said don't worry about it. Do I look mad?" Autumn smiled sincerely.

Cecelia looked deep into her eyes, searching for her emotions through her face. "No," she said at last.

"There you go. You got all that stuff to do like that paper and running the store. I understand and know it's stressing you out. Those assholes don't help much. You know, the ones from earlier? Our Christian friends?"

Cecelia relented. "Okay then," she said smiling. "I'll take your word for it." Running her own business was easily within Cecelia's capabilities, but coinciding with her basic duties she had to get this lengthy paper finished, run the store, perform the other tasks of financial, commercial and legal issues and with the Samhain event quickly approaching, she had to get advertisements out and planning finalized for the store's biggest event. Lately things had been worse than hectic. Life grew more stressful each passing day. After completing this letter and the extra tasks to keep her business running, things would hopefully calm down. Cecelia had saved enough for a nice vacation. Perhaps she would see Paris or maybe Tokyo. A trip to Southeast Asia would be nice, or maybe a sojourn in the Austrian Alps was in her future. She might even settle for a visit to her roots in Terrebonne Parish.

Autumn and Cecelia closed shop. Though Cecelia wanted to have a simple meal for dinner at home and finish her paper. Autumn persuaded her to take a break from work and join her for dinner away from the shop. The two walked aimlessly into downtown, searching for a restaurant. They passed closing shops and crowded bars. Cecelia looked into their open doors, getting a glimpse of the early evening's bar scene. These places were filled with melancholy people, having two or three or four before going home to their spouses and children. A row of gloomy, drooping faces lined the bar, each hanging languidly over a stein of beer. Most of these faces belonged to men, darkened by sadness, lit by neon signs in the bar. At their necks the top button of each shirt was unbuttoned and their neckties were slackened. They delayed the inevitable commute home, a place of awful mistakes. Premature marriages, unwanted children, shackles of responsibility and obligation awaited these men. Low morale and sadness was the atmosphere of happy hour, the universal concoction of stress, hopelessness and misery served cold at the bottom of a bottle in bars nationwide.

Cecelia and Autumn came upon a Chinese restaurant and decided to feast there. The sign in the window claimed it served authentic Chinese food. Cecelia thought that was a strange thing to claim. Though Chinese food was quite popular throughout the nation, most Americans had presumably never been to China. It provided an argument that there were so few people to judge its authenticity. She wondered if American restaurants in China lumped hot dogs, fried chicken, tacos and gumbo onto the menu in one place and labeled it as authentic American cuisine, though the spices and ingredients would surely disappoint any American. She had heard of Cantonese as a class of Chinese food in the sense that Cajun was a style unlike other native dishes to America, but assumed there had to be a much wider spectrum to their homegrown foods. The friends sat and awaited their order as the cooks in the back fixed their food while conversing in Spanish.

Autumn fetched the food when they called their number. There was an order of vegetable lo mein for Autumn and fried rice for Cecelia. Each got an eggroll and fortune cookie with their meal. Autumn fumbled with a pair of wooden chopsticks, cursing loudly as she lost her grip on them. It caught the attention of some of the workers and somewhat embarrassed Cecelia. "I don't see how Chinese people eat with these goddamn things anyway." She picked up her plastic fork and ate with more ease.

"They probably say the same thing about forks," Cecelia said jabbing at her plate of fried rice with her spoon.

"Cecelia, you okay?"

It was strange. Autumn almost always called her "Sissy." She only used the formal if she knew something was wrong or had some reason. "I'm sorry."

"I mean lately you've been all distant. Something bothering you?"

Cecelia sighed. "It's this whole office project. I know they'll give me money to move my business, but it's not enough. That place is my house too. Not to mention how much I love our neighbors." She bit her lower lip and fought back tears. "I think part of what makes our shop so successful is its location. I'm scared it will be torn down. I don't want to lose my home or business. I could move, but it wouldn't have the same feel. You know?"

"I'm sure you'll do fine." Autumn put down her fork and leaned closer to Cecelia. "All of ya'll are fighting these pricks. Maybe you're right though. I mean, right to be scared." She put her hand comfortingly on Cecelia's. Cecelia looked away from her meal and up to Autumn. "Sure, they're going for homes and businesses, and your voices may not be enough, but maybe you need to get your clients involved. All of ya'll should."

"You mean, you think we can get people outside of the area to support our cause?"

"I don't see why not." Autumn brought up an excellent point. After taking so much time to progress her letter Cecelia had nearly finished and could easily create a memo to encourage people in the neighborhood to enlist the help and support of friends, relatives and customers.

"You're right Autumn," Cecelia said straightening up, a sound of hope at last appearing in her voice. "I'll write something up tonight. I'll see if we can't get fliers up in all these stores."

"You know I'll be there for you." Autumn stirred her steaming noodles and said, "hell, they want to take my job too. I don't want to drag my ass halfway across the city when I only have to walk ten minutes now."

The two friends smiled and spoke of other, more enthusiastic, less stressful subjects over a meal of mediocre, greasy, allegedly authentic Chinese food. They focused their conversation on lighter subjects and future hopes. They finished their meal and walked each other out. Downtown had become nearly desolate with only a few pedestrians and homeless people on the streets. The buildings towered above them sitting quietly and derelict. Red lights atop the roofs blinked on and off to signal their presence to the airport's air traffic. The two walked side-by-side toward the shop, but parted ways once reaching it. They gave each other a parting hug. Cecelia unlocked the door and turned off the alarm then reset it. She went upstairs with the food sitting heavy on her stomach and took a shower.

She put on her nightgown after drying herself and once again sat before her computer to finish this paper. After an hour of typing she at last finished. She printed her argument and then instantly began her memo. The memo took a mere fifteen minutes to type. Cecelia felt a sense of accomplishment after finishing this consuming task. She upheld her commitment to write the letter and took an extra step to fight the incoming corporation. She turned on the television and crawled into bed feeling the burden lift from her shoulders. She lay there drowsily, drifting to sleep. She snapped back to full consciousness when a loud noise came from the television. She felt around for the remote control and turned it off, then rolled over to sleep.

Just as she began to fall asleep, she awoke hearing a loud crash outside. She propped herself up and looked around her dark room. It sounded as though her flowerpot outside fell. Out the window she saw the tree in her front yard. It stood motionless, indicating there was no wind to push the pot off the porch. She figured it was a stray cat. She had seen some around her house before. She wondered what would draw the cat to the vase. Only asphodel grew in the pot. Cecelia got up and went to investigate the disturbance. She put on a robe and walked downstairs, peeking out the window. She noticed the pot was missing and decided to clean it up now so that she could tend to her opening duties in the morning. This was just an annoyance in the night keeping her from sleep. She turned the alarm off and unlocked the door.

It was nearly eleven now and Cecelia just wanted to lie in her soft bed and sleep. She found the broken pot smashed on the steps leading to her porch. Greenery, petals and black soil laid strewn about the stairs and base of the steps. It was a complete mess. She would need a trash can and a broom to clean this. She shook her head and mumbled, then turned to enter the house to get her cleaning tools.

She gasped as a heavy blow hit her in the back. She fell to the wooden porch and could not breathe, much less scream. She looked up, writhing in pain. It was difficult to make out specific features, but she saw the shape of the offender's head. He knelt close to her and at that moment she recognized him. It was one of those Christian protestors from earlier. He said something loudly, calling to others. His two cronies joined him and stood huddled over her body. Cecelia could not summon the strength to cry out for help.

"Looks like we got ourselves a witch," one of the men said hovering over her.

"Come on," said another. "Let's get out of here."

Cecelia felt relief through pain. She would be spared her life though would suffer this horrible pain. The men shuffled around and grabbed parts of her body, then lifted her from her spot on the porch. They quickly moved her to the street. One of the men let go of her and left. Cecelia could not see where he went. She could hear him unlocking the trunk of a car. She saw the trunk open as it rose into the air. She grew more afraid. The other two men dropped her into the trunk. Through frightened eyes, she saw the men standing over her, backlit by the orange glow of the streetlights. One reached up and gripped the trunk cover, then slammed it shut. The dull lit sky and all physical features disappeared. All was dark. Cecelia was trapped in a dark, confined space, tight and black like a coffin's interior.

She squirmed and twisted in the trunk like an insect in a chrysalis hoping to break free and fly away to freedom. In the utter darkness she heard the car start and the doors slam shut. She could feel the car lurch forward. The pain in her back became less intense. She found she was able to again move her limbs and speak. She wailed incessantly, calling for help and pounding any side around her she could. She cried, fearing her fate. The trunk was hot and the virtual blindness in the dark was terrifying. She was trapped in this vehicular prison.

The car jostled her about as it careened through the city. She could somewhat tell where she was based on feeling the car move. It constantly slowed and stopped, presumably at red lights. She felt her prison dip and accelerate, signaling that they had entered the freeway. Being in this place was maddening. There was little room to move, thus it cramped her in the dark, hot space. The air grew thicker, hotter, becoming harder to breathe. Frustration and panic overcame poor Cecelia, overriding logical thought and problem solving skills. She needed a way out of here. The most she could do was scream in the dark and pound on the roof of the trunk.

The car followed the freeway's contours, making curves to the left and right, speeding up and slowing down depending on what the physical obstacles unseen from the trunk were. To Cecelia it was a nightmarish ride in a deadly carnival. Where were they taking her? What were their motives? In response to the flurry of uncertainty and terror now consuming Cecelia, her mind fabricated beautiful images, inspiring hope, promise and comfort in this dire situation. She fantasized of the police capturing these vicious brutes and then getting the chance to confront them. Her story would be heard by sympathetic ears, captured in print and on television. Newspapers and magazines would run her tale on the press. Televised media would afford her a spot on national news and a seat on a talk show or two. Her experience would inspire women and witches everywhere. It would be her fifteen minutes of fame, sending a message of courage in the face of adversity and the human will to survive against all odds. First thing was first: she had to get out of this trunk.

She would not give up, but the car continued moving. She pictured herself fighting the men with her bare hands. Perhaps she could summon kung fu, tae kwon do or some form of martial arts by willing it. Although it was relative considering the situation of being kidnaped and stuffed in a trunk, the trip seemed unusually long. Cecelia figured she had to be in a distant suburb or even out of the city by now. It made her more curious as to where they were taking her. The moving cell had maintained a constant speed, suggesting less traffic wherever she was now. Cecelia could not tell which direction they were now heading. It was hard to breathe in the stuffy trunk. There was no use trying to escape. If she did manage to get the trunk open, the car was going so fast she would be killed on impact after jumping out of the mobile cell. However, while feeling around in the trunk she came across a tire iron, which would be a useful weapon once the trunk opened.

The car slowed down considerably. It bounced and rocked now. Cecelia heard the popping and grinding of gravel and sand beneath the car's wheels. It was apparent they were on a country road. She realized they were away from civilization and these men could do as they pleased without anyone noticing. Thinking of that made Cecelia grip the tire iron tightly, preparing to strike the men down with it. She would have to hit them hard and fast, then take the car and try to find her way back into town. The car slowed down more, then stopped. The engine shut off and all was quiet and still. The sound of three doors opening and slamming shut surrounded her in the darkness and shook the enclosed space of the trunk. Cecelia breathed quickly and her heart beat rapidly. She held her weapon behind her back and waited like a spider waiting for its prey to come to its web.

Her heart raced now as she heard the men outside walk around to the back of the car. She heard the keys jingling outside and the click as the trunk unlocked. It swung open and three dark figures stood over her. Behind them, all the night sky's stars shone brilliantly, not one dulled or blocked from the city's light pollution. Despite the situation it was a beautiful place, a pleasurable aesthetic of nature amidst the misfortunate human element. One of the men leaned in to pull her out of the trunk. Cecelia swung the tire iron at the man, hitting him in the shoulder as hard as she could. He yelped like an injured dog and fell to the ground. Cecelia scrambled to her knees, but her body hurt from the earlier assault and the cramps from being crumpled in the small space. It made her escape difficult.

She pulled herself out, searching for the closest man to strike with her potent weapon. A blast cut through the rural air. Cecelia dropped the tire iron as a sting overcame her right shoulder. She grabbed the afflicted area, feeling a wet, warm blotch on her nightgown. She toppled to the ground writhing in pain. One of the men walked to her, holding a pistol in his hand. "I guess witches can feel pain," he said grinning wickedly in the night. He pointed the gun at her. "I wonder if a bullet can kill one too." Cecelia stared up at him in fright.

"No," the other said, helping up the man Cecelia managed to hit. "That isn't part of the plan."

"What are you gonna do to me?" Cecelia asked, with suffering strangling her voice.

The man with the gun kicked her. "Shut up, witch."

"We...told you," the hurt man said through his own pain. He held his shoulder and said, "you...are...a tool of...Satan." He stumbled and dropped to his knees.

"I am not," Cecelia said holding back tears.

"She lies!" one of the men shrieked.

"We warned you, witch," one of them said, "we heard you can float if we put you in water, but let's see how you like a little of this." He pulled something out of the back seat of the car. It made a metallic screech as he dragged it across the pebbles. Cecelia could hear some liquid sloshing in the container. One of the men helped the other lift the heavy object. Together they poured the contents on Cecelia. It was gasoline. It soaked Cecelia from head to toe. After this Cecelia knew her fate. There was nothing more she could do to protect her life.

Quickly she concentrated on another plane of existence, trying to launch herself there from this body. Projecting herself to another realm of being was her solution to coping with this very painful way of death. There was a snap as one of the men lit a match. It hissed as it flared in the dark fields. It twirled downward, touching Cecelia's body, igniting her at once. Her hopes to leave her body failed. It was quite excruciating.

She rolled in the dirt, screaming in agony. Her skin blistered and her blood oozed out of her body, simmering in the flames. The body of the burning witch lit the dark field with a bright orange glow. The effervescent fire cast light upon the three smiling Christian faces. The chorus of crickets all about became muted by her screams of pain and the roar of the fire. The acrid smell of charring human flesh displaced the fresh air outside the nearby metropolis. Cecelia stopped moving. Her body lay there, still engulfed in the hot fire. It was a horrible way to die. The men stayed, feeling the heat from her burning remains warm them in the chill autumn air. They waited until the flames subsided. Feeling accomplished in the Lord's work they returned to the city.

Sensing something was wrong with Cecelia, Autumn reported her absence to the police immediately, though they acted days later. Investigators combed the area for clues, finally discovering an ATM across the street with a security camera angled toward Cecelia's shop. After analyzing the tape they found the car in front of Cecelia's house on the footage from that Tuesday. They located the car by its license plates and registration. They found one of the three men, who without hesitation turned in his accomplices. The three were taken to prison and executed as their trials and judges found them guilty of first degree murder. They all divulged the exact location of Cecelia's remains, which, whatever was left was brought back to the city.

Autumn bought the store and ran it alone, though mourned the loss of her friend, sinking into a deep depression for nearly three years. Often times Autumn felt as though Cecelia had left her only in her physical form, but her kindred spirit stayed with her, always watching and comforting her and stubbornly refusing to part with her. Autumn often cried in her sleep missing her friend, though through her tears and desolation swore she felt Cecelia's warm, spiritual hand stroking her face, calming her, telling her it would all be okay and that she would wait for her in death until they were reunited as spirits and born again as dear friends.

Sympathy poured in from their close-knit community. Pagans and witches gathered to celebrate her life. Margaret painted a series of Danse Macabre works in love, honor and memory of Cecelia. However, upon finishing them she could not bear to part with them. In a stroke of guilt and understanding, the corporation having heard of Cecelia's murder quickly withdrew its plans to raze the neighborhood and erect an office building. Having read Cecelia's letter, which Autumn submitted, they too posthumously recognized the late witch and chose a vacant lot several miles from downtown proper. After media coverage of the full story, the men who were once commended by their church for service in God's name were condemned to save its threatened grace. Soon the story faded, forgotten by many, but still a gaping wound in the heart to Cecelia's friends and family, thus concluding the gruesome tragedy of Cecelia Reeves, the ill-fated witch.

Gorgon

As Cecelia and Autumn dined at the Chinese restaurant that fateful Tuesday, a large event elsewhere in the city brought in a large crowd. Far from downtown stood a large arena, capable of seating over a thousand people and supporting major venues. Most days it sat quietly, bearing a few caretakers, silent halls and a vacant parking lot. Nights with scheduled performances made the place lively, loud and colorful. One could get a feel for the entertainment simply by looking at the crowds. Sometimes they wore tuxedos or suits, evening gowns and anything designed for class and culture, suggesting opera, classical singers or a ballet was scheduled. Some nights rendered hundreds of young girls, indicating a group of young men or a teen idol would sing. Cowboy hats usually meant a country singer was in town. Whatever the event, the arena easily drew in a large crowd.

Tonight, spotlights touched the night sky, swinging back and forth, promulgating a great show. Traffic inched through the parking lot, each driver searching for a place to leave the car. It snaked through the lot and out onto the street causing gridlock. People wandered up to the great building to wait in a long line to enter and enjoy the show, which would start in just over an hour. The teeming masses at the concert dressed primarily in black. Overall it was a young crowd, most in high school or college, though many more ranged in age up to their forties. Most everyone in the arena, regardless of gender, had multiple piercings. Silvery rings and studs adorned ears, eyebrows, noses, lips and various other parts of the human

Robert Liles

anatomy, some unseen to the public. Also regardless of gender, most had long hair.

Tonight's show featured a largely underground, British gothic heavy metal band just recently making a name for themselves in America, though they were quite well-known in England. They had a smaller cult following in North America and other parts of Europe. The band, known as Darkest Folklore, sang songs of life's darker side in contrast to the more popular singers of today's music scene. Each of the band's six members bore a name rooted in horrible creatures of mythology. The drummer took the name Kraken, so named for his talent in percussion as though he had many arms. At the keyboard was Gremlin, who played maniacally with the fast pace of Darkest Folklore's music. The band had two duos of male and female partners. There were the guitarists, Goblin the female and Hydra the male. One of the other pair was Siren, so named for her allure and versatility as a female vocalist. Her counterpart, Gorgon, the group's lead singer and virtual face of the band now put on a thick coating of black and white cosmetics.

The other members had already prepared to go on stage. The men all wore black, leather suits with boots and metal accessories. The women wore scantily-clad costumes comprised of corsets, fishnet stockings and glossy black stilettos. Unlike the men, they had a bit more color to their wardrobe with red lining and colored garters. Goblin had hair dyed bright white and Siren's was a deep purple. The opening band took the stage and began entertaining the crowd. Their loud music blared, reaching every ear in the arena. The door to a private annex to this dressing room flung open and in the doorway stood Gorgon.

His hair was somewhat long, but spiked upward four inches. It was black with streaks of dark green. He was thin and his skin was pale, coated by white makeup, giving his skin the pallid color of a corpse. His eyes, usually green, had

164

contact lenses in them making them yellow. He wore a black body suit, which took him twenty minutes to adorn. It was covered in straps and rings, looking somewhat like a mental institution's dark fantasy. Each of his spindly fingers had a massive ring, every bit of jewelry with a dark image. One was a skull of a human, another a skull of a bird. One was a marbled eyeball with elaborate designs around it and several other eerie figures carved in stainless steel decorated his hands. He stood at the door rigid and appearing serious.

"Well then, ladies and gentlemen," Gorgon said in a moderately accented, deep voice, "shall we?"

"Please," Siren said, smiling devilishly. Members of the band scrambled quickly through their bags. Goblin pulled out a case. Inside sat six glasses, one for each of the band members. Gremlin presented a large spoon and a bag of sugar cubes. Siren fetched the crowning glory of the ritual. In her hand was a large bottle of emerald green absinthe. She held it seductively and handed it to Gorgon as though she were passing him an infant.

Gorgon stared deeply at the bottle of French absinthe, espying in the drink the pure essence of Paris. There was a couple sitting at a café over coffee. An accordionist nearby played a melancholy tune beneath a streetlight on the corner. An artist packed away paints and his unfinished painting of the Parisian landscape as seen from Montmartre while a man on a bicycle with fresh baguettes in his basket rode by on the cobblestone streets. A one-armed veteran of de Gaulle's *Résistance* ran a small shop with a scratchy record hissing and playing *La Marseillaise*, in honor of the dignity and pride of France. Lovers kissed over the Seine beneath the stare of a Notre Dame gargoyle. All entwined harmoniously. The sights, sounds, smells, tastes and feelings of Paris blended together in a vibrant, cosmopolitan mix of history, culture, sophistication, art, love, beauty, swishing together in a green mixture, bottled to share with the world.

"Well," Kraken said impatiently, slicing the mood like a guillotine.

"Right, right," Gorgon said, breaking himself from the hypnotic spell over him. He poured the absinthe over a sugar cube on the large spoon for Kraken, who then poured in water from a silver pitcher. The crystalline green became cloudy. Kraken drank it as it was, unpolluted with sugar and water, preferring the drink this way over the customary flame added to the contraband cocktail. Each member had a glass and then a second prior to performing. Two glasses of absinthe before the show became a ritual for Darkest Folklore. They were told to get ready to go on stage after their guests finished. The audience now had half an hour for intermission before these headliners sang.

Having shopped for merchandise and visited the booths, bought refreshments, smoked cigarettes or used the bathroom, the crowd returned to the main theater, screaming and cheering in a deafening roar. Eerie, fast-paced music blared and lights flashed on the stage. There stood Darkest Folklore before their instruments, or in the case of Gorgon and Siren at the microphones. The music rocked the arena, sounding of gothic thunder, tantalizing the ears of the fans. They raised their arms in praise, trying to match the voluminous blast of sound from the massive speakers. Gorgon sang, his fast words in perfect cadence with the beat. Siren had limited lyrics and acted as a sex symbol on the stage for the fans. The song played on for just over four minutes. The audience cheered wildly.

"Welcome to our show," Gorgon said in a menacing, deathly voice, "here we shall chill you and please you with our wicked tunes. Hear the pain and atrocity of love in our next song, written for the helplessly lovelorn. We call this number *Hemlock and Punctured Hearts.*" Though apparent in his speech, Gorgon's British accent was nearly imperceptible while singing. The song began with Siren singing, then switched to Gorgon. The audience cheered to the song's gruesome lyrics.

Outside, the halls were relatively empty, though vendors still watched over their booths. A young woman walked amongst them, standing as a stark contrast to the dark ambiance and prevailing theme and imagery of blasphemy, death, pain and sexuality. She was in her mid-twenties, had blonde hair tied into a ponytail, a carefully made-up face and tan skin. She wore a hot pink shirt, jeans nearly as tight as the flesh on her toned body, a rhinestone belt and white sneakers. She was quite colorful in comparison to the prevalent black clothing around her. Hanging from a belt loop was an identification tag with her picture and the name of the weekly entertainment newspaper for which she worked *Out Spoken*. Next to her picture in bold black letters was her name, Kimmy Alexander.

She scribbled things she saw in her notepad, taking notes for her big review on Darkest Folklore. There was a booth selling T-shirts with the band's logo and various pictures. Another sold memorabilia to this subculture. Kimmy cringed at a sado-masochist booth displaying a banner with big, red letters reading "Pussy Eating Contest." Disgustedly she wrote this feature into her notepad. There was a concession area as well, though it was of little interest. It was a permanent part of the arena, selling high-priced, low-quality foods and beer. Hearing the music inside, Kimmy wrote her final notes and hurried inside to observe the band and the audience. There had been an announcement in *Out Spoken* for the Darkest Folklore American Tour, but Kimmy had been assigned to cover the venue and interview the band, as she was one of three journalists who covered concerts and the local music scene. Kimmy, however, was forced into this review. She knew she would not like it and presently felt uncomfortable in this place with these people.

The seating area was dark, thus making it hard to take notes. Kimmy watched as Darkest Folklore played on the stage with intense chords accompanying Gorgon's harsh, heavy metal voice. Kimmy could barely understand the lyrics because of the volume of the instruments and speed of the singer's eerie words. The members moved about the stage in any way they could. Kraken beat the drums wildly, the image of his swift arms appearing to be many more than two and lithe like tentacles. Gremlin worked the mechanics of his keyboard like demonic magic, his nimble fingers scratching the keys with surgical precision. Goblin and Hydra, the dual guitarists, speedily played their instruments, rocking and walking back and forth unlike their stationary colleagues Kraken and Gremlin. Due to the electric cords, however their movement was restricted to a small area. Siren pranced about the stage like a nymph, moving and posing sexily, bringing forth erotic appeal to the grim side of life. Gorgon had the greatest freedom of movement, running about the stage doing his part to visually entertain the crowd. Patterns of light flashed on the musicians. Behind them was a large statue, seemingly made of plaster of a martyred devil hanging from a cross.

The crucified devil chilled Kimmy. It had a skull for a head with curved horns like an ox. It had two holes rather than a protruding nose and long, sharp teeth like a Jurassic carnosaur. It had sockets for eyes with two glowing, yellow lights inside. A crown of thorns sat atop its head. The body was emaciated, its arms spread outward on the cross with its ghastly claws nailed to it. It wore a loincloth and below were two bestial legs ending in cloven hooves. Kimmy took a picture of the hideous behemoth and scribbled in her notepad that though Darkest Folklore was quite animated on the stage and brought with them the blasphemous eyesore, the band lacked in theatrics.

She did not care for their type of music, but tried to stay neutral, understanding that many people did. Rather, Kimmy chose to focus on the aesthetics of the concert. It was visually stimulating, despite absent theatrics and the crowd seemed quite absorbed in the show. She took note of the rapport and continued her observation. The music was extremely loud.

The floor trembled beneath her. She felt each pulsing wave of the heavy metal beat pass through her body. The sonic booms blasting from the giant speakers left no part of her body untouched. She felt the music in her ears, on her skin, in her blood and through her bones. All in all, Kimmy would call this a great show, though it was hardly her taste.

After the show, the crowds filed out of the arena. Some went to purchase a souvenir by which to remember the show. Others lined up for an autograph session. Most, however, spilled out into the parking lot to create another traffic snarl. As the band signed whatever object was presented to them, CDs, posters and even parts of the body, Kimmy made her way through the red tape of the entertainment bureaucracy, fighting with security, arena employees and others to find the band's room backstage, so that she could interview them. She already had approval to do so, but now it was made difficult. At last, she found their room backstage and waited for the band to arrive.

"Hello, young lady," said a deep voice behind Kimmy. She turned around, startled. "May I help you?" It was Gorgon with the other band members behind him.

"Um, yes," she said nervously, searching for words. "Kimmy Alexander. *Out Spoken News*." She extended her palm for a handshake, but Gorgon kept his arms crossed and stared at her. She withdrew her arm. Gorgon stared at her blankly. "*Out Spoken*," Kimmy said, "you know, like out on the town and spoken in our..."

"Yes," Gorgon said sneering, "I get it. What exactly do you want?"

Feeling uncomfortable by Gorgon's deathly appearance, stern tone and austere aura, Kimmy said, "um, we called about an interview. And, well, here I am." She laughed nervously. She did not like Gorgon.

Gorgon continued to stare, searching her face. "Yes, yes. I remember." He moved to the door and opened it. The band gathered behind her, making her feel quite nervous as though they would sacrifice her to the Devil. She embraced herself to provide comfort. Gorgon held the door open and waved her inside. "Please, won't you come in?" A slight smile cracked in the corner of his mouth. He led the way for her. Kimmy entered the room and took out a tape recorder. "Have a seat," Gorgon said, offering the lovely lady a cushioned chair. She sat down promptly and Gorgon pulled up a chair across from her. "What would you like to know?"

Kimmy was surprised he seemed so cordial now. She clicked on her tape recorder, slouched forward and held it out to capture both of their voices. "First, how does it feel to be on your first American tour?"

"It feels wonderful, actually." Gorgon smiled. "We are pleased that our music is gaining popularity in North America. As I'm sure you know, our tour also includes some Canadian cities, such as Montreal, Toronto, Vancouver...oh damn. Siren, where else are we going?"

She looked upward as she thought. "Calgary. I think that's all."

"Right then," Gorgon replied. "You see, we were big in Britain and Germany years ago, but we're growing in popularity in the States and Canada, as well as France, Russia and Romania. We appreciate this opportunity and are excited that people here and elsewhere worldwide listen to the messages of our music."

Kimmy nodded her head and drew from that, "what message do you want your listeners to get from your music?"

Gorgon put his fingertips together and stared deeply into Kimmy's eyes and beyond, seeming to search for her soul. He was silent for a moment, then replied, "our messages are quite clear. We illustrate the pain of loss and love, advising people to take caution. It truly is a rough world and people must watch out for themselves. Our song *Ghosts and Seas of Tears* is about one's loss of his lover. He goes mad from the heartache, dying miserable and lonely. We also like to just tell stories and in the case of our latest album, we speak out against hegemonic fascism and totalitarianism."

Kimmy stared at him, lost in his words and voice. Gorgon was indeed eloquently spoken and a highly intelligent man. She could feel by the way he carried himself that he was an intellectual. "I'd like to get back to the other two messages you ended with, but first I would like to ask who writes your songs."

"It's a group effort," Gremlin said. Kimmy looked over at him. He sat on a couch distanced from Kimmy and Gorgon. She scribbled it in her notepad fearing he was too far from the recorder for it to capture his response.

"Indeed," Goblin said.

"For the most part, I write the majority of the songs," Gorgon said, "though everyone has written, at least in part, a few songs." Gorgon crossed his legs, making the leather pants squeak. "Sometimes someone will write the music and we'll come up with words, but usually we'll make the instrumental music follow the meter of our lyrics."

Kimmy was a bit confused, but said, "how did you all form a band?"

Kraken, who was sitting next to Gremlin on the couch, began, "we owe it all to London."

Gremlin said, "Gorgon and I were close mates in Birmingham, but left for London in the mid-'90s to make it in the music scene."

"Then," Kraken said, "in a club they came upon a talented drummer from Liverpool." The band members laughed at that remark, but Kimmy did not react.

Siren said, "Hydra and I were close. We both come from Kent and moved to London and heard about this forming band. By this point, the other three had already started, so we auditioned and they liked what they heard, so we joined."

"Then they sort of stumbled across me," Goblin said. "I

was in a small band from Wolverhampton that got a gig in London. I knew it wasn't going anywhere and they offered me a spot in the band."

Kimmy cocked her head, "just like that?"

"Just like that," Goblin replied.

Kimmy licked her lips, "but how did they actually find you?"

"Oh," Goblin said, "did I forget to mention that part?"

"Yes," Kimmy replied, nodding.

Goblin completed the story. "Well my old band performed at this little place and the others just happened to be there that night."

Gorgon said, "this was all over a two-year span. But as you can plainly see, we all came from different parts of England and met together in London, thus forming what you see before you."

"Interesting," Kimmy said, "but now I'd like to go back to what you said about messages in your songs. You said that sometimes you just like to tell a story. Could you elaborate on that for me?"

"Certainly," Gorgon said. "As you can plainly see and as you heard earlier we like the dark side and choose to bring a face and voice to it. Some of our songs sing of monsters, some of people, some of famous figures from the annals of history. However, people have an affinity for the darker side of life. We represent the death to life, the night to day, the black to white. You see it in all forms of entertainment, though we concentrate solely on this topic." Kimmy appeared confused. "My point is there is something about the dark side of life. People are drawn to it. We exemplify it."

"And how do you relate that to telling stories?" Kimmy asked, feeling a slight chill down her back.

"As tried and tested by entertainers throughout history," Gorgon said gesturing with his hands out and palms facing up. "*Oedipus Rex* is one such example. The poor man did nothing wrong, but a misfortunate fate plagued him. In his case bad things happen to good people. Shakespeare wrote on it as well. *Othello*, *Hamlet* and *Romeo and Juliet* were love stories in a sense, yet they were tragedies. Think of how many of these fools in love died by the end and the others that fell with them." Kimmy stared at Gorgon, bewitched by his soothing voice. "When cinema arrived people like Bela Legosi and Alfred Hitchcock used horror to entertain. Not to mention, if you listen to most of the music that comes out today you'll find that the lyrics are really quite depressing, though the actual music so falsely appears to be cheery. People dying, hearts breaking, catastrophe wrecking lives...it's all the same. It's the sadistic side of humanity few are willing to admit they like. Audiences follow these stories and find pleasure in someone else's pain."

Gorgon's words brought clouds over Kimmy's sunny disposition. She figured this was enough of this subject, but only a small piece for her article. "Okay," she said, "what about your positive message you mentioned earlier?"

At first, none of the six members would answer. "Which would that be?" Hydra asked, breaking the silence.

"Speaking out against the world's dictators and fascist governments," Kimmy replied with great curiosity.

"Ah," Gorgon said, "yes, but if I may object, we said nothing about dictators. But I believe you're asking about hegemonic fascism. By this we mean those culture–controlling devices around the world that benefit some, yet oppress many others." Kimmy looked intrigued, nodding her head. "We disagree with religion, for example. Actually, I should say organized religion. Culturally, religion influences the way a person thinks, thus it grips and affects everyone in the culture. As you may have heard, our latest album *God Save the King* criticizes the theocratic state and the religious influences on people. I can speak for us all in saying that religion not only restricts the freedom we as humans should have, but also others not of that religion within that culture."

The last part of Gorgon's argument seemed cryptic. Kimmy sought clarification and inquired of him, "so, in this regard of human freedom, religion acts as a dictator?"

"Correct," Gorgon replied. "Religion is not merely just a belief in a god, but also a philosophy as how to live life. It transcends those in power and affects the greater population. It's quite problematic, you see. Let us examine Christianity. It is what I call an umbrella religion. It's a term used loosely to describe one who follows Christ. Under this umbrella are countless sects of Christianity, each with a similar, yet different philosophy on how to live life." Gorgon stretched and twisted his back, making a loud cracking noise. "Forgive me if I am wrong, but I have a little understanding of American government and if I'm correct, in the Legislative Branch, both the Senate and Congress are essential. It goes without saying that they will act politically not entirely in the people's interests, but in their own. On the whole, they will bring in religious philosophies into your government buildings." Kimmy stared at him, adoring every word out of his mouth. "Let us create a fictitious Congress. Here we will have a small sample population. One shall be Catholic, another Mormon, one Buddhist, an atheist, a Muslim, a Jew and a Hindu. These seven politicians are a small group, but for the sake of brevity, let's assume each member of Congress is of a different religion. It would be difficult to pass laws with this conflict of faith."

"So you're saying religion will hurt the government," Kimmy asked.

Gorgon looked at the ceiling. "I suppose hurt would be an applicable term, yes. Many people base morality on religion, not reason. In creating law and policy, political leaders often rely on religious teachings over what is truly the right decision."

"Give me an example," Kimmy said, growing more interested in the singer with every question he answered.

Gorgon thought for a moment. "Let's take two somewhat similar issues: abortion and euthanasia. A moral conflict arises here. Many people see them both as murder considering both end a life early. Lawmakers will fight to keep or make them illegal. On the personal side, both issues come down to being someone's choice. In America you may live where you choose, drive any car you choose and so forth. You value your freedom to choose what you want in life. Why should life decisions such as these not be available?" Kimmy nodded her head and stared at him intently. Her discomfort had disappeared as she realized now that Gorgon was an intelligent man beyond the character she saw on stage. "If a baby will ruin a woman's life it should be her decision to carry it or not. If the mother considers it murder, then she won't have the abortion. It isn't right to make a human being live in a world where it won't be wanted or loved. If someone has terminal cancer, AIDS or what have you and they choose not to fight the sickness it should certainly be their right to end their life peacefully and comfortably, rather than suffering until their last day."

Though impressed with his knowledge and analytical thought, Kimmy was growing a bit frustrated with his long-windedness. His speeches were long and straying from her point. "But this is political. How does religion play into this?"

"Quite simple," Gorgon said gesturing with his hands, "in either case a death's involved. Christian religions, Jews, atheists and others will understand that death is forever. Other faiths however would see it simply as throwing a fish back into the sea. A death does not matter if the soul will be reincarnated. How would these people vote in Congress? Referring to atheists and Christians, the atheist will rely on his or her logic while Christians will see either case as legalized murder."

Kimmy felt patronized, quickly searching for an error in

his logic she said, "but there are Christian lawmakers now who support abortion and euthanasia. How does this fit into your argument?"

"I won't deny that," Gorgon said, "there are always exceptions to the rule, but I will say that on the whole, their faith intervenes with reason. Some may break through those dogmatic barriers for the good of the people, some may not. An atheist could be raised by Catholics whose conservative way of thought may influence standings on such topics. If he's against gay marriage, then why? He might argue something without using God. If he's against euthanasia, then why? He might argue something without using God."

"Could you be more specific?" Kimmy asked.

Gorgon sighed. "The religious teachings from his parents could ultimately affect his ethical and moral standings, though he abandoned religion. If his parents find homosexuals to be inferior people because they were told that in church, he will grow up with that bigoted frame of mind and stand against gay rights. If they call abortion and euthanasia murder, he will grow up thinking that. In any case, though an atheist it is possible for religion to dominate his thinking."

Kimmy asked, "does this apply to all atheists or religions?"

"Certainly not," Goblin said, cutting in amidst Gorgon's long streak of speaking. "I have mates in England that are godless and grew up in Anglican households."

"Yes," Gorgon said stepping back into the spotlight, "and this is a general look on the situation. Some policies may have a direct conflict with religious beliefs. Some politicians do act in the best interests of the people, though many do not. Referring to our rather diverse Congress we mentioned earlier, look at the ludicrous policies some may want to enact. What if the Jewish man wanted to outlaw swine and shellfish for consumption? What if the Mormon wanted to legalize polygamy? What if the Catholic wanted to do away with prison and give mandatory Hail Mary's? That is, of course, absolutely stupid. Why should atheists give up ham and lobster? Why should Buddhist women share a prurient husband? Why should Muslims do a Hail Mary? They shouldn't." Gorgon actually appeared flustered by this tangent. He seemed to be working himself up into a rage. "In a nation diverse in religion and culture such as America, no group, minority or not should have to be subjected to the religious doctrine of a dominant religion."

"Interesting," Kimmy said. She looked at Gorgon, mesmerized by his intelligence and eloquence in speech. Though she did not care for his extremely long-winded, detail-oriented manner of speaking she found his outlook fascinating. Kimmy was agnostic, perhaps saving her from becoming offended by this man's staunch philosophy. "Okay, moving away from politics, I have to ask, because of your appearance, sounds and lyrics a lot of people associate you with Satanism. What would you say to that?"

"My dear," Gorgon said smiling, "as I mentioned before, I do not adopt Christian teachings or believe in God. To believe in Satan would mean that I believe there is a God as well. Likewise, believing in the Christian God means believing there is Satan. I believe in neither."

Kimmy shrugged, "good point. But what would you say about your dark clothing and music, which most associate with Satanism?"

"I mentioned before that we embrace the dark side," Gorgon said. "What you see now and what you saw on stage was our personification of such an abstract idea. We think of what is dark and apply aesthetics. Satan symbolizes darkness in Christian mythology and I'm sure you're well aware we have a running theme of mythical creatures. Thus darkness transcends us as vessels and appears in all aspects of our band."

"You mentioned before that people are allured to darkness,"

Kimmy said. "You do represent it well and to a greater extent, seem to embody death."

Gorgon sat silently, summoning words. Kimmy knew to expect another long speech from him. "Death varies by culture," he said. "Of course we all die in the end just the same. How death is perceived and the ritual commemorating one's passing is regarded differently around the world. It is, however, one of the darkest aspects of life. It is beautiful, yet so frightening. People worldwide wish to ignore they will die one day. They think of what is to become of them after their passing, though do not think of the actual death itself." Gorgon leaned forward. "Religions around the world have fabricated what happens after one dies. Some see a heaven, or to keep people in check while alive, a hell. Others believe they will come back in another body. Some feel their spirit will wander the Earth freely. The concept of an afterlife requires either a lot of imagination or unhealthy religious dogma. Who can say what happens after death? No human being can return from the grave and frankly discuss the pleasures or horrors of the afterlife. Those near death experiences are quite questionable if you wanted to argue in favor of that. People who believe in reincarnation believe you have feelings, but no memories from a past life. In truth, no one can give concrete evidence of life after death." Gorgon reclined and put his fingertips together. "Existing beyond life is an idea to cope with the inevitable loss of the self. Since humans first walked the Earth we knew death was a part of life. As culture developed, it became interpreted and viewed differently in different parts of the world, thus explaining a natural phenomenon we all must face one day. Death is mysterious."

"I see," Kimmy said, unsettled by this discussion. She rubbed her arm and grimaced.

"When you contemplate the notion," Gorgon continued, "death is a bit chilling. It is ceasing to be. There is no more sensory or ideological interpretation of the world on behalf of the self. There is only nothingness. The human mind cannot fathom a concept so abstract."

Kimmy was speechless. She too had not thought much about death, though the thought occasionally crossed her mind. However, death usually crossed her mind in second or third degree ways. She avoided heavy drinking and smoking, ate a relatively healthy diet and aside from marijuana once in awhile, she stayed away from drugs. Unhealthy lifestyles equated to a body in deteriorating shape, eventually taking a physical toll and leading to death. This death was premature. Living the way she did only prolonged her life, yet like an alcoholic, smoker or glutton she faced the same fate. Having no particular religious affiliation, Kimmy believed in a higher power and trusted her spirit would be placed in a beautiful, alternate plane of existence accordingly. She felt she was a good enough person. After he said these words, Kimmy made the attempt to concentrate on nothing. She pictured white, then black, both colors and likewise something. She tried to think of clear, but only managed to think of a color behind it. Then again, clear was still something. Nothingness was nothing. It was not even a frame of mind. Try as she might, Kimmy could not think of nothing and could not picture such a state of being.

"Well," Kimmy said breaking free from her trance, shaking her head, "you mentioned that you sing about some historical figures as well. Who is it you write about in your music?"

Kraken began, "one song we have that I wrote is dedicated to Elizabeth Stride. I called it *Clitoris and Jugular*." Kimmy looked at him, her face revealing her shock of the vulgar title. "She's such an obscure historical figure," Kraken continued. "She was a prostitute in London and one of Jack the Ripper's victims."

"I wrote one as well," Goblin said. "It's called *Harlequin Carrion*. It's all about the American serial killer clown, John Wayne Gacy."

"I've written several," Gorgon said, "but my favorite is about Marquis de Sade in our song *Perversions of the Bedroom*."

"Understandable," Kimmy said. The topic was a bit unsettling, but after the earlier discussion she felt surprisingly at ease. "It suits your genre of music. Now tell me, you said this is your first North American tour. Now have any of you been to this side of the Atlantic before this?"

"Once," Hydra said, "but only the Northeast. I visited Boston, New York and Philadelphia. It's interesting to see more of the country now. Unfortunately, with our schedule we only see the city through the bus. We have only a few stops that will let us get out and explore more."

Gorgon spoke, "I've come to America twice. I've been able to see more of the country though. I've visited everywhere from Boston to Washington, as well as New Orleans, Chicago, Las Vegas and cities along the California coast." The rest of the band was silent, revealing they had yet to have visited the North American continent.

Kimmy realized it was a rather dull question to ask the band, yet asked a follow up, "what do you think of our country?"

"It is beautiful," Siren said, "I have to admire the natural landscape and significant differences in the way the cities look."

Gorgon spoke next, "England is home and always will be, but I love to visit here. New York has to be one of the greatest cities on Earth."

Kimmy thought it was odd of them to say this given the dark nature of the band members and the course the interview had gone so far. She followed this question by asking, "how do you like life on the road?"

The band was silent for a moment. They appeared distant and dipped their heads. Gorgon lifted his and said, "I think I speak for us all in saying that it's interesting to tour the continent, but it does get lonely. We all are friends, yet all have friends and lives outside the band. After returning to England we will have a two week hiatus and then we will begin a four month European tour, beginning in Britain and ending in Moscow." Kimmy dreamed of a life like theirs. "It sounds glamorous to a lot of people. This whole year we'll be seeing New York, San Francisco, Rome, Paris, Milan and many other cities a lot of people only dream of visiting. But we will only be going to perform. We will not have the chance to enjoy the cities we visit for the most part. After the touring is complete we only want to stay at home, not travel. This is how we make our living though and the fans want to see us perform, but being away from home can be tiring and lonely. Shortly after the European tour we need to begin construction on our next album. It's all about pleasing the fans."

"You sound busy," Kimmy said. "When do you have time to write songs and record them?"

Hydra answered her question. "On tour."

Gremlin, breaking his long silence said, "sitting on the bus between cities is a great time to work. There's little else to do on the bus for so long and without something to occupy your time you'd go mad."

Kimmy kept interviewing the band members, recording this question and answer session on her small tape recorder. She found the band members to be an interesting group of people. Her initial reaction to the booths, fans, music and band members was quite negative, though she felt guilt for thinking of these people as aberrations of humanity. It was not often that people she interviewed challenged her to think so much. Even more than that, they opened her eyes to things before her she could not previously see. Concluding her interview she thanked the band for their time and walked out to her car sitting in the open parking lot. Gorgon's refined manner of speaking and charming British accent lingered in Kimmy's ears. Despite his disdain of being out around the world, Kimmy envied his quasi nomadic lifestyle. She had visited Mexico once on a Spring Break vacation in college, but had otherwise never left the country. She closed her eyes, still hearing his words, picturing London the way her mind saw it:

A cool night sat upon the old English city with a silent fog settling on the streets and buildings. Big Ben chimed in the late hour, sending bell tones through London City, Town and Court. A flaccid Union Jack hung over Parliament overlooking the Thames, inky in the night. Small cars cruised through the streets and circled the city's roundabouts. Monuments and landmarks glowed in the city lights. Guards in red coats and tall, black hats stood as statues before Buckingham Palace as bobbies dressed in blue strolled down the streets, twirling night sticks. The ancient Yeoman Warders stood guard over the Crown Jewels and ghosts at the Tower of London, while ravens sat securing Britain's livelihood. A likeness of Sherlock Holmes stood in Bakerloo and trains roared beneath in the Underground. Piccadilly Circus glowed in vibrant colors, pigeons flocked in Trafalgar Square and shoppers filled prestigious Oxford Street. Centuries of history all clustered into one metropolis so many miles away, yet as close as Kimmy's mind. Awaking from her daydream, Kimmy stepped into her car. It saddened her that her only exposure to London was a travel book she bought and read many times, hoping to one day visit the old British city. Kimmy sighed looking at the arena from the driver's seat of her car and left.

Kimmy's article made it in the following week's edition of *Out Spoken*, though she abridged the full interview into the choicest parts. After the interview, Kimmy found herself to be a fan of Darkest Folklore, seeing more in their music than the average listener. The lingering wanderlust remained in her head, inspiring Kimmy to use her vacation time the following year to visit Great Britain. Over time she left the local paper to work for an acclaimed travel magazine in New

York. Her expenses to see the world were paid, though after a short while, Gorgon's words were at last understood. She was constantly on the road, seeing the world. She loved the job and the opportunity to travel, but could not help but realize the loneliness of the lifestyle of always being somewhere but home. In turn, Kimmy sacrificed her friends, family and potential for marriage and family life to feed her craving to see the world. Though it was a lonely life, Kimmy would never trade it for anything else.

Darkest Folklore's popularity increased somewhat in North America, Europe, Australia and a few Asian nations. After their first American tour, they released four more original albums before retirement. In that time they toured America twice, Europe three times and Great Britain once per year until they split apart. Having made millions from worldwide record sales they were able to live quite comfortably without the pressure of forcing art and inspiration. Unfortunately the band remained large only in Western Europe, never becoming mainstream in the other areas of the world, despite an increase in listeners. Even after official retirement Gorgon found the retired life too slow. He became a solo artist, releasing several more records. Feeling the same, Gremlin and Kraken played their instruments for Gorgon to keep from depression and boredom in retirement. In time, the band faded from memory though their music was occasionally played in clubs and venues for future generations of this subculture.

III

It had been six days since the bombing at the mosque. It was Wednesday, the day after the Darkest Folklore concert. City officials fretted over perpetually growing tension. People sympathetic to the tragedy were to gather at a downtown plaza for a vigil on Friday. Likewise, the Fundamental Center for Families made a last minute plan to hold a demonstration at City Hall to promote their organization. They had often used a major event such as this to promote their values and ambitions with a Christian bias, though never before had they been so bold with their move as to appear amidst a tragedy. Feeling as though the FCF's demonstration on Friday manipulated the loss in the Muslim community to push their own interests, members of Islam and activists in the name of Allah planned an urgent protest against the right-winged group. Feeling their liberties threatened by such a callous act, other organizations launched separate campaigns to deride the FCF, all in unity against their common enemy, though unfortunately many of these groups were in opposition to each other. Members of an organization supporting the separation of church and state were to protest, as well as a liberal organization standing adamantly against the FCF and conservative values. A Jewish group made arrangements to show and it was rumored that members of the Ku Klux Klan would attend.

Hearing of the FCF rally and the diverse mix that may follow was to be just outside his office, the mayor issued an alert for people at City Hall and the ambient areas. The chief of police was contacted demanding that he send officers to the area in full force before the rally began and well after it ended. The mayor fretted, fearing this event would explode into catastrophe, devastating his career in politics and worse yet, devastating the city and those that worked and dwelled within it. With this one potential cataclysm looming a mere two days away, the higher powers of civic government cut through red tape and bypassed bureaucracy to prepare for an urban disaster. A violent riot tearing through downtown at the end of the work day would surely be a massacre. As of now, they could only prepare for the worst and attempt to save as much property and as many lives as possible.

Peggy-Rae

Miles from downtown was a neighborhood of housing dating to the early 1960s. It was many square miles of cookie cutter housing from the Golden Age of white flight, emptying the urban core and conformity. In its glory days it was luxurious living. It was an escape from diversity in the central city and somehow it was once declared a slap in the face to the Cold War Kremlin. Each house bore wooden exteriors, shingle roofs and green yards. In the era of the Red Scare these were affordable notions of the good life. In the early 21st Century they were merely older houses, not as spacious, modern or distanced from the urban core as newer tracts of housing.

Though old, this Vietnam-era neighborhood stayed in relatively good shape. The homeowners were in the upper portion of the middle class. It was in a good school district and crime, though higher in this neighborhood now compared to the 1960s was still low in contrast to other areas of the metropolis. It had significantly diversified since the Civil Rights movements, though was still largely white. The neighborhood had character, though that had developed through time. Architecturally these were still cookie cutter dwellings though paint jobs, annexations, landscaping and other forms of housing upgrades made each house unique and prevented this neighborhood from falling to urban decay. Homeowner associations far removed from the urban core regulated identical housing in color and appearance, intolerant of expression and personalizing the home the way the owner wanted. This neighborhood was spared of such fascism.

In one of these houses lived Peggy-Rae Wilkinson. She was a Texas-transplant who brought a piece of her homeland into this house and her workplace and any conversation with any new person she met. Her house was easily identifiable with the large Texas state flag hanging from a pole attached to her house. She always felt it necessary to boast her Texas heritage and force all others to know of the wonders and glories of that state. She proudly told people that her ancestors lived in that state before it was even its own republic. Tracing her Lone Star pedigree to the Mexican-owned era, she could not brag that a relative fought at the Alamo or battled in Sam Houston's brigade. These relatives of a time long ago were simple ranchers, raising livestock to make money with no interest in the ultimate future of Texas. Regardless, Peggy-Rae vainly detailed her Texas bloodline.

She was a rather large woman standing at six feet tall. She added to her height when she donned her precious boots. Her collection of rancher footwear came from an extensive list of places. She had a pair from El Paso and one from Amarillo. Her closet housed three fancy pairs from Dallas, two from San Antonio and a single boot missing its partner from Houston. Her less classy pair of sneakers was purchased at a local mall and had little mileage. She loved her boots, feeling like a real cowgirl when she wore them. Peggy-Rae was even bigger in weight than she was in height. The area of flesh on her body rivaled the square mileage of the great state of Texas. Her rump made for a snug fit in two airplane seats and her breasts were large enough to bludgeon a cow. On top of her head sat short, curly red hair, not the least bit faded though she was two years away from turning fifty.

Originally from Midland, Peggy-Rae met her husband Wilbur Billy Bo Wilkinson at a high school football game when they were seniors. His team represented a school from Odessa, hers from Midland. They shared a forbidden love split by rival high schools. It was a Romeo and Juliet tale from central Texas. However, both discovered that they would be attending Texas Christian University after graduation and thus continued their relationship in college. After school they married and Wilbur Billy Bo got a job that required a location transfer, thus bringing Peggy-Rae away from Texas to this house. Oddly she came here after once claiming she would choose death before leaving Texas.

Peggy-Rae moved about the kitchen that Wednesday morning. She was on vacation from work this week and attended to domestic duties. As a pot of coffee brewed Peggy-Rae fried bacon and eggs for breakfast, using a pound of bacon and the entire carton of eggs to feed her family of four. On a skillet next to the pan of frying animal products she cooked a batch of pancakes. Usually the family ate at different times and always separately, but Peggy-Rae grew worried of this dissipation. She felt America today was becoming a decadent place losing its moral value. She wanted to do her part to salvage what she thought was the breakdown of her family. She felt having them eat together was a step toward saving them and preserving her family.

Only Peggy-Rae attended church regularly and wanted to force her husband, son and daughter to go each Sunday as well. Her children stopped going though still believed in God. Her husband attended only if she nagged him to go. In her heart she thought Jesus could save her family through her. Her daughter Trish came downstairs first. "Hey mom," she said cheerfully. Trish lacked the thick accent her mother had. "Smells good."

"Well you can wait," Peggy-Rae said. She spoke slowly with her thick Texan drawl. "We're gonna eat breakfast together as a family the way God wants us to." She did not look at her daughter, but rather attended to the sizzling food. Trish rolled her eyes and opened the refrigerator. Peggy-Rae turned around and put her hands on her hips with the flipper in her hand. "What did I just say?" Trish looked at her mother with the refrigerator door still open. "Now go sit down at the table." Trish sighed heavily and slammed the door, then took a seat at the table and huffed.

Minutes later her son Tyler came downstairs. Groggily he walked to the pantry and took out a box of sugary cereal. "Boy," Peggy-Rae said glaring at him, "take a seat at the table. You know we're gonna eat as a family from now on." She turned back to the stove and put the last batch of sunny-side up eggs, crisp bacon and fluffy pancakes onto plates, then set them on the table. She fetched a bottle of maple syrup and put it on the table where her hungry teenagers sat. She walked to the stairwell and called out to her husband, "breakfast's ready." There was no answer. Peggy-Rae heard silverware scratching on the plates and turned around to see Trish and Tyler eagerly eating breakfast. "Hey," Peggy-Rae said as she lumbered to the table, "wait for your father."

"We're gonna be late for school," Trish said with a mouthful of pancake.

Peggy-Rae was upset, but relented. Wilbur Billy Bo was still upstairs defying her wishes to eat together as a family. She sat with her children and piled several pieces of bacon and five eggs onto her plate. She added a tall stack of pancakes, coated each with a thick veneer of butter and doused them with maple syrup. She poured herself a cup of coffee and added a heaping spoonful of sugar and enough cream to pale her beverage to the shade of tea. She licked her lips looking at the meal she had prepared and feasted ravenously like a bear. She fit an entire fried egg into her flabby jaws and chewed. Her husband ran down the stairs fully dressed for work. "Have a good day. I'm gonna be home late tonight," he said as he walked quickly out the door.

"But wait. I made..." Peggy-Rae said calling out to Wilbur Billy Bo. He walked out the door without looking back. "Breakfast." Peggy-Rae felt rejected and ate quietly, that is, without speaking. She was quite a noisy eater, smacking and slurping her food and snorting as she ate. Following her piggish mastication was a loud gulp. Her children left half their food on their plates, bid their mother goodbye and left for high school. Peggy-Rae sat at the table alone and finished her plate of food, as well as everything else she cooked that morning that no one else had eaten. She then stood over the sink and washed the dishes.

Standing over the sink Peggy-Rae reflected on her life. She was raised a Southern Baptist and raised her children with the same faith. Her husband shared conservative ideology and religious doctrine with her. She had no doubt in her husband's beliefs and virtue, but feared her children were straying from her beliefs. They never talked to her anymore and both spent a lot of time away from the house. Whenever she had the opportunity Peggy-Rae liked to snoop on their lives. She had ample time today and would do some detective work in order to find clues and understand her children better. She thought about her husband. How she missed him. The past few months he had been staying at work late more often because of a massive project. Luckily his job required little travel. Peggy-Rae grimaced as she remembered the last disaster when he had to travel for work.

Two years ago he had business to attend to in Tokyo. He insisted on going alone, but Peggy-Rae plead to let her tag along for the trip. He at last let her come with him. She complained about the seemingly unending plane trip across the Pacific. Once there she saw no trace of Texas and very limited American influence. The culture was thus alien and she took it upon herself to let the Japanese know she was Peggy-Rae Wilkinson of Midland, Texas though she had left the state years earlier. She cringed at Japan's high prices, felt the bustle of Tokyo equated to the people as being rude and found the food to be inedible. The large presence of noodles, rice and fish could not satiate her massive appetite or please her palate. The oceanic taste of seaweed made her gag each time it touched her tongue. She settled for Western fast food chains and had Japanese food only once while there. One day she requested to meet with her husband after work in the Shibuya District. In her travel guide she read that the Statue of Hachiko was a great meeting place. She dressed herself in a large cowboy hat and her black and red boots from Dallas. She put on a black shirt and a vest sequined red, white and blue to resemble the Texas flag. The blue rectangle with a single star was on one side of the vest's front and the red and white rectangles on the other. She wore a denim skirt and a massive, brass belt buckle making her an eyesore of a cowgirl beneath Hachiko's patient stare. Peggy-Rae waited for hours as Tokyo passed her by. Eventually she returned to the hotel. Her husband joined her an hour later, having never gone to Shibuya.

Peggy-Rae pondered that memory as she dried the dishes. She remembered being upset about that, but never asked why he had been truant at their rendezvous and so late to the hotel. He had said that she knew how his job was. Peggy-Rae, having finished the dishes walked into the den and turned on the television to Channel 5. She tried her hand in interior decoration in both the den and living room. Both rooms had a Texas-theme. She had hung up decorations with the shape of her homeland as well cowboys, boots and chili peppers. On a mantle in the den sat a stuffed armadillo with a cow skull hanging from the wall over it. She laid a colorful Mexican blanket on the wooden floor to accent the room. Both rooms had chairs and sofas in earth tones. She checked the time on the VCR clock, which blinked and read that it was midnight. The wall clock read 9:50. "Just in time," she said happily. She removed a stack of unread books from the chest that sat in the corner and opened it. She pulled out a large bottle of vodka. This chest was her hiding place for her little secret. She unscrewed the cap and took a swig from the bottle.

She sat in the recliner with the bottle and watched television. Her husband was always at work and this habit helped her to cope with her loneliness. She drank more from the bottle. At ten her favorite show aired. It was called *Gloria*. It was a talk show with a target audience of housewives. Usually Peggy-Rae watched it later in the night when it aired a second time, though because she was on vacation this week she could watch it during the day. Today's show featured concerned mothers and their children. There were four parties on the show today. The first mother brought out her son, who had become a thug. The boy dressed in clothes two or three sizes too large. He had a nylon piece on his head and wore three gold necklaces, making him look more like a rapper than a high school student. He spoke like a gangster, using slang and violent speech about his mother and Gloria. Peggy-Rae laughed at him. "You're a white boy," she shouted at the screen. She drank more vodka from the bottle.

The second mother came out with her daughter, who dressed lasciviously. The mother was concerned her daughter was involved in lewd behavior. "Your daughter's a whore," Peggy-Rae said laughing. The next guest brought out her lesbian daughter. The daughter cried and begged for her mother to accept her, though the mother seemed more intent on embarrassing her daughter on national television and changing the young girl to her liking. "Get that filthy dyke off there," Peggy-Rae screamed. "Them homosexuals all going to Hell." She drank yet another mouthful of vodka. The final guest had a son who joined political groups and spoke out against conservatism. The mother complained that his ambitions and outlook contradicted the family's beliefs and that for which their household stood. "You're right to fix that anti-American little asshole," she shouted again. "Ungrateful little bastard." She stood up and set her bottle down after the show.

Peggy-Rae stood behind the government and questioned people's loyalty to the flag if they spoke out against its actions. That was of course if the government leaned to the right. Otherwise a leftist America meant all was in disarray. Under

Democrat leadership she felt her way of life was endangered. In this case the government was wrong. Abortion, gay rights and anti-war activists and all the other sinners and anti-American traitors had no room in America she thought. Likewise she denounced immigration. She felt the solution to most of America's problems would be solved if the government would seek out and deport all immigrants. Regardless of the nation's rich cultural diversity she believed there was no room for the foreign-born here. The question of the deportation of all American-born citizens including those of European descent was presented to her once. A former co-worker asked if all people not of any American Indian tribe or lacking any of their blood should leave as well, thus returning America to the indigenous people. Peggy-Rae angrily dismissed the remark as anti-American and made quite a scene expressing this. Soon after she fabricated a sexual harassment suit to chase the young man out of her office. The administration made a decision in her favor and the man was fired soon afterwards, though he never sought revenge against her or an investigation into his erroneous termination.

Peggy-Rae wobbled as she walked. It was just after eleven and she had finished half the bottle of vodka. A woman of her large proportions and high tolerance of alcohol could handle such an amount with ease. She was in a state between tipsy and drunk. It was that pleasant moment of intoxication with the pleasure of alcoholic influence without nausea. She stuffed the bottle back into the chest and put the short stack of books back on it. It was a mix of the Bible, books on Christian philosophy and reason and one book of conservative, socio-political commentary. One day she swore she would finally make the time to read them. As of now they sat on the chest only as a way to allow guests to believe she lived in a family of readers. She upheld the household with the utmost values and morality. At least, it was her subjective morality. She saw to it the house was run under God and that nothing undesirable by her strict standards would ever enter this house.

Peggy-Rae left her bedroom having at last changed out of her nightgown. She wore a mammoth pair of sweats that fit her body like paint on a house. She wore a faded red T-shirt with yellow lettering reading "Don't Mess With Texas." Her stomach showed symptoms of hunger. Her mighty breakfast had passed on and now the great cavern within began to lightly bellow. She loved food almost as much as she loved Texas, but would wait for the time being. Before lunch, she wanted as much time for spying on her children's questionable lives as possible. She stood at the corner in the hall with her hands on her hips. She looked at Trish's door and then to the adjacent door, which led to Tyler's room. She felt something was amiss in both their lives, but presently could not decide which to intrude first.

She sighed and arbitrarily made her decision, flinging open Trish's door. Her sides scraped the doorjamb as she entered. The room seemed ordinary, but she had seen it before. On the walls hung many posters of men Trish found attractive. The bed was not made. The yellow comforter and blankets sat upon the queen-size bed disheveled. Otherwise the room was neat and smelled of perfumes. Trish had several brands, which blended together into one sweet, feminine smell in her room. Pictures of her friends sat in frames on the dresser. Peggy-Rae picked one up and focused on her daughter's image amidst her friends. Her daughter was slender and had long, red hair. She reflected on the close relationship they once had. Her daughter's lust for her independence saddened her. Peggy-Rae no longer had as much control or influence over Trish. She stumbled a bit as a wave of the vodka swelled over her. She set the picture down and looked around the room. Rather than diving into the closet, Peggy-Rae decided to begin with the dresser before her. She opened a drawer and sifted through it. They were all T-shirts and nothing she had not seen before.

She closed it and moved down. The second drawer down housed nothing but socks. She searched the final drawer and found undergarments. She dug through the bras and panties, ultimately finding a clue into her daughter's secretive life.

She pulled out a handful of strings. At least Peggy-Rae thought they were strings. They looped around into a confusing knot. She separated them into three separate pieces. There was a red bunch, a purple bunch and an orange bunch. Through the vodka's influence she tried to discern what these were. She fumbled with one, trying to make sense of the fabric. It had two strings and a triangular piece of fabric. Finally it hit her. These were skimpy pairs of underwear. She dropped it and grimaced. "Ugh," she grunted. "I couldn't get one leg through that." She looked at them disgustedly. "So that's what Trish spends her allowance money on." Despite the provocative sight before her she was curious. It upset her that her daughter would wear something so sexual, but perhaps she could learn from this. Wilbur Billy Bo barely touched her anymore, let alone fed her sexual desires. A bit of revealing lingerie in her wardrobe could solve this problem. But where would she find so much material for her size covering so little of her flesh?

Peggy-Rae wadded the thongs and stuffed them back into the drawer. She stood up, stumbling as the feeling of vodka sloshed in her head. She looked in the closet seeing her daughter's vast collection of clothes. She fingered through them and found articles she never knew her daughter had. There was a leather mini-skirt and shirts with decorative sexuality. A pink shirt with a low-cut to reveal to males a gracious view of cleavage read in red-sequined letters, "Slut." Another blue T-shirt with words in yellow block letters read, "Eat Me" with an arrow underneath them pointing downward. The blatant sexuality revolted Peggy-Rae, though she took a mental note of these suggestions. She was shocked her daughter wore such clothes. She closed the closet door and turned around shaking her head in disbelief and disappointment. She felt shamed.

She espied a book sitting barely tucked under Trish's bed. Peggy-Rae looked at it, her vision somewhat scrambled from the vodka. She observed the nondescript blue cover. It was Trish's diary. It was the sort that any curious pervert could pick up and open, as it lacked the little lock and latch to secure her daughter's innermost secrets and the mysteries of her adolescent life. Without hesitation, Peggay-Rae opened it and read.

After skimming through several entries, Peggy-Rae gathered that her daughter was more emotional than she had presented at home. Her daughter revealed in an entry dating back to September 14, 2001 that she had been heartbroken after her boyfriend of a week and a half took her virginity at the age of thirteen and broke up with her. There was much sadness between that date and the middle of November, when the entries abruptly stopped temporarily. Peggy-Rae thought about this, but could not remember. She felt that she did not remember because she was preoccupied with feeling America should vaporize the Middle East with nuclear weapons, as this was only three days after the fall of the World Trade Center.

The entries resumed almost a year later, beginning in August of 2002, just after Trish's fourteenth birthday. She had met another boy and the two had been together a week. She wrote of her giddiness and love for him. "Aw," Peggy-Rae cooed, "you don't know what love is." She smiled, amused by her daughter's emotions. After two weeks, Peggy-Rae disgustedly read that her daughter had engaged in sex for the second time. The break-up came another week later, followed by several entries of depression, loneliness and suicidal thoughts. Peggy-Rae scratched her head. "Why can't I remember this?" By Christmas of that year she had tallied two more boys to Trish's list of sexual experience.

Reaching spring of 2003, after a diary hiatus following the holidays, Trish wrote that she had met another boy. Peggy-Rae read about their relationship lasting a month. Unlike the previous four boys, this pairing seemed more sexually compatible, as Peggy-Rae counted a dozen instances written in the journal as well as reading that her daughter admitted to having performed fellatio and received cunnilingus for the first time. Peggy-Rae gasped, trying not to picture this in her mind. She did not want to read any more of this degenerate filth. She noticed a break until Halloween of 2003. She continued reading. Trish had gone to a party that night and wrote a harmless entry about it before attending the party. November 1st told of the boy she met there and the pleasure they had in the closet. "Trish," Peggy-Rae lamented, "you were only fifteen." Her eyes burned and started to tear.

There was a long absence in her daughter's escapades. There was nothing until May of 2004. Trish wrote that she found herself more interested in sex than love. She wrote that she believed she did not want her heart broken again, but craved the carnal pleasure of the phallus. "Men," Trish wrote, "are disposable. I don't need them or they're bull shit." Peggy-Rae stopped and thought about "they're." She knew that was a grammatical mistake. Was it "there" or "their" in this case? She shrugged, struggling to think of the proper use of the homophone and continued reading. "I swear," Trish wrote, "if I could have a man without a brain who could just fuck like a rabbit I would keep him chained in my room and be happy." Peggy-Rae shuddered.

Weeks later in the diary Trish had met another boy. Oddly Trish had sex with him, but left him because he could not pleasure her. She admitted that he in honesty wanted a girl to love. The roles had reversed and Trish had become the heartbreaker. Surprisingly the entries had become more frequent. Very few of the entries had been about anything other than her relationships with boys. Beginning in July of 2004 Peggy-Rae had counted up one new boy until the end of that year. January 2005 saw two new boys and February bore four more. Peggy-Rae read with a scowl that Trish had sex with three men every month until the present. It was forty-three by her count and Trish was only seventeen now. The inebriation had worn off during the sobering moment of realizing her daughter was a nymphomaniac. Her stomach bellowed and she went downstairs to fix lunch.

She felt like having a sandwich and dropped three slices of bread into her toaster. They owned one capable of holding four slices. She stood before the refrigerator pulling out foods and condiments for her sandwich. At first she wanted tomatoes, turkey, pepper jack cheese and mayonnaise to make up her meal. She felt it would merely whet her appetite so she pulled out the roast beef as well. To compliment it she took out bologna, salami and pastrami. There was a virtual slaughterhouse on the counter now. Peggy-Rae thought it would be best to balance it with more than just meat. She took out the cheddar and Provolone as well, though realized she had only one condiment. She settled with yellow mustard and horse radish. It seemed to be too much now. Peggy-Rae promptly put the tomatoes back in the refrigerator. The toast popped up, crispy and hot. She fetched a plate and began to construct her behemoth of a sandwich.

She sat before the television to have a sort of live theater to accompany her meal. "That damn Muslim hell house again," she said as the news covered more of the bombing story. Peggy-Rae hunched over the plate bearing her massive sandwich with a moat of oily potato chips surrounding it. It was a dedication to the state of Texas in size and ingredients. The lion's share of the hulking lunch was stuffed with slices of cow corpse, though pork had a considerable presence as well. Surely the money she spent on meat benefitted some Texas ranchers very well. She lifted it to her jaws while watching television. "Damn liberal media," she snorted. The sandwich could have been a formidable opponent to most anyone as it measured eight inches high. She pulled the great sandwich closer to her mouth. Her jaws opened wide like an anaconda and bit hungrily into it. Her incisors sliced through the layers of bread, meat, cheese and dressing and she chewed ravenously like a hyena, smacking the mouthful of food.

Peggy-Rae finished the sandwich and potato chips with little effort. The meal had satiated her appetite for now. She looked over at the chest and debated finishing the bottle of vodka, as the effects had left her. She was now sober. She shook her head and decided to wait until after she completed her investigation of her son Tyler's room. Peggy-Rae lifted herself from the sofa, using all her lower-body strength to raise her immense body weight. She held her back, as it ached from the burden of carrying the many pounds in her gut and breasts. She had tried many kinds of diets, always experimenting with the latest weight loss trend. Atkins, South Beach and so many others had failed her. Once it had been suggested to her to eat less and exercise more. She snorted and replied, "like that will do any good." Peggy-Rae believed these publicized diets over the word of a non-professional. She walked into the kitchen and set the plate in the sink, then returned upstairs to finish her spy work before her children got home.

Entering Tyler's room made Peggy-Rae nervous. Trish, she had discovered, had an insatiable appetite for sex and Tyler had drifted from her over the past few years. He was a quiet boy who either spent his time alone in his room or at his friend Eric's house. Surveying his room Peggy-Rae hardly understood why he would willingly spend time in here. The room was a sty. Clothes lay strewn about, dirty and clean alike. Papers from school mixed with the clothes. Underneath the bed was a cache of various objects crammed to capacity. There was a television on the floor with a video game console attached. Soda cans, candy wrappers and other bits of garbage lay about this landfill of a room. The air was stale and Peggy-Rae found it somewhat hard to breathe. Looking around she had no idea where to begin her search.

She scratched her red hair and figured Tyler's dresser,

much like Trish's, would be the best place to start. She opened the underwear drawer and found nothing except wadded pairs of her son's boxers stuffed messily in the drawer. She opened a drawer of wrinkled shirts and discovered one subject of interest. Tyler had several pornographic magazines hidden in here. "Oh my," Peggy-Rae said. She had two perverts in one family it seemed. She leafed through one of the magazines with a grimace on her face. How could women make a living doing this? There were women exposing their vaginal interiors, groping themselves and acting sexually with other women. She shook her head and stuffed it back into the drawer. How could she bring this up to Tyler? She thought about how to talk with Trish, but Tyler would be far more difficult. The pornography, however, only piqued her interest.

Peggy-Rae looked through the sock drawer and found a piece of plastic barely concealed by the socks. She tugged at it and pulled it out. At first she could not tell what was in this plastic bag. It looked like tea. Why would he hide tea though? She smelled the dried leaves and a college flashback hit her. It was marijuana. "Oh, Tyler," she said nearly weeping. "How could you?" She looked in the drawer again and found a box of papers. In her own house he was using drugs and rolling joints. She looked at the alarm clock by Tyler's bed. It was one-thirty and the kids would be home in about two hours.

Peggy-Rae sat outside in her backyard. She had patio furniture for the whole family, though they rarely used it together. She sat on a stool with a back as the armrests of the chairs would not permit her to fit. It was a brisk autumn day and partly cloudy. Peggy-Rae sat in the sun, which shone on the city in a break between drifting clouds. She looked at the white stick in her fingers and licked her lips. Using her son's stash she rolled a bulging joint. She put it between her lips and lit the end with a long lighter intended for the outdoor barbecue grill. She forgot what a strange taste this had. She had not forgotten the burn in her throat or that she had to hold the smoke in her chest. Each time she inhaled the smoke irritated her throat. She held it in her lungs until the caustic feeling forced her to cough. It had been a long time since she last smoked pot. She sucked more of the burning cannabis into her lungs. It crackled as the fire drew closer to her lips. The taste seemed to grow worse and Peggy-Rae began to feel a little sick.

After several minutes she felt something in her head. She could feel her brain inside her head. It felt as though her skull was racing forward and her brain was packed tightly in the back of her head. Some force weighted her body, fastening it to the stool. It felt as though she were on a high-speed roller coaster with no support around her. She felt dizzy. The world around her looped and spun. A sickly feeling filled her stomach. Despite the cool autumn air a flash of heat warmed her body and lingered, making her feel feverish. Tiny droplets of sweat formed. Peggy-Rae could feel each one, though they numbered in the thousands. They felt like small ice crystals forming in her pores. This was a different experience from what she remembered.

She sat looking at the tree in her backyard. She never realized how beautiful and fascinating it really was. The leaves were different shades of yellow, orange and red. Her jaw hung open in awe as she marveled at this fiery-colored tree. The trunk was magnificent, holding a vibrant sunset in its branches. A light breeze tickled the leaves and made them dance. They rustled and swayed in the autumn air as Peggy-Rae sat gorgonized on the porch. The hypnotic movement held her gaze in a mesmerized trance. She felt something at her fingertips that made her jerk. She looked at her hand to see it was the half-smoked joint. She had never let go but had just now felt it. In a moment of clarity she said, "I'm gonna kill... um...that...boy." She forgot her son's name. "Bringin' them... drugs...in my...house." Peggy-Rae giggled. She forgot what had caught her attention and stared at the wooden fence as it suddenly captured her interest.

"Mom," a distant voice called. "Mom are you okay?"

"Oh shit," Peggy-Rae shrieked. The kids were home looking for her. She tried to stand up, but felt heavier than usual. At that moment she noticed her daughter standing next to her.

"So you can smoke, but I can't?" Trish said looking at the object in her mother's hand. Trish was referring to the time her mother caught her smoking at the mall. She had been punished severely, as her mother said that smoking was a sin.

"What do you want?" Peggy-Rae said awkwardly.

Trish stepped back. "What?" she said aghast.

Peggy-Rae rubbed her face. "Just get me the...the...pizza."

"What's wrong, mom?" Trish asked concernedly. Something odd was happening. "Have you been crying?" Peggy-Rae stared blankly at her daughter. "Your eyes are red. Are you okay mom?"

"Yeah, yeah," Peggy-Rae said. "Now get me... that...um... pizza. It's in... in the, uh...that... cold...thing." Trish backed away looking at her mother with a confused expression. She went inside to heat the frozen pizza her mother requested. Peggy-Rae lounged lazily, leaning on the table. How long had she been out here? She felt as though it had been only ten or fifteen minutes, though her daughter's presence suggested it had been well over an hour. The world seemed more animated and life felt much better. She used the barbecue igniter to light the end of the joint and inhaled more smoke. As she held it in her lungs, the damning thought of Jesus' disapproval entered her mind. She knew drugs were a sin, but where exactly in the Bible did it say that? Peggy-Rae struggled for the verse and gave up trying.

Trish came out with the large pizza on a platter. "Here mom." She sniffed the air like a curious dog. "Mom, what's that smell?" Peggy-Rae looked at her lazily and unresponsive. "Is that a cigarette or something else?"

"Give me... the... pizza... and get... to...your room." The marijuana toned down the anger in her mother's voice.

"What?" Trish said clearly upset, though unclear to her mother. "What did I do?"

"I said get," her mother snapped in a mellow tone. Trish huffed and put the pizza down on the patio table. She stomped away. "You're in... big... big... trouble... missy." Peggy-Rae yelled out. "Don't be... um..." She fumbled for the word. It was something about her daughter's sex life. She spaced out, lost her train of thought and looked at the pizza. Trish forgot to slice it. Peggy-Rae rolled it into a large cylinder of tomato sauce, crust, cheese and pepperoni. She ate it rabidly, finishing the entire pizza in ten minutes.

A few hours later Peggy-Rae had completely sobered. She remembered why exactly she was upset with Trish and headed toward her room to confront her. She was also upset with Tyler for keeping his room a mess and for keeping drugs in her house. She saw not the least bit of hypocrisy in her action earlier though. However, she would deal with him later. First thing she wanted to prevent her daughter from fornicating anymore, at least until confined in wedlock. She walked upstairs, gasping, feeling heavier with the large pizza sitting in her gut. She stopped at the top and paused to catch her breath. She wheezed and clutched her chest. Her doctor told her the great mass of fat pressured her heart and her cholesterol was killing her slowly. Another way to say it was that Peggy-Rae had already entered the dying process. Now was not the time for her to contemplate such matters.

Having regained her breath she headed toward Trish's room, which had music blaring from behind the door. As she approached it she heard a click and stopped. Tyler's door opened slowly and he poked his head out, not immediately seeing his large mother standing there. He came out a bit farther. His head turned and he saw Peggy-Rae standing there. He jumped, startled and let out a quick shriek. "Mom," he said. "You scared me." His mother eyed him with an intimidating stare. He was at an obvious loss for words and appeared paranoid and frightened.

"How was your day?" she asked sternly.

"I, ah, well I..." Tyler tripped clumsily over his words trying to think of something sufficient to say. "It was...um... was... was okay." He stood motionless searching his mother's face for an expression telling him that everything was all right.

Peggy-Rae stared him down like a tiger. Tyler gulped. Both knew the issue here. Something in Tyler's drawer had gone missing. The mother and son stood there in tense, uncomfortable silence. At last Peggy-Rae spoke. "You seem a little off today."

"Oh?" Tyler responded.

"Well, we can talk later." A devilish grin overtook her face. She reveled in the torture. It was an understood pleasure of parenthood, as sadistic as it was. Tyler crept back into his room and Peggy-Rae focused on Trish's door. She approached it and stood there silently, deciding how exactly to discuss this. This was one of the understood pangs of parenthood, as difficult as it was. At last she knocked on the door. After several seconds she knocked louder. The blaring music shut off and Trish answered her mother's knocking.

"Oh," Trish said feeling a sinking sensation, "hi. Did you enjoy the pizza? It's all over your face."

Peggy-Rae felt embarrassed and wiped her mouth with the back of her arm. It left a smear of grease and tomato sauce on her skin. "We need to talk," Peggy-Rae said austerely. It was hard to take her too seriously with the orangish stain about her lips.

"What about?"

"I was looking in your room earlier and found that diary and those little panties of yours. And those disgusting shirts."

"You what?" Trish responded in shock.

"Is that what you spend your allowance money on? Your father and I..."

"I can't believe you looked through my room," Trish exclaimed angrily.

"And that diary."

"What gave you permission to read through my diary?"

"I'm your mother," Peggy-Rae said pompously, crossing her arms. "That's what."

"It's my business. Not yours!"

"Trish, I am very upset with you for this. And when your father finds out..."

"You're telling him?"

"Of course I am. We can have a nice, long..."

"I hate you," Trish shrilly screamed. "You're a... a... a fat-ass, nosy pig!" She slammed the door in her mother's face.

An intense surge of anger grew in Peggy-Rae. She jiggled the handle to find that Trish had locked it. She slapped both hands on the door and screamed through the locked barrier. "Now you hear me you little slut, Jesus said to honor your mother and father. We both deserve it. Your father and I are good people who..." The music blared again drowning out Peggy-Rae's angry voice. She hit the door and stormed away angrily.

The rest of the afternoon was quiet. Tyler and Trish stayed confined in their rooms. Peggy-Rae steamed in anger on the couch downstairs. When Wilbur Billy Bo got home she would discuss her revelations with him. She would at last have someone on her side. Her thoughts occupied her mind for hours. She was so deep in thought that she did not notice the sunset outside. She grumbled, "this never would've happened if we just stayed in Texas." She hated everywhere she had ever been except her home state. In her eyes, the entire state was heaven and all Texas cities should be the standard for all other cities worldwide to follow. She glanced at the clock on the wall. It was just past seven. Unusually, her stomach did not announce the time. It usually worked like clockwork, telling her it was mealtime every few hours. Initially she thought it was strange, but after realizing the time with her own eyes she quickly became hungry.

She stood in the kitchen with the microwave humming. It was heating a frozen dinner of chicken fried steak with a peppery, white gravy. Peggy-Rae looked at the timer. It had only two minutes left. That was just enough time to finish the pot of pork and beans simmering on the stove. This meal reminded her of Texas. She was in the mood for barbecued ribs, but did not have the time to prepare them and felt ribs at any restaurant in this forsaken city could never compare to even the worst ribs in Texas. She set the microwaved food on the table and poured the hot beans into a bowl. She set it next to the plastic dish containing her chicken fried steak. The hungry woman ate her food like a scavenging beast. Bits of her meal dribbled down her chin, splattered on the table and fell to the floor. She devoured this meal faster than any other she had that day. Still not satiated, Peggy-Rae served herself a heaping bowl of strawberry ice cream. She realized it was twenty minutes until eight and her husband was still not home. He had told her before that he often had to work late once in awhile, though it seemed more frequent the past couple years. She wished he were not such a slave to his job.

Sitting on the sofa eating ice cream and watching television, Peggy-Rae reflected on her greater ambition. She felt the family was disintegrating and after the day's unsettling knowledge she felt it was imperative to pull them closer before they lost each other permanently. She wanted to use the church as a cornerstone, promoting the good Christian values she held dear and swore she lived by each day. There had been waning interest on her family's part in attending church. Perhaps they needed the refreshing words of the Bible to set their lives straight again.

At a quarter to nine Wilbur Billy Bo came home and the kids had yet to come downstairs since this afternoon. The house's patriarch walked in looking annoyed. Peggy-Rae walked over to greet him. "Hi dear," she said. "How was work?"

"What's for dinner?" he asked curtly.

Peggy-Rae looked at him silently. "Anything you want I suppose."

Wilbur Billy Bo grunted and said, "never you mind. I'd figure you would've had something ready for me. You know I work long hours."

Irritated Peggy-Rae snapped back, "well if I knew when you'd be home exactly I could fix you up something." Her husband ignored her and went to the kitchen. She followed him and watched him make his own dinner. The man had never learned to cook, feeling it was the woman's obligation to nurture her man and children. The few instances he actually cooked anything turned out to be something simple. Tonight he threw a few hot dogs on a skillet and turned on the stove. "Don't you want to know what happened today?" Peggy-Rae asked. Wilbur Billy Bo kept his back toward Peggy-Rae and would not answer his wife. "Turns out Trish is a little whore and Tyler smokes marijuana."

Wilbur Billy Bo quickly faced his wife. Not a word was spoken. The only sound was the sibilant hiss of the hot dogs cooking on the skillet. "What?" he asked at last. "How did you find that out?"

"I went lookin' in their rooms."

He sighed and turned around again. "Shit," he whispered angrily. Peggy-Rae felt uncomfortable by his cold silence and went upstairs to their room. She lay on the bed and turned on the television. Her husband's distance had been worrying her, but she always kept quiet about it. She thought about sitting him down and discussing the issue, but never had the courage to do so. They were married, thus all had to be well. When she was a little girl in small town Texas she dreamed of the ideal man who would be her soul mate. She figured everyone had one and God blessed her with Wilbur Billy Bo many years ago. She thought he may just be under stress, but not hearing it from him only titillated her curiosity. She twisted the wedding ring on her stout finger and thought. Enough was enough. She had to go downstairs and get answers from her husband. Peggy-Rae walked downstairs determined, yet apprehensive.

Wilbur Billy Bo sat there with the television on in a dark room. He had apparently finished his meal. "Bo," Peggy-Rae said, "I want to talk to you."

He jumped up and shrieked as though those words gave him the final push into insanity. "You know what Peggy, I'm sick of this. I'm fucking sick of it."

She stepped back, frightened, but knew she had to talk with him. "What are you sick of?"

He counted the reasons on his fingers. "I'm sick of this house. I'm sick of the kids. And I'm sick of you."

Her jaw dropped as her feelings shattered, "but why?"

"You're fat. You're ugly. You're a pain in the ass. I hate being around you. The sex sucks." He looked at her without the least bit of remorse and delivered another blow. "And you're a bitch. There. I said it. You're a fat-ass, ugly bitch." He glared at her angrily, feeling relieved to vent it to her at last.

Peggy-Rae held back her tears. "Can't we work this out? We can talk about it in bed."

"Oh, I'm not going to bed with you." Wilbur Billy Bo had a sickly expression. "I'm not touching your blubbery body ever again." Peggy-Rae stared at him with wide eyes. Her jaw quivered. "I'm leaving you," he said walking past her. He stopped at the bottom of the stairs and looked at her. She was frozen in place, still staring at where her husband had just stood. Her broken heart grounded her. She could not move from the spot. Wilbur Billy Bo saw that she was hurt and felt he had to say something. "I don't know if you picked up on it, but I've been having an affair for the past few years." Her head dropped. Wilbur Billy Bo could not see her face. "You mean you didn't pick up on it?" She did not respond. He shook his head and walked upstairs. "Figures," he snorted. "You always were a dumb bitch."

Peggy-Rae stood in shock and disbelief. How could she have been so naive? Her world, her foundation, everything fell apart around her. The emotional entropy broke her initial shock, shattering her heart. It relented to a lump in her throat and burning eyes. Her face crinkled. She pouted. Peggy-Rae could do nothing but stand there and attempt to make sense of the situation. She could not accept it. She would not accept it. Christianity did not tolerate adultery and her husband was a Christian man. Rationally he must have said that out of stress and did not mean it. She felt her duty as a wife was to go upstairs and comfort him. Her ulterior motive was to discuss the marital issues they both suffered. She walked toward the stairs still hurting from his comments, yet she was determined to resolve all that was wrong. She uttered a quick, yet sincere prayer to God for strength and her desired outcome.

When she entered her bedroom she saw her husband cramming clothes and belongings into a suitcase. She stood there shocked. Had God not heard her prayer? "What are you doing?" she asked.

"Packing," he replied coldly, not even looking at her.

"But why?"

"I told you downstairs," he said. "I'm leaving you."

"Can't we talk about it?"

"Nope." He callously continued packing his things.

"Surely we can work something out."

He grunted and looked at her. "Look at you Peggy-Rae. You're a pig. You smother me too much. I can't grow any more with you. You're more interested in that damn TV. This marriage was done a long time ago."

Peggy-Rae felt as though she had done everything right. She admitted that after having given birth to Trish she put on some weight. "But I love you. That's why I want to be around you so much. It's why I call you at work."

"Well," he said packing his suitcase. "I don't love you. Not anymore."

Frustrated and feeling defeated, Peggy-Rae moved to the offense. "How can you call yourself a Christian?" He stopped and looked at her. "How can you... have... sex with some other woman when you're married to me? You have a wife and kids."

He scowled at her and said, "I can call myself a good Christian just fine. Jesus would want me to be happy. You don't. I can never be happy with you." He stuffed one more shirt into his suitcase and pushed down hard on the cover to seal it. He put all his weight on the suitcase and latched it shut. Using both arms he lifted the suitcase off the bed and set it on the floor. Then he dragged the heavy load to the door where Peggy-Rae stood. "Out of my way," he said aggressively.

"No," she said, folding her arms. "I want to..." he lunged at her with his shoulder, knocking her out of his way. Without bidding her with even a simple goodbye he walked downstairs, into his car and drove away. Peggy-Rae went downstairs just as he pulled out of the driveway. From inside the house she heard the tires screech as he left the house for the last time. It was too late for her to ever again see her husband. She breathed heavily as it settled in and as she realized it a flood of tears soaked her cheeks. She moved quickly to the den. With one swipe of her arm she knocked the books off the chest and then flung it open. She grabbed the bottle of vodka, unscrewed the lid and put it to her lips. She tossed her head back and chugged the drink as though it were water and she had spent a day in the desert summer sun. Having finished the bottle she looked at the wall, then fell to the floor. She lay there huddled in a fetal position crying uncontrollably.

Peggy-Rae mired the rest of the week. She did not eat and left the house only twice, going only to the liquor store.

Robert Liles

She neglected her children and did not see them at all after that fateful day, remaining locked in her room. The following week she abandoned her situation and moved to a trailer in Lubbock, Texas, leaving her house and children behind in that city she hated so much. She never saw them again. She found work in retail and in time healed to a point that she could live life as normal, though always carried with her a piece of pain in her heart. However, she died of cardiac arrest only four years later. Wilbur Billy Bo, following the carnal advice of his penis fell for a stripper and met his horrid end in her world. The children fended for themselves, becoming citizens in society forced into dead-end jobs. After having been abandoned, the house was seized and sold to another family, bringing another tale its rooms could tell.

Winston

The city, like all other major urban areas found ways to diversify its economy and increase its prestige. It sought to entertain and educate its citizens simultaneously with centers for the public to gather in the quest for knowledge and aesthetic pleasure. Museums and libraries attracted people to their halls for the population to learn of literature, art, science, history and all the factors of the continuity of culture, those elements of humanity that perpetually expanded generation after generation as they had since humans first moved toward unity through common culture.

Like the handful of museums and libraries in the metropolis, academic centers of higher learning functioned as educational establishments that brought the city's population together in pursuit of knowledge. The city had its main university, as well as several smaller, less prestigious institutions. Community colleges offered students a bargain in price at the sacrifice of a lesser-known name. Many students chose to attend for two years only, just to complete general education requirements. Tuition was more affordable at these academic centers, though every college and the smaller universities stood in the shadow of this metropolis' grandest center for education: its primary university. Regardless, ideas, knowledge and theory were exchanged almost daily in all of these centers.

The very Thursday after Peggy-Rae's life crumbled a man pulled his car into the visitor parking of one of these colleges set in the suburbs. This man was Winston Townsend. He visited this college once every two weeks in order to pass his knowledge and theories to the student body. He was in his mid-fifties and age had definitely taken its toll on him. His skin was pale and wrinkled with several unsightly blotches scattered over his body. His hair had thinned and grayed. His stomach bulged and sagged. Time had not been good to Winston's body, though in his mind the spirit was the most essential form. Today he volunteered his time and spirit to educate the young men and women of this college to enrich their spirits. He would stand alongside the booths of student organizations to capture the interest, ears and minds of these students. Winston pulled a sign mounted on a thin, wooden post and a black sack out from the backseat of his car.

Winston carried his sign and sack onto the campus. Only a few students walked about, as it was twenty minutes until noon. Most students were in class at this time, but a large rush came at twelve. Students on their lunch breaks fled class and sought food. With the huge numbers of passers-by Winston could capture the attention of enough to draw in a crowd, as he always managed to do. He would impart his knowledge to this young generation. He found a spot next to the Young Republicans booth. Winston hoisted the sign and planted it into a muddy patch in the grass flanking the sidewalk. Written in red and black lettering, his sign displayed a plethora of messages. One line read, "Stop Abortion" and was surrounded by eight lines forming an octagon, mimicking the common traffic sign. Below this line read, "Homosexuality is a sin." The phrase lacked in creativity, but the message was clear. He added a rainbow rectangle with a red circle surrounding it and a line slashing through it. Under this read, "Sinners, repent or burn in Hell." Following this was the predictable reference to the trite verse, John 3:16. Wiggling the sign to test that it would remain in the earth, Winston smiled as his sign was displayed for all to see. He felt the adjacent political group would boost his power while they in turn would benefit from his vibrant energy.

Winston stood there proudly. He watched over the campus, which seemed nearly derelict. Noon was quickly approaching and with it the flood of potential listeners would overcome this pedestrian thoroughfare. His sign was a tried and tested attention-getter. It never failed to bring a crowd of listeners. He saw himself as a warrior. He was a mercenary of God put on Earth to save America from its sinful path away from Christ. He was likewise a sheep in the flock, conveying the messages he heard in church each and every week and twisting them to his own liking and interpretation, spitting them out with his razor tongue to the students. Rarely did he spread the love of God, but rather he focused on the Lord's wrath and hatred. It often caused a small-scale controversy. Many students did not agree with Winston and would express their conflicting beliefs. It was this breed of people that convinced Winston that speaking to the public in this way was his raison d'être in this world. It was his sole duty to convert these sinners. He had to halt their wicked lifestyles and ways of thinking so that they may adopt his beliefs and way of life. He felt his life was ideal and nothing short of perfection. It was a life all others should be forced to live. The Word of God was mandatory. There was no choice in faith.

As noon chimed in on the Student Union's campanile bells, Winston began preaching to the student body. He waved his Bible in the air to flag down passing students. So many passed by without eye contact or attention of any kind. These were the horrible sinners Winston sought to help. Amidst these repulsive atheists and other non-Christians Winston saw some of the youth stop and read his sign. Some continued on their path, but others gradually clustered around him, giving Winston his much desired audience.

"America today is full of sinners," he screamed. "Your generation must find the path to God. Without the love of Jesus, America will crumble." He paused for applause, though received none. "God watches over this great country of ours.

He has chosen us to do his work. He has asked our president to do his work in the Middle East. We are acting in the name of God to erase those sinful nations of Islam."

"Hey," a young man shrieked angrily. Winston saw the young man gazing at him furiously. He had black hair and dark skin. "We are not sinners. Islam is a religion of love."

"Son," Winston replied, "if your religion is about love, why do your people blow up buildings and kill innocent people?" Some young men laughed at the argument, hoping to see a physical fight between Winston and the young man.

The young antagonist scowled and barked back, "why do yours?"

Winston pointed his finger at the young man. "This man is an evil sinner. He fights Christ in the unholy name of Islam. When America lets these awful people practice their religion in our country, it angers God." The young man grew more agitated. "God has asked our country to rid the world of the Muslim menace. This young man says his hateful religion is based on love. The only religion based on love is Christianity. If you do not accept Jesus, you cannot love your fellow man."

"Where does the Bible promote love?" a voice from the crowd called.

"The Bible is love," Winston replied. "The Bible is full of love."

The same voice shouted back, "the Bible is full of killing and encouraging persecution. How can you ignore that?" Winston could not find the speaker, as the face was hidden somewhere in the crowd. The young Muslim stood back talking with a group of what seemed to be others of his faith. The small group looked angry. They seemingly were plotting something at the back of the crowd. Winston suspected it was an act of terrorism against him. He felt their faith was belligerent and hateful. Surely these men were angered by Christ and were finding a way to violently strike at God, even if it was through Winston. "Well?" the voice called out again.

Confused after diverting his attention to the Muslims, Winston replied, "what?"

"With all the persecution and hatred in the Bible, how can you say it's about love? You can't just ignore those parts."

"Son," Winston said pretentiously from his pulpit, "there is no bad in the Bible. There is no persecution except for that the Romans used on Christians. If you say that speaking out against Islam, abortion and homosexuals is persecution, you're wrong. The Bible tells us how to live our lives and none of these disgusting things are supported in God's words."

"Excuse me," a young woman said angrily, "my brother's gay and he's a really good guy. I take offense to that. How can you say he's so evil if you haven't even met him?"

"Homosexuality is a sin," Winston snapped back. "Those people purposefully go against God. Jesus hates homosexuals."

"I thought Jesus loved everybody," the girl said, growing angrier.

"Jesus only loves those who follow his teachings. Homosexuals defy the Word of God and reject the teachings of Jesus. They are sinners who must be punished. America gives homosexuals more advantages than normal people like you and me. If America wants to support their wicked lifestyle then we will see our society fall as God will no longer love and support us."

Several people laughed at Winston. Others including the clique of Muslim men and the girl glared at him, offended by his hateful words. A girl approached him. "How can you say this stuff?" Winston searched for an answer. "Look at how crazy you are," the girl said before he could reply. "I mean, do you actually believe the words you're saying?"

"Yes," Winston said in a condescending tone. "Young lady, I have read the Bible many, many times. I am convinced that if our country allows sin to happen freely and we legalize all these things the Bible forbids, it means our government is recognizing it while putting a burden on moral Christians like me. Then God will smite us all. For the sake of our country we must ban these immoral practices. Stop abortion! Stop homosexuals! Stop sin!"

Winston felt a bit despondent. He was raised in the religious revival after World War II. When America engaged in religion, God smiled on the land and helped it to defeat Russia decades later amidst scares of espionage, infiltration, nuclear war and spreading communism. He felt he must resurrect Christianity as best he could to preserve its definitions of morality. If the younger generations accepted sin and considered ignoring the Bible to be "tolerance," then in years to come God would bless a more devout country. He prayed that China would not adopt Christianity, as God would surely favor it and allow it to dominate the world. Despite its growing power, he felt it would never grow stronger than America without the grace of God.

Although he knew he had to answer questions to convert these non-believers, Winston had to address the bigger picture and preach the Bible. He saved the worn book in the air and screamed verses and ideology maniacally. Some members of the group left, though others joined. Soon the lunch crowd thinned and his audience dwindled to a few students who admired him and relished every wise word from his mouth. They praised his intelligence, courage and dedication. It brought a smile to Winston's face. There was hope in this generation after all. These young men and women were the future of God's tenacious grip on American society and law. These were the faces of tomorrow. They would be the ones to battle the sinful agenda that so many sought to battle in courts and high government offices. These were the people who had to preserve the death penalty to prevent murderers from walking free while fighting to eliminate abortion, fight infidels in foreign lands in the name of God and keeping the teachings of Christ alive and enforced.

After bidding these listeners goodbye, Winston plucked his sign from the dirt and returned to his car. He felt accomplished and hoped his words lingered in their minds. It was the only way to make change. He opened the back door to his car and put the sign on the seat. The Bible always sat in the passenger seat next to him. He held it close to his chest as he put away the demonstration sign and his makeshift pulpit. A pop sounded and Winston's head was knocked forward as something hard and wet slapped into the back of his head. The shock made him drop his Bible. It fell to the asphalt and Winston was horrified, as though it had been made of fine crystal. The juice from the projectile dribbled down his neck and soaked his shirt. Slime slowly oozed down amidst the juice. Winston touched it and looked at his fingers. Chunks of red with pale pods sat on his fingertips. Someone had thrown a tomato at him.

Winston turned to face the assailant. He discovered that it was not a single philistine, but rather a daunting group of them. One he recognized instantly as the Muslim man in his audience earlier. He presently stood with a group of his friends. They stared at him menacingly. Winston gulped. This was the risk of being one of God's chosen warriors. When sinners felt threatened by the love of Christ, they would lash out at the flock. It was proof of the persecution of Christians in America today. Allowing Muslims to share the nation, offering services for sexuality such as free testing for sexually-transmitted diseases were amongst the many aspects of oppression against Christians. Now the Muslims stood before him. These enemies of Christ and the Christian way of life threatened him. They stood still and angry, like gargoyles in the flesh. They said nothing with their mouths, but their eyes spoke to him. They warned him. They asked him to leave before he became a martyr. As steadfast as he was in his beliefs, Winston's survival instinct beckoned him to flee. He did not look away from them, but felt for the door handle. He grasped it, but it was locked. He turned quickly and stabbed at the lock with his key, finally inserting it. He unlocked the door, flung it open and dived in the car. The tires screeched as he peeled out of his space.

He breathed a sigh of relief reaching the street. He now headed home, driving his old car. It was a car in the sense that it had a motor, wheels and needed gas to move. In actuality, Winston's car was more of a mobile church. A large cross dangled from the rearview mirror and a Bible always sat in the car. The car was white, but patches of paint were missing, leaving metallic spots exposed all over the car. Little of the car's rear was visible. Only the lights, windshield and a few spots of the car's body could be seen, as Winston had plastered so many bumper stickers on the car the back had become a mural of pious messages. There was a Jesus fish and a Jesus fish with an open mouth eating a fish promoting the non-Christian value of evolution, as the smaller fish had a pair of legs. Some bumper stickers displayed his love of God, some demanded fellow motorists accept God and the others demonized people the church dubbed as inferior. This monastery-on-wheels always captured passing eyes, though because of the ridiculous amount of messages it was impossible to read even half of them at the city's longest red light.

En route to his house, Winston smiled with one of the city's Christian radio stations playing in his car. The station alternated between music and airwave evangelists. It was the station to which Winston tuned in the most, though if the mood struck him he would listen to the heavy beats of Christian rock on another station. That music, however, could become too intense at times and Winston would set the dial back to talk shows and choir music. Coming to a red light, Winston slowed his car and stopped behind a smaller car. His eyes widened as he read the bumper sticker before him. One had a picture of Jesus' face, complete with the crown of thorns. A caption next to it read "Jesus Hates It When You Drive Too

Slow." Another sticker on the car read, "Professional Simoniac on Board: One Way Ticket to Heaven Only $19.99." Deeply offended Winston accelerated his car and rear-ended this heathen.

The driver jumped out and ran to his window. It was a young man with long hair and black clothing. "Dude," he said, "what gives?" Winston just scowled at him. The man waited for an answer, but finally said, "you were stopped. Why would you step on the gas? We were at a red light you asshole."

"Son," Winston said through clenched teeth, "that was a wake up call."

"What? Wake up... how is that... why?" Winston's comment had irritated the man.

"Your un-Christian lifestyle will take you straight to Hell."

The man threw his arms in the air and gestured angrily. "That's why you ran into me?"

"Yes."

"Dude," the man said, "you got problems. You're fucked in the head."

"Don't talk to me that way." The car behind Winston began honking. The light had turned green during this confrontation. "Now kindly move and learn to accept the love of Jesus."

"I'm not going anywhere you dick." The man leaned toward Winson's window. "Give me your information or I'll call the cops." The man pulled out a cell phone from his pocket. The car behind this altercation continued to honk impatiently, now joined by the growing caravan of traffic stuck in the right lane behind this fender bender. "You're holding up traffic, man."

Winston threw his car in reverse, slamming into the car behind him. The honking ceased. He turned the wheels and cut into the left lane and in turn, clipping the young man. An approaching car in the right lane swerved into oncoming traffic, causing a collision. Winston drove away victoriously.

The Father and Son would be proud of him for doing their work and not bowing to that face of evil. It was a great way to spread their love and message. Winston did it because he cared.

About fifteen minutes later he reached his house. He parked his car in the driveway and got out. The exterior of his house was not sanctified as his car was, but the interior had been colored in shades of brown and white only. The extent of interior decoration he undertook in his house was an ample supply of crosses, crucifixes and portraits of Jesus: at least one of these on every wall. It was a small house, having only two bedrooms, one bathroom, a den, a living room, a kitchen and a laundry room. There was also a basement. It was a place Winston kept his highly personal belongings. He had no family and had never been married, thus the basement had been seen by no one other than him. Winston entered his small house and locked the door behind him. He had done the Lord's work for the day, but had another major message in store for Halloween, which was coming soon. All the planning was in his basement, where Winston now headed.

He flicked the switch on the wall and the single, dangling lightbulb over the creaky, wooden stairs illuminated. Winston walked down into the house's abyss. His footfalls echoed in the concrete cavern below his home. Each step he took made an eerie creak rise from the wooden planks. He reached the bottom. It was a dark, musty, quiet place. He flicked on another switch, lighting his basement in full. Before him sat the Lord's war room. Weapons against the sinners filled the basement. Large drums of explosives sat in one corner. City guides, pamphlets and phone books lay on a table. These sources of information were a guide to the metropolis' dens of sin. On full display on an easel was a map of the city complete with the suburbs. Colored tacks were pinned on the map marking the exact location of each horrible place he loathed. The tacks were color-coded. Blue tacks marked the university, colleges and places with high volumes of pedestrian traffic in the city. These were ideal for public demonstrations. Yellow tacks marked institutions, businesses and organizations supporting vice and sin. On the map was a single red tack. Winston touched it gently with his index finger and smiled. It marked the address of the devastated mosque.

Winston smiled wickedly and picked up a packet of papers with names, addresses and dates on them. The mosque topped the list, dated last Thursday. A red line scratched through it. Below it was the name of a popular gay club, dated for the coming Halloween. Winston set the ream down and picked up an advertisement for this club. It was an advertisement torn out of a local magazine. There was a picture of two men, both bare-chested. One wore white pants and angel wings. The other wore black pants and devil horns. It promulgated the upcoming Halloween party at the club. Winston researched this particular dance club. It was a popular place under normal circumstances, but the Devil's holiday would bring these sinners here in even greater numbers. Winston smiled at the thought. He would do God's work and make these sinners pay for their unnatural crimes on Halloween night. He glanced over at one of the large barrels. That night the club would become a fiery hell storm of God's wrath. He would kill hundreds in the name of the Lord. It was, after all, what Jesus would do.

The mere thought of the looming massacre made him smile. It would please God to send these people to Hell. The list of targets continued, promising to eradicate the city of abortion clinics, the genetics research facility, a Buddhist temple, other gay bars and numerous other establishments the church found to be undesirable. "Soon," Winston said. "Soon the Devil's work will be cleansed from this city." He was passionate about his work and vowed to aid an ailing America. He hoped his deeds would inspire others to fight in the name of God across the United States. He wanted to preserve the moral values and assuage an angered God. He had further plotting, but first he had to leave his armory to fetch a glass of apple juice and a sandwich from the kitchen.

Winston left the basement, leaving the door open so that he could carry his late afternoon lunch downstairs. As he approached the kitchen, he heard the doorbell ring. He stopped and turned to the door. He had a wooden door with a peephole. Winston peered out and saw a young man. His face was distorted by the curve of the lens. "Who is it?" Winston asked with his face pressed against the door.

"Hi," the man replied cheerfully, "I'm Garrett Flynn with the New Church of Jesus Christ. I was wondering if I could speak with you."

Through the curved glass in the peephole the young man appeared dressed well enough to be a mild-mannered Christian. Winston always relished the opportunity to speak with a fellow warrior of God. People like young Garrett endured the arduous task of going from one house to another to speak to others about God. "Well," Winston said opening the door, "come on in." Winston smiled, realizing he could be a mentor to this young man.

"Thank you, sir," the young man said. He was a bit shorter than the average male. His skin was pale white, his hair was innocently messy and blonde and he had little muscle mass. "I saw your car out front and wanted to talk to you especially."

"Oh?" Winston said, flattered. "I must warn you, son, I don't think there's a lot you can teach me." He held his head up pompously. "You see, I'm a man of God myself. I've made it my life's purpose to spread the Word. Perhaps there's something I can teach you."

"Why, I bet there is," the young man said. "The way I see it, America's losing its touch with God."

"Indeed it is." Winston gestured that Garrett should sit on the couch. Garrett sat and Winston took the chair facing the couch. He grunted as he sat. "All this rampant sin is tearing us apart."

"I couldn't agree more," Garret said, "I think..."

"All this homosexuality, drinking, drugs, abortion...it just makes me sick. It's a relief to see a young man like you with a good sense of morals."

"That's right," Garrett said after Winston stopped, "the way I see..."

"And that's not all," Winston said with a surly expression, "this feminist movement and women doing a man's job. What has happened to us as a nation?"

Quickly Garrett blurted, "and what do you think of women's rights?"

Winston sighed and reclined in his chair. "I don't see why they want to drag our country further from God."

Garrett smiled. "I know just what you mean. I think..."

"I mean," Winston started, leaning forward, "the Lord wants them tending to their men. They think they have to go out and make a living." He shook his head in dismay. "That's not a woman's role. You see son, women are to give birth to babies, take care of the children, cook the meals, take care of her husband, clean the house... you know, that woman stuff. Women are taking the roles of men and that must be stopped at once."

"It's great to meet someone like you," Garrett smiled. "So few understand."

Winston enjoyed his ego being fed by this young man. "It's great to meet someone like you as well," he replied, pleased. "Frankly son, I thought your generation was lost. The Bible makes women's roles clear. I'm upset that even Christian folk won't recognize that these days."

"Exactly, sir." Garret nodded as he spoke. "By the way, what's your name?"

"Winston."

"Well Winston, what are your thoughts on polygamy?"

Winston recoiled. "Son, it's wrong and disgusting."

Garrett frowned. "But the Bible clearly supports polygamy."

"It does not."

"It does so. Think of the story of King Solomon. His son also had many wives. Also it says so in Exodus 21:10, as well as…"

Winston grimaced and interrupted him. "Well the church has denounced that. Polygamy is for Muslims and Mormons. A man should have only one wife."

Garrett smacked his mouth as though he had bitten into the most foul tasting morsel. "The church can be wrong."

"The church is not wrong. It is never wrong. Take weddings for example. Ministers correctly credit God for creating marriage and it is between one man and one woman. Not two men or two women and not one man and more than one woman." Winston had considered ceremonies in other cultures before Christian colonization or resistant to Christian doctrine to be invalid marriages. Winston knew they had been heathen mockeries of the Lord.

Garrett became more intense in his speech. "Sir, let me tell you about why I'm here. I firmly believe Christians today must embrace the Bible more and I have come to spread the word as it is written."

"We do," Winston replied confidently. "Preachers read the Bible and tell us what it says and how we must live our lives."

"The Bible says we must not eat shellfish, pigs and rabbits, yet Christians eat that without regret."

"That's for Jews," Winston snorted.

"It is in the Bible and Christians today do not follow the Bible as it is worded. It is great that they know homosexuality is a sin and many know drinking and gambling are sins. However a lot of Christians, too many actually accept all of those awful sins. I would like to change that. That is why I am here."

"Drinking and gambling are sins," Winston said in the

fashion of a wise sage. "But son, Christians will do what they will. They will stray from the path to God. No, they shouldn't gamble or drink. They reject the words of Christ, but he still loves them for loving him. They can simply ask for forgiveness." Winston smiled warmly.

"We must protect our Christian brothers and sisters," Garrett replied sternly.

"If they reject the Word of God, they will pay in Hell."

"We can help them."

"Son," Winston said, reclining again, "you have a long battle ahead of you."

Garrett scratched his head. He was happy that Winston had at last stopped interrupting him, but was angered by his liberal ideology. "And what about the Ten Commandments."

"What about them?"

"Well," Garrett put his fingertips together, "the forbidden foods are in the Old Testament, so are the Ten Commandments. You said the forbidden food applies to Jews only. Do you feel that way about the Ten Commandments as well?"

"Certainly not, son," Winston said, appearing offended. "They tell us in church that the Ten Commandments are sacred. They even put them up in courthouses to remind people what is wrong. Our government can recognize that and we *are* a Christian nation."

"That's not important," Garrett replied, "they're in the Bible. That's what really matters. So are many other laws people refuse to recognize."

Winston chuckled. "I adhere to the Ten Commandments."

"Oh?" Garrett inquired. "What are they?"

"What are what?"

"The Ten Commandments," Garrett said appearing stolid in expression and posture. He shrugged. "What are all Ten Commandments?"

"Well, you know," Winston said nervously. He cleared

his throat. "Have no one before God because He's jealous. Ah, jealousy is there too. Or coveting I guess as it's worded." Winston began to sweat lightly. "Um, adultery, honor thy mother and father." He wiped the sweat off his brow. "How many is that?"

"Four," Garret said holding up four fingers, showing Winston he had been keeping track.

"So, six more, huh?" Winston's face reddened in embarrassment. "Graven images," he said slowly. Garrett stared at him in silence. "Oh, what does it matter?" Winston said relenting. "Ah, killing and stealing are forbidden on the list. Anyway, they're good Christian logic. That's all you really need. Am I right?" He laughed nervously. This young man had made him feel idiotic.

"I see," Garrett said quietly. "What you're really telling me is that you call yourself a devoted man of God who cannot even name all Ten Commandments. Is that correct?"

"Hey," Winston said, trying to turn the tables on this young man. "You don't agree with the church's interpretation of the Bible. Do you not go to church? I know that's a sin."

"I attend church every Sunday. Do you?"

"Of course I do. Then I go to work downstairs."

Garrett raised an eyebrow. "You work on Sundays?"

"I," Winston started, but paused. "Yes...I mean, no. Yes, I do, but it's work for God." Garrett just stared at him coldly. Winston had never felt more uncomfortable in his whole life and this shame struck him in his own home. "Before you came knocking at my door son, I was going to get some juice. Excuse me." Winston hurried to the kitchen.

He washed his sweaty face with a cold dishcloth. He looked out the window, staring at the drifting clouds in the sky, hoping to espy the face of Jesus Christ in Heaven looking down on him. He needed strength against this adversary. Never before had Winston come across someone who had been more knowledgeable of Christ or had been better suited to debate it than this young man. Despite it all, this young man would surely join him on his quest to eradicate sin from this city. All he had to do was to make the proposition. He poured himself a glass of apple juice and returned to the living room.

"Well son," Winston said, "I have an offer that I think you might..." Winston stopped, seeing that Garrett had left. He saw the basement door standing wide open as he had left it. He hoped Garrett had not ventured down there prematurely. Winston wanted to show him personally. "Son," he called out. There was no answer. He poked his head in the basement door and said again, "son." It was still quiet. Winston turned around and tried to find the young man.

The attack came quickly like a lion blended in the tall grass pouncing on its prey. Garrett threw his weight into Winston. A sharp pain surged in Winston's abdomen. Garrett stepped back enough for Winston to peer down at his stomach. He had been stabbed. Garrett's hand tightly gripped the knife's handle and a steady flow of blood streamed out of the wound. Winston knew enough anatomy of the human body to understand the blade had penetrated his liver. Winston looked at Garrett. Winston's face revealed his shock and physical pain. His eyes were wide and his mouth hung open as though he was screaming. Only grunts and coughs came from his mouth. A moment such as this led to blurred thoughts. Winston focused on the shock of being stabbed and the pain that came from the assault. He could not think of anything else.

"I bet you're wondering why I did this," Garrett said, still holding the knife in place, standing close to Winston. An evil look of satisfaction sat on his face. "I mean, I am a warrior of God after all." In truth, that question had not entered Winston's mind. Of course, such a pious young man should not commit such a lowly act. "You are not a man of God. You may say you are, old man, but you're a fake. You are corrupting people further. The punishment for betraying God is death."

"Where," Winston gasped, "where...does it...say that... in...the...Bible?"

Garrett chuckled, "a so-called warrior of God like you should know that." With a quick jerk, Garrett tore the knife out of Winston's liver, sending a flood of crimson blood pouring down his body. Winston stumbled toward Garrett in a pathetic attempt to attack him. Garrett merely darted to the side to avoid him. Gasping and holding his bleeding gash, Winston looked at Garrett searching for answers. He laughed at Winston wickedly. "Maybe you've heard of me in the papers. They call me a serial killer. They think I single out Christians to murder. Some call it a hate crime against Christians. The journalists couldn't be more wrong, old man. I act in love." Garrett lifted his head nobly. "People like you pervert the name of Jesus and I must stop that. You're the third wicked man I killed." Garrett stood there victoriously, as Winston barely stood at all. He was hunched in agony. The knife in Garrett's hand had been coated completely red. Drops of blood gathered at the blade's tip and fell to the carpet.

Winston moaned and felt dizzy. It appeared that Garrett would not leave until Winston drew his last breath. Again Winston lunged at Garrett, though he could barely move. Garrett, however, stepped back instinctively and mockingly. A step backward was all he needed. A step backward was all Winston needed as well. That single step backward was the entrance to the basement. Losing his footing, Garrett dropped the knife and threw his hands in the air. He grabbed for something, but grasped nothing. Garrett rolled quickly down the stairs and lay on the floor of the cold basement. He lay spread out in the darkness. A gash on his brow leaked blood and his eyes stared into nothingness. A shocked expression sat frozen on his face. The vertebrate in his neck bent sharply outward, leaving a visible lump of broken bones poking out from the soft skin on his neck. Garret lay there dead.

Giving into pain Winston collapsed to the floor. The pain

subsided and he barely noticed the sticky, wet pool of blood that soaked his floor. He lay there breathing, taking comfort in the thought he would soon see the end of the misery that was life and venture to Heaven. The thought of Jesus complimenting him on his good deeds as a street preacher and an exterminator of the undesirable made him smile. Winston knew he was dying. It felt like falling asleep for the first time in years. His eyes closed and shot back open, still seeing his house, his blood, his life surrounding him. He swore he saw two shadows at the window. His eyes closed again. They opened to a sound, otherwise loud, yet muffled by encroaching death. He saw four legs with blue pants and black shoes. He heard voices, but could not understand what they were saying. It was the police. Perhaps God sent them to help him. The Lord worked in mysterious ways. Hitting that man with his car in the street earlier must have led to their arrival now. One stepped over Winston and turned on the light to the basement. He would be known as the mosque's bomber. He would be known as a hero to Christians everywhere. God would help him live. He had to live. He had more work on Earth that needed to be done. At that, Winston died.

Charles

This city, like all major American cities, supplied a prevalent presence of government institutions. The state capital was many miles away in another, smaller town and the stately national capital was even further, but federal, state and local establishments representing the government and serving the people had a sizeable appearance. Immeasurable lengths of red tape coursed through bureaucracies, linking and dividing the various offices. It was part of the pulse of the city. Politicians, lobbyists, civil servants, judges, bureaucrats and scores of other workers toiled each weekday morning to the early evening to keep the system flowing smoothly.

It was within the walls of these places that democracy tried to function. Gridlock slowed the efficiency and many projects and interests sat on hold as issues and proposals ventured through the labyrinth of in and out boxes, emails, memos, fiscal watchdogs, legal matters and innumerable other obstacles in the maze of government. At long last a traffic light may be erected near a school zone or repairs on a busy street may finally commence. It was the drudging way of government. City Hall was constantly bombarded with requests, criticism and complaints. It had to carefully balance the city's budget, the citizens' desires and progressing the city to become the next great American metropolis. The city's prestige and size also made it an unfortunate target for social unrest.

It was now Friday, the day after the slaughter of Winston Townsend. It was the day of the vigil in memory of the innocent who died in the mosque. The nationwide organization the

Fundamental Center for Families sent representatives and alerted its members in the area to join their counter-event near the vigil. The most prominent figure in this demonstration was the organization's director Charles Aeble. He had led the organization for over a decade. He was in his early forties, was married to a loving wife and had eight children, ages six through fifteen. He was the pious leader who led Christians in America on a holy war against the filth and sub-humans all across the nation. Their war drums would beat, calling for generous donations in sight of legislation contradictory to their right-wing values. The religious, political organization would blitz government buildings and officials with an army of lobbyists and lawyers to block what they saw as evil from being passed. The FCF was the sworn enemy of pro-choice supporters, gay rights groups, separation of church and state advocates, gaming institutions, left-wing organizations and a long list of others with opposing values. The organization issued propaganda to its members and potential members, buying advertisement space to bring in more funds to fight for their holy cause. Charles came to this city to sound his battle cry and motivate his dedicated followers in the face of the tragedy at the mosque.

Charles had blond hair, blue eyes and fair skin. He considered himself to be an ambassador of the Lord, sent from Heaven to enforce God's rules on Earth. The nationwide organization had a few million members and ample finances. Charles took advantage of the membership fees and extra donations to boost his family into the upper class. He had politicians in Washington and state governments at his command like marionettes. Several high officials supported his appearance in this city today. He currently sat in a posh hotel room, preparing for his speech to the crowd at City Hall. This man of God busily amended his speech to defend Christianity and the need to incorporate it into law and society, as the media reported Winston's ambition to enforce Biblical law after his body was discovered the previous day. Questions and attacks immediately followed the news. It was up to Charles' cunning to defend the name of Christ and move forward with his political interests.

Charles edited his speech, keeping a close eye on the clock. He had two hours before he had to be at City Hall. The stress gnawed at his head and put a sting in his back. He knew the message was essential, but the theatrics of public speaking could motivate the audience more than the actual words. Charles was a natural public speaker. His fiery speeches captivated his audience every time. He worried more about the message regarding Christian fundamentalism than the quality of the speech in these added parts he now quickly wrote. He could, after all, make up for the rushed writing with passionate speaking.

There was a knock at the door. "Yes," Charles called out from the desk. Maddened by his power, Charles swore the left-wing conspired an assassination. He was cautious to screen for this cabal at all times.

"It's me, dear," a feminine voice called out, muffled by the door.

He stood up and cautiously approached the door. "Who?" His voice was demanding.

"Your wife. Helen." The woman's voice said from the other side. Still fearing it was a woman with a gun on the other side of the door he crept to the door so that the potential killer may not hear him, thus knowing his location in the room. She could shoot through the door if she knew he were there. He spread his fingers on the door cautiously and leaned to the peephole. It was indeed his wife. He unlocked all four locks and opened the door for her. "I just met with Lynn," she said walking briskly into the room, passing her husband.

Charles quickly slammed the door and locked all four locks after she entered. "Who?" he asked uncertainly.

"Lynn. Lynn Jacobs. She's the director of our local chapter." She looked at him, surprised he had no idea who Lynn was.

"Oh," he said. "How is she?"

Helen rolled her blue eyes. "She's fine." She walked to the bed, sat down, taking off her shoes. "She's concerned about this whole...ugliness. That word works, doesn't it?"

"This mosque thing?" Charles asked. "What's she so worried about? That's why we're here."

"Oh, dear don't get me wrong." Helen was now taking off her jewelry. "She supports this speech one hundred per cent."

"Good," Charles said, still standing there. "That's what we're paying her for." He walked back to the desk to finish modifying his speech.

"Well she said this whole speech thing we're doing with the vigil tonight has brought even more people."

"More people?" Charles did not look away from his speech.

"Well, as you know we planned for our rally to happen near that gathering." Helen was now undressing. "I think you were right to do it. Maybe we can get some of those horrible Muslims to convert and be on our side."

"That was the plan," Charles said monotonously, carefully perusing his speech to find places in which he could add more words to gain support.

"She's worried about some other groups that want to protest us." Sitting in her bra and panties Helen stood up and reached around to unhook the bra. "Well, after the news this morning that they found that bomber died in his home, a lot of those Jesus-hating liberals want to protest us. I mean, some were going to do it before, but now it's like, huge. Even more people plan on showing up."

"I'm not worried about it," Charles said, not looking at his nude wife. Deep inside he was a bit paranoid that the left would have him gunned down at this speech.

Helen smirked. "I'm hopping in the tub before we go out." She turned and walked to the bathroom.

"Make it quick," Charles yelled out. "We have to be there in a couple hours." Saying that he became more conscious of the time. Stress burned through his body. From the bathroom came the sound of water filling the tub, followed by the door closing and the click of the lock. Charles muttered the words to the speech as he read through it. He added insults to the undesirable groups and erroneous facts in random place to stimulate paranoia and manipulate their latent fears. He knew he had to, by any means possible, motivate the crowd. News networks and the press were scheduled to capture the vigil on tape and in written word. Charles hoped for a piece of the attention. Now was the time to elevate Christianity and seize the day. He aspired to lead God's army into social-political victory. He wanted to rally fellow Christians in the face of tragedy and advance the culture war in God's favor. His ambition was to gather support, so much support that his followers would carry him to a victory in the White House in the future. The FCF indeed had the buying power to support his future campaign and best of all he had friends and bought-out politicians in the ranks on Capitol Hill to ensure his administration could carry out its agenda. He aimed for a presidential victory in 2012.

Charles broke from the speech for a moment to daydream of that glorious day. He hoped the conservative shift in American politics would allow him to carry out his policies. He would launch a new Golden Age of Christianity and claim America as the new Holy Land. He would support Christian groups and offer financial aid to churches in need. He would then seek to eradicate all he considered indecent and lewd. The pornography industry, sex shops, strip clubs and all areas of sexuality in business would crumble. He would usher in a stricter governmental stance on alcohol and shut down all gaming operations in the United States. He would increase censorship on television and radio, then push to clean the internet, cable television and satellite radio of vulgarity. A war against Muslim nations would begin in his presidency. From there he would use fear and Christian pride as a catalyst to promote his administration and support for the war. All his rivals and critics would be subdued. Islam in America would become extinct. He would advocate homosexuality as a growing problem and teach Americans to fear and loathe it. Soon there would be camps for these sexual deviants and they would be exterminated. Abortion and euthanasia would never again be issues. Prayer would return to schools and creationism only would be taught in science classes. Likewise he would see the demise of biotechnology, stem cell research and genetics technology. With help in Congress and the Senate, he would sweep America into this fantasy of his. Charles returned to reality with a renascent attitude and complacent expression. It would be beautiful. The time to act was now.

Charles and Helen exited their rental car. They walked hand-in-hand out the parking garage downtown. In Charles' other hand was a folder bearing his speech. He squeezed it tightly in his fingers, terrified it would fall from his grip. He held it closer to him than his wife in the other hand. The two walked out to the street in silence, headed toward City Hall. As they came closer they saw that the media had already arrived. A crowd had gathered for his anticipated speech. A few hundred yards away, the crowd gathered for the vigil curiously at their nearby gathering. The local chapter of FCF had set up a table and followers had arrived bearing signs. Small gatherings formed somewhat distanced from City Hall. A middle-aged woman with a leathery face ran eagerly up to Charles. "Oh," she said with a wide grin, "you must be Charles. I'm so glad to meet you." Charles looked at her blankly. "I'm Lynn Jacobs, director of the local chapter. I met with your wife earlier."

"Oh yes," Charles said, extending his hand to shake hers. "You're new aren't you?"

"Of course," she responded, shaking his hand vigorously. "I started a few months ago after Gerald retired."

Charles grinned widely. "Just from FCF. We have high hopes that he'll make it into the State Senate. I trust you're backing him?" Charles winked at Lynn.

"Oh, we are. I think he'll make it. Polls show he's leading against that lady running against him. I forget her name, but it's early in the race." Lynn appeared nervous. She spoke to Charles as though she were speaking to her Lord God in the flesh.

"I appreciate your hard work and dedication."

"Thank you," Lynn stretched her arm out behind her, presenting the venue to Charles. "Why don't I show you around? I'll let you meet a few people." Lynn escorted Charles and Helen around the area, introducing him to the more prominent members of the FCF and showing him who would be giving speeches before his grand delivery. A member of the city council would speak, as well as the pastor of one of the city's largest churches. Following them, the wealthiest and most generous benefactor to the FCF bought his way to the podium. The director of a separate organization with similar goals would follow him, then Lynn would make her voice heard before introducing the organization's esteemed president. Charles knew his speech had to be somewhat short, yet motivational. With so many speakers scheduled they ran on a tight frame. Charles shivered. It was a chilly day with overcast skies. The forecast called for a forty per cent chance of rain.

Dusk came quickly and candles from the nearby vigil flickered in the light breeze. Charles prepared himself as he stood to the side, watching the others give their speeches. He had glanced over at the vigil and noticed some members of that crowd had continued to look over at his. The plan seemed to be working. He thought that this would pull people from the wretched grip of Islam and boost his organization.

He only hoped they would be moved enough by his sincere words to forever abandon Allah and join the loving forces of Christ. Many of the previous speakers gave poignant, moving speeches, which could help elevate Charles to the highest position of American government.

"And now," Lynn said excitedly from the podium, "I would like to introduce the president of the FCF, Mr. Charles Aeble." The audience applauded and Charles took his place at the microphone as Lynn stepped aside to let her master speak.

"Thank you," he said smiling and waving. "Thank you. It's so nice to be here. As Lynn mentioned, I'm Charles Aeble, President of the Fundamental Center for Families. It is my privilege to be here with you this evening. I know it's a bit chilly and they say it might rain tonight, but you have all come out here to show your devotion to God and to our noble cause." The crowd applauded. Out the corner of his eye, Charles noticed the crowd from the vigil began dwindling, some coming closer to his group.

"Friends," Charles began, "I have come here tonight with this ugly incident at the mosque looming over us. It was just last Thursday and without a doubt, fresh in all your minds." At that moment, Charles summoned the strength and power of influential speech and persuasion that was his talent and let these divine forces transcend his mortal body. "If that disaster can tell us one thing it was that now more than ever we must stand together and fight. America is facing tough times these days as we stand in the middle of a cultural war, economic uncertainty and widening rifts."

Charles glanced down at his paper. He felt a bit nervous discussing the next item, which he had just written in the hotel earlier that day. "The left is accusing organizations such as ours, though we have only the best intentions, of fueling people such as Winston Townsend." The audience remained silent, awaiting their exalted leader to make his point. "For those of you who may not have heard, he was the man who destroyed the mosque last week. He was found murdered in his home just yesterday. I am here to reassure you that the FCF does not condone acts of terrorism such as these." The crowd applauded him. Much to his delight, Charles noticed that the media had focused its attention on his group, leaving the vigil, which was still in progress. Charles smiled, hiding his anxiety well. He noticed the police force relocating and the distanced groups nearby had grown significantly.

Charles cleared his throat and began to speak with steadfast words and gestures. "The Muslim community does not understand our way of life and now is the time to stand up and fight." There was a murmur at that statement. "Violence carried out by Muslim extremists threatens your way of life and your beliefs. They want us to bow down to them and repeal our faith in the Lord. Such acts drive men such as Mr. Townsend to such acts. I am here to say that the FCF will not fight Islam with terrorism." The people clapped again. "We, as I said before, are in a culture war. We must stand strong against Islam. We must stand strong against the homosexual agenda. We must stand strong against the godless left. These people all seek to destroy *our* family values, *our* society, *our* morality and *our* faith in God." The audience reacted strongly. Charles knew he had hooked them with his words.

"These horrible people find our way of life offensive and disgusting. The hate-mongering words of the Koran, the sexually deviant homosexuals and the entire left will not stop until they have eradicated this great country of ours of all that is moral." The audience murmured again. Charles saw that the vigil had now slowly moved closer to his demonstration. "Well, ladies and gentlemen, as President of the Fundamental Center for Families I will not allow that to happen in America. I will not let that happen to you, our loyal supporters. I will not let this happen to your families. Most of all, I will not let these heathens do this to our Lord." Charles had now thrown his body into the speech, gesturing furiously. He nearly screamed the words to his speech now. "The time for us to end this is now. We must strengthen our values and moral conduct in opposition to the left. I would like now to propose my solution." It was essential to say this loudly, as he had to be heard over the din of applause and cheers.

Charles paused, seeing the eyes of his audience, knowing they wanted an answer on how to end this culture war with their side as the victor. His work was not yet accomplished. He had to further rally his troops to secure their support. He also saw others gathering around the group. More police had arrived on the scene. It was imperative that he hurried through the rest of his speech to protect his endangered life. "We must be vigilant. We must gather as we have this very night routinely. We must tell our elected officials how this country should be. We must stand up against the left and keep them out of our homes and cities. Hollywood has infiltrated our cinemas and television sets with deviant, anti-Christian content. Governments at all levels are growing more accepting of sinful lives. Ladies and gentlemen, if we allow this to happen to our nation, it will fall under the wrath of God." The audience clapped with a feeling of fear and uncertainty. "Fear not, for we as Christians can stand together and not allow these Muslims, homosexuals, abortion advocates, atheists and all other Christ-hating filth in our society to defeat us." The audience cheered his words.

Charles relished the audible praise, but noticed a looming menace approaching his group. He hoped his words would get through to them, but seemingly his speech was becoming more like gasoline on a fire. He feared for his own life, but hoped that he could convince some to quickly join his side. At the very worst, he thought he would only anger the crowd of non-believers. Continuing his fiery speech Charles cut short the endearing applause. "The incident at the mosque should set an example. It was a reaction to Islam's hatred of us. Today should be the cornerstone. Nationwide the FCF is calling for support to reclaim this country from the clutches of sin and debauchery. We are taking a stand against abortion. Never again will you have to fear another woman killing her baby. We are taking a stand against indecency. Never again will you have to suffer that slime tainting our country." The crowd cheered loudly.

Charles smiled knowing he had such an impact on the crowd of loyal followers. "Now ladies and gentlemen, let us take arms against these impurities. We can push for a nation free from sin and vice and make a wholesome, clean life for all Americans to enjoy. With your continued support, with your voices, with your power... we can make this dream a reality in the very near future. Before long we will have prayer back in school and the holy words of the Bible put into the government." The people cheered the future Charles painted for them. "However, we can do this only if you are willing to fight for it. Good citizens, let me hear your voices fill the air. If you are willing to join us in our greatest move to date; to vanquish the immorality and scum tarnishing our nation; if you are willing to rescue America and bring it back as ours, let me hear you... let God hear you." Having finished his speech, Charles received the greatest ovation he ever had before, even at the illustrious banquet they held annually. Though the praise was sweet music in his ears, there was an ambient boo from surrounding crowds. Charles noticed the entire crowd from the vigil had relocated near his. Members of his crowd were protected by a barricade of police officers dressed in full riot gear. Then, at that instant, all life slowed to a crawl and all went completely silent.

The faces of the FCF crowd smiled brightly, some people still clapping. They were pleased to hear of their potential future. One elderly woman toward the back smiled and spoke to her husband without taking her eyes off the podium where Charles still stood. She was unaware of the large rock hurtling toward the back of her head. The boos from the vigil crowd became angry threats. Arms reached out from the sea of people as a wave of human energy easily broke through the line of police. More angry chants came from all sides as rival groups at last advanced on the FCF and each other. The Christian group had been completely surrounded. Officers screamed into their radios. Frightened people screamed and pushed against the violent masses, desperately trying to escape the riot. Helen looked frightened. Lynn ducked away. The other speakers huddled and backed up, trapped by an angry mob before them and the granite walls of City Hall behind them. It happened so slowly, Charles could see it all. Each detail of the unfolding chaos appeared in his view. He saw fear strike his followers as they became aware of the situation. He saw one man take a fist to the head and fall to the ground. He saw the old man in the back holding his wife, whose head was bleeding profusely from the projectile rock. He saw police striking people with clubs. He saw smoke from tear gas rise over the mob. He saw fear and anger collide like deadly fronts, creating an unbridled human storm of raw, primeval power of anger in great numbers. He did not see the bullet that penetrated his eye and pierced his brain.

IV

The riot raged on for hours. The present police force was easily overcome by the violent outburst. The citizens revolted against the law, though special forces were called immediately to the scene. The fights quickly escalated as others found themselves engulfed in the chaos. The mob split in divergent directions, leaving a bloody mess before City Hall. Innocent and guilty were swept into the violence, moving throughout the urban core as one organized religion fought another. Their rigid rules and regulations had conflicted for too long and now the breaking point had been reached. Joining the holy war were other groups who came tonight only to promulgate their existence and continue their fight for equality, recognition and tolerance.

The peaceful gathering became a grisly battle. Christians fought Muslims. Gays fought straights. Men fought women. Americans fought Americans. Human beings fought human beings. The death toll steadily rose and the numbers of wounded grew faster. The financial district became one battleground, a dilapidated neighborhood outside downtown became another and a nearby retail district was the third. Soon, violence toward each other became directed on the city. The mob turned over cars, set homes and businesses ablaze, smashed windows, looted and destroyed their city in any conceivable method of civil unrest. Sounds of explosions, alarms, emergency vehicles and distant human screams rose above the central city. Fires consumed properties as the financial cost of the riot dramatically grew. Despite it all, the money needed to rebuild the destruction could never account for the human loss.

Police forces from the suburbs were dispatched to quell the insidious riot. Finally, in the early hours of Saturday morning the violence ceased. Paramedics and firefighters flooded the central city to resolve the state of emergency. They battled the flames and gathered the dead from the disaster area. They gathered people coated in blood, people lying nearly dead, people crying in pain and disbelief. Hospitals were instantly flooded and a refrigerated trailer was used as an overflow morgue until the victims of this horror could be properly identified. Amidst the wounds on the city's infrastructure were stains of spilled blood on the streets and sidewalks. Survivors anxiously awaited news on missing loved ones, waiting all night for the phone call. At around sunrise the clouds from the evening before had not dispersed. The rains at last fell, cleansing the city and aiding firefighters in their battle against the blaze. Blood and ashes mixed with the rains and drained drearily into the gutters and storm drains, flowing into the city's bowels. The news spread coast to coast. Photographs, sound bytes and footage spread across the nation and soon across the world's oceans, showing a global audience the unfolding terror. The violence caused many to question the government, society and themselves. Other governments worried that the violence could hit home, though the incident was contained in this city, leaving a hideous scar and ugly part of its history.

Numerous charred buildings left large black pockets of ash and rubble in the urban core. Luckier buildings patched their broken windows, though small shards of broken glass before the buildings twinkled in the lights. Further away, other areas of the central city were spared, as the battleground had not ventured to these streets. The different neighborhoods and suburbs distanced from the urban center sympathized with the victims of this nightmare, yet scoffed with their haughty mentality that it could only happen in a poorer neighborhood as that of the central city. Further from the central city the population became sparser and the urban density declined, lessening the shock and effect on the population as the distance from the suffering metropolis became greater. One lonely highway connecting the big city to rural towns cut through the hinterlands and out into the countryside, leading to another town with other stories.